The Riddle of Riddles

Thomas McGann

Copyright © 2007
Thomas McGann
All Rights Reserved

Agapi tis Glossas Publishers logo is a registered trademark
of Agapi tis Glossas Publishers
ISBN: 978-0-9906241-1-0
LCCN: 2014916416
Published by Agapi tis Glossas Publishers, USA
57 Moffitt Blvd., Islip, NY 11751

Cover art by Roy A. Mauritsen

Thank you W.W. Norton & Company for permission to quote selections from The Divine Comedy by Dante Alighieri, translated by John Ciardi. Copyright 1954, 1957, 1959, 1960, 1961, 1965, 1967, 1970 by Ciardi Family Trust. Used by permission of W.W. Norton & Company, Inc

For my wife Donna
For believing in me

ACKNOWLEDGEMENTS

This work was a long time in coming, and the fault is mine alone.

Many people believed in me, and encouraged me to publish this book. First, and foremost, is my wife, Donna who stuck by me when things got tough. Thanks, Babe. Thank you, Kathleen, Brian, Gregory, and Peggy. A special shout-out goes to my sister Susan who, not only typed my manuscript for me, but also believed in this work enough to read it to her sixth grade students.

An early pioneer was Brian Lyzer (author of *The View*) who stepped up numerous times with pithy observations and unending enthusiasm. Others include Mark Panek, (award winning author of several books including *Gaijun Yokozuna, Big Happiness,* and *Hawai'i.*) and Kevin Dineen. Thank you Judy Bland, another author (*Legacy, Escape*) and her husband, Ray, for proofreading, correcting and critiquing this work.

Pam Chiarizzi showed her talent with the logos she created both for the book and publishing company, and with her marketing artistry.

I would also like to thank Roy A. Mauritsen for the incredible artwork on the book cover and trailer. I also owe him a debt of gratitude for his advice and encouragement during this project.

Ordinarily, this book would have been dedicated to my Mother and Father. Unfortunately, they are both gone now and the world is a lesser place because of it. Nonetheless, I owe them a debt that can never be repaid. Mom gave me the courage to attempt a task of this magnitude and Dad gave me the quiet assurance that I could do it. They engulfed me in clouds of love that keep my dreams afloat to this day.

FOREWORD

Three matters need to be addressed up front.
First: This book was written to be read aloud.
Second: This work *is* a riddle about a riddle containing riddles. It also contains Brainteasers, Enigmas, Hints, Equations, a Rebus, Epigrams, Numerology, Observations and Whatnots. There are games for children, games for adults, and games for those who have worked hard at remaining a bit of both.

Examples of some of these games are:
1. On what page does this work actually begin?
2. Can you assemble the puzzle pieces?
3. Can you find and unravel the anagrams presented?
4. What role does numerology play?
5. Can you solve the Kryptographeme (cryptogram)?
6. Can you find the hidden names of the members of a certain rock music group?
7. How many of that rock group's song titles can you find?
8. Who wrote/performed the books/lyrics quoted?
9. Have you discerned any games yet?

Third: The Afterword (if you must peek) provides the answers to the riddles contained in the text. There are, in addition, many other hidden allusions for those who are paying attention.

I hope you have as much fun taking this work apart as I had putting it together.

The Writer

Table of Contents

CHAPTER 1 – BOREDOM 4
CHAPTER 2 - THE WISHFUL WISH 8
CHAPTER 3 – BELVIDERE 15
CHAPTER 4 – KNORBERT 22
CHAPTER 5 – RIDDLES FOR BREAKFAST 31
CHAPTER 6 – CHOICES 44
CHAPTER 7 – DETOURS AND SHORTCUTS..... 52
CHAPTER 8 – BOGS OF DISCOURAGEMENT .. 58
CHAPTER 9 – KNOTHEADS 66
CHAPTER 10 – SAPIENTIOPOLIS 73
CHAPTER 11 – THE KORTEXTIUM 76
CHAPTER 12 – CAFÉ AVANT GARDE 82
CHAPTER 13 – THE TOO-GOODERS 96
CHAPTER 14 – THE INTERIOR 100
CHAPTER 15 – CAUSE OR EFFECT 108
CHAPTER 16 – WHAT BIRD IS THIS? 114
CHAPTER 17 – MORE RIDDLES 118
CHAPTER 18 – AN OLD MAN 121
CHAPTER 19 – THE REAL TEST 129
CHAPTER 20 – BELVIDERE – AGAIN 132
CHAPTER 21 – MOUNT KNEVEREST 140
CHAPTER 22 – WILLI-NILLIES? 144
CHAPTER 23 – A LOCOMOBILE 148
CHAPTER 24 – INNER SPACE 159

CHAPTER 25 – THE PLEASURE PALACE 164

CHAPTER 26 – DEEPER INTO INNER SPACE . 195

CHAPTER 27 – MAN HATIN' ISLAND 199

CHAPTER 28 – DEEPER AND DEEPER INTO INNER SPACE 220

CHAPTER 29 – THE WEB AND THE PIT 225

CHAPTER 30 – WHO IS IN CONTROL? 238

CHAPTER 31 – THE RIDDLE & ANSWER 241

CHAPTER 32 – RACING WITH THE SUN 245

CHAPTER 33 – BIRTH DAY 247

AFTERWORD 253

PART I
THE READER OR THE WRITER

Once upon a time, not that long ago really, and not all that far from here either, if the truth be known…
 Oh no!
Not that "Once upon a time…" sentence again.
Why do so many stories begin with those words?
And why am I reading these words even as am I thinking these thoughts?
It's like I'm the writer instead of the reader.
In fact, all of this now seems, somehow, strangely familiar, as if I knew even these words would be here.
It is as though by my thinking these thoughts, these words are being written even as I am reading them.
I am being swept along in an ongoing flood of déjà-vu.
What is going on here?
 Am I the reader?
 or
 Am I the writer?
Reading…

PART II

ADVENTURES IN THE REALM OF REFLECTION

CHAPTER 1 – BOREDOM

Once upon a time, not that long ago really, and not all that far from here either, if the truth be known…there lived a boy named William Woodew who everyone knew as Will.

Will was about as ordinary a youngster as ever lived, as ordinary as you or I. Oh, maybe he was a bit frailer than some, but that frailty never really affected Will much—never affected him, that is, until the day he first heard about Willi-Nillies.

Will did, however, differ from everyone else in one most extraordinary way. Will was, you see, immortal. He was going to live forever and ever and ever. He never really understood how it came to be that he was going to live forever. He just knew it was so, and he never questioned why. It just *was* and that made him different. And special.

Yet as wonderful a gift as this was, it did create a bit of a dilemma. Since there was just so much time in which to do everything, Will never got around to doing much of anything. There was, after all, no hurry.

Consequently, Will was constantly bored. Days went by, and weeks went by, and years went by, while Will whiled by, idle and

Chapter 1 - Boredom

bored,

The Riddle of Riddles

bored,

Chapter 1 - Boredom

bored.

CHAPTER 2 - THE WISHFUL WISH

It was a day just like today that Will first heard about Willi-Nillies. It was a gray day, as gray as a Kansas prairie before a cyclone, with Will lost in the deep silence of his room pacing

                                                                                 back

                  and

forth

                  and

                                                                                 back

                  and

forth, wondering if—just, maybe—he should be doing something, *anything*, when, out of the corner of his eye, he spotted movement. He turned quickly in the direction of the movement only to burst out laughing. There, staring back at him from the mirror across the room, was his own reflection.

    Will approached the mirror, still laughing, with that countenance in the mirror laughing back at him. He got so close his nose almost touched the cold glass, and began studying himself as he never before had. He gazed intently into his eyes, and as he stared, the image of his face began to sag like melting wax.

    First Will noticed that his right cheek began to droop a bit. Then his left eyebrow began sagging until it halfway covered the eye. His nose broadened and then twisted like a question mark. His lips swelled and turned a purplish black. He wet them with his tongue, which was thin and slick and frightened him.

    The only parts of him that remained his own were his eyes, but even as he watched, their color began draining away. The pupils shrank until they became pinholes. Then they suddenly expanded and began spinning; spinning and contracting, spinning and expanding. Spinning, spinning, spinning, the pale discs beckoned him in, bottomless cones sucking him into the very center of his being.

Chapter 2 – The Wishful Wish

A hint of the scent of violets dusted the air.

Will blinked.

The mirror-imaged apparition blinked back.

The looking glass got soft like gauze, turning into a sort of vapor. The glass began to melt away into a bright, silvery mist, leaving his image totally exposed in the surrounding void.

Will grew increasingly frightened, terribly frightened, of this image of him standing in that empty, silvery void; frightened of those swirling eyes; frightened of those swollen, blubbery lips that began to purse and twitch as if possessed of a mind all their own. He was afraid those lips would speak.

And they did!

"What will you do with your wish?" the lips mouthed, contorting slowly, familiarly over each word, words which struggled up out of the depths in a slow hoarse whisper Will could barely hear.

The mirror-imaged apparition stared into Will's eyes. Will stood transfixed, trembling, unable to speak.

"What will you do with your wish?" the image asked again.

"What?" Will blurted out, half horrified, half terribly intrigued. "Who are you and what are you doing here?"

"I am Lou," his image-twin replied. "What will you will do with your wish?"

"What wish?"

"Your wish. Everyone gets a wish, one wish to do with as one pleases."

"Are you telling me I have a wish, a wish just like in children's books?"

"Of course," Lou replied. "Children's books are often quite perceptive."

"But those books usually grant three wishes."

"Those tales are for the very young, for children who have not yet come of age."

"And I've come of age?"

The Riddle of Riddles

"You are here."

Lou paused. "You have to decide what you want to do with your wish to make it come true. However, I caution you to wish wisely, for once wished your wish cannot be unwished. All are so forewarned, but still many waste their wish."

A wish! A real wish just like in fantasies Will had read—but this was no fantasy. This was real. He really had a wish, his one wish to do with as he chose.

Will gulped.

He had actually thought about a moment such as this. Suppose, just suppose, that one day he really was granted a wish—just one wish—what would it be?

Will knew.

He knew his wish. He had figured it out a long time ago, never really believing this moment would ever come but…it had.

"I-wish-for-all-the-wishes-I-wish," Will wished-just-like-that.

Lou stared out at Will, a look of weary sadness overcoming his face. "You have wished the Wishful Wish." Lou's voice was slower now, deeper.

Will hesitated. "So?"

"So," Lou continued, "the Wishful Wish is a selfish wish. Since you would have all your wishes in one wish, you must prove yourself worthy."

Will's voice quivered. "How…how do I do that?"

"You prove yourself worthy by earning it, and to earn your wish you must complete one of the Nine Noble Tasks."

"What nine noble tasks?" Will asked, his eyes held captive by Lou's eyes.

"The Nine Noble Tasks are…" Lou began,

"One-Solve The Riddle of Riddles.

"Two- Deduce the Common Denominator.

"Three- Forge a Handleless Handle.

"Four- Map the Unseen Way.

"Five- Tame the Twin Dragons.

Chapter 2 – The Wishful Wish

"Six- Record the Music of the Spheres.

"Seven- Build a Bridge of Understanding.

"Eight- Capture Imagination.

"Nine- Drink from the Fount of Satisfaction."

Will's mind reeled. He asked Lou to repeat the tasks and then to repeat them again, a third time. His mind raced up and down the list: riddles, dragons, handleless handles. He did not like the sound of any of the tasks. They were all so far beyond his understanding, to say nothing of his capabilities.

Lou broke the ensuing silence. "You must choose."

Will breathed rapidly. He could not speak.

"CHOOSE." Lou's voice was louder. "Choose your Noble Task."

"I pick the first one, number one," Will blurted out before he even realized he was speaking.

"You have chosen to solve The Riddle of Riddles."

"Yep. Yes I have."

Will was unsure about what was actually happening to him. This whole episode seemed surreal, as if it was happening and not happening, both at the same time. He could not stop fidgeting, shifting back and forth from foot to foot, clenching and unclenching his fists.

Lou nodded. "So be it."

Will's mind was all agallop. "What is this so-called Riddle of Riddles anyway? I mean, if I'm supposed to answer a riddle, I guess I should know what it is, right?" He was unable to keep from speaking, as though his tongue had suddenly acquired a will all its own. "I mean, if you are given a task to do, you are told what that task is, right? So I must know what my task is. I mean, I do know what my task is—to solve The Riddle of Riddles—but I don't know what that riddle is and if I'm supposed to answer it I should know what it is, right? I must," he gasped, "know what it is, I mean..." his breath finally giving out.

"When is the riddle the answer?"

Will cocked his head. "That's what I'm asking *you*."

The Riddle of Riddles

"When is the riddle the answer?" Lou repeated slowly.

"I don't understand." Will shook his head. "When *is* the riddle the answer?"

"Exactly," Lou replied. "When is the riddle the answer?"

Silence, that was not a silence at all, fell into the empty hollow in which Will stood.

"Oh!" Will swallowed. "Oh…of course, yeah, I get it. *'When is the riddle the answer'* is The Riddle of Riddles."

"Correct." Lou nodded.

"Oh boy!" Will swallowed again, harder this time, and dropped his gaze to the floor. "When is the riddle the answer?" he repeated. Then he cleared his throat. "Oh, boy…"

"A logical approach can help you solve the riddle, Will. Do you play chess?"

Will looked up. "As a matter of fact, I do, but why do you ask? "

"I thought you might know how to play. The ability to play chess can be a valuable tool."

"I know more than just how to play." Will rolled back his shoulders and puffed out his chest. "I am in the process of perfecting the game of chess, one where white will win every game because white goes first."

Will looked at Lou for a reaction, but Lou remained silent.

"I know that there are an almost infinite number of possible combinations in any chess game, but in the perfect game white will win no matter what moves black makes. White always mates, always without exception."

"That's an interesting concept."

"It is, isn't it?" Will smiled. Then he grew silent for a moment. "This is just an idea for now, but it makes sense logically, don't you think?" and he shrugged. "White has the initiative and will compel black, move by move, into checkmate."

"The game of chess does require logical thinking" said Lou, "and logic can help you solve The Riddle of Riddles. There will be clues to the answer to the riddle that you will encounter

Chapter 2 – The Wishful Wish

during your search. You must pay attention. You must look for these clues so you do not miss them, and then put them all together to help solve the riddle."

"OK. Thanks for the heads up."

Then Lou raised his voice. "But do not dilly-dally because you must bring me the answer before the sun goes down."

"What sundown?"

"Sundown today. You must bring me the answer to The Riddle of Riddles before the sun goes down today, or face the consequences."

"Consequences?" Will squeaked. "What consequences?"

"You forfeit your life."

"Forfeit my life!" Will choked on the words. "You mean...*die*?"

"That is correct. Die unfulfilled."

"But I am immortal. I am supposed to live forever."

Lou's face registered no emotion.

Time slowed like a motion picture projector with the power running down. The light dimmed. The lens zoomed away. Will's vision went dark. Silence vacuumed his ears.

The answer before sundown or...

Will did not want to consider his alternative. He had to answer The Riddle of Riddles before sundown or...or die...die unfulfilled.

He took a deep breath.

Like flight turned to fight, Will's mind was suddenly aflutter with wishes. Everything and anything he ever wanted could be his, his very own, including those new video games he wanted so much: *Grand Theft Automatic, White Ops,* and *Super Superior Superb Brothers*. He could even become big and strong if he wanted, maybe ever a Quidditch champion. He could...

Will shook his head. There he was, being his usual greedy self again. How about wishes for others? Sure, special wishes for friends, and family, and all those less fortunate than himself. After all, he was going to have as many wishes as he wished for. All

The Riddle of Riddles

these wishes could be his once he found the answer to The Riddle of Riddles, wherever that might be.

Will returned his attention to the mirror. "Where do I begin looking for the answer to this riddle?" he asked.

Will's question was answered with silence.

"Where do I start?" Will repeated, louder this time. He looked for Lou.

There was no reply.

"Lou!" Will's eyes darted about the mirror. "Lou!"

But there was no Lou. Only Will's reflection remained, staring back at him out of the mirror, mouthing the words he was speaking. Will put his fingers up to the impersonal glass, glass no longer misty, glass now solid. His image mimicked his every move; one thin thickness separating his warm, warm fingers from those in that cold, cold glass.

Will stumbled backward into his room. His eyes welled up, his hands trembled, and his knees quivered. He steadied himself momentarily against the wall as he let the recognition of what had just happened sink in.

"*Uh-oh!*" Will's stomach roiled. "*What have I done?*" The sudden realization of some uncompromising, prophetic knowledge he had just acquired abruptly filled him. "*Where am I ever going to find the answer to The Riddle of Riddles?*"

Behind a hand held over his eyes, Will searched his mind. He turned over this thought, then that thought, hoping to scare up any ideas with life enough to scamper across his consciousness.

By George, of course! Will remembered this book, this book he is reading that deals with riddles and tasks and, hopefully, answers.

Will realized this book was in hand and he was reading…

CHAPTER 3 – BELVIDERE

Once upon a time, not that long ago really, and not all that far from here either, if the truth be known ‥ •

Will marveled as he watched that third dot, the one right there at the end of the last sentence, start to grow larger than the others. It continued growing until, much to his bewilderment, that big black dot drifted up off the page and hovered in the air halfway between the page and his eyes.

It kept expanding slowly, expanding until it was larger than the book from which it had come and completely blocked it from view. Still, it continued growing, and as it did, it swallowed up all of Will's surroundings

one

by

one

until Will found himself engulfed in utter

DARKNESS

Yet…not quite *utterly* dark, for overhead Will could just make out the twinkling of stars.

He threw back his head to drink in their grandeur, and as his eyes adjusted to the darkness, he could see that the sky was ablaze with stars.

Whaaat?

Will was suddenly giddy, as though he had stepped into a rabbit hole and was falling, falling, falling. His mind wheeled about, taking the heavens with it. He threw both arms straight out from his sides, palms out, fingers spread to steady himself. "Where am I? What am I doing here where I don't even know where *here* is?"

Will focused his mind, first on his room and the mirror, then on Lou and the Wishful Wish, then on the Riddle and this book, and then...then...here, wherever here is or was or whatever.

Will shook his head, half expecting to hear all the unconnected fragments rattle about inside: here—there—is—was—whatever!

As he groped for a reference point, any reference point, Will's eyes fell upon the unbroken horizon, the laser-sharp edge of a clear, black sky resting on calm, blood-red sea. He locked onto this new reality like someone stunned coming to consciousness.

Beyond the stretch of that limitless sea, the cloudless sky had just begun to lighten. The heavy black of night was giving way to slate-gray, as overhead the stars slowly began fading from view.

A blue tinge soon brushed the slate-gray sky as shafts of gold spoked their way through the e-ver-so-slow-ly-fad-ing-black-of-night.

Each moment seemed to have an extravagant moment in which to reflect itself, like mirror facing mirror—moment reflecting moment reflecting moment—adding a dimension to the sunrise quite unlike any Will had ever before experienced.

A golden dot appeared at the rim of the sea, a slight sliver of light that began painting color onto the day. The sliver grew slowly until it became an arc, an arc of gold that illuminated a sandy shore and the gently surging sea. The arc continued to balloon until it became a golden globe as the sun broke free of the horizon, suffusing the morning with its warmth.

Will took a deep breath. *"Where am I?"* he wondered, looking around at the unfamiliar surroundings.

He took another deep breath, and then laughed out loud. "Wherever I am, at least this day has just begun, and I have all of today to find the answer to The Riddle of Riddles. But which way do I go? I'm lost in a lost world. If only there was some kind of sign."

Chapter 3 - Belvidere

Will's eyes swept around like a beacon searching for a passage between unfamiliar shoals. The beach on which he stood stretched far off into the distance in either direction, washed by the waves of the deep crimson sea. On either hand, back across the sparkling sands, ran set after set of dunes. Off to one side the dunes gave way to the gradually ascending cliffs of a headland, until they too dimmed from view, lost in the distance and the white haze of a growing morning mist.

"Straight ahead is as good a direction as any." Will shrugged, but when he attempted to step forward he discovered that his legs would not move.

He looked down. He was half-in and half-out of the sea. The foam on an incoming tide licked at his feet, licked at the sand beneath him, undermining him before receding. He was stuck.

He pulled again, harder this time, still to no avail, each sea surge depositing more and more sand over his feet, trapping him.

Will's immediate reaction was panic. Knowing how frail he was, a picture of him sinking into the soft sand as the tide came in to drown him abruptly took on very real dimensions. So, he mustered his energies and pulled harder.

Slowly his foot rose. Slowly it began its escape from the suck of the soft eroding sand, slowly, until—finally—it broke free with an audible slurp. Then Will had to free his other foot, even as the sea renewed its siege on the first. Then, having freed his other foot, he had to free the first foot again, and then the other, one foot after the other, each time more and more rapidly.

He smiled as he gained momentum.

Then smiling at his smiles, Will broke out into laughter and a run all in one, leaving empty footprints in the sand where he had stood just moments before. He stopped and turned. His footprints were being filled by the sea-driven sand until—soon—there was no trace that he had ever stood there.

The gradually warming day was giving rise to a fog which thickened as he walked. Its mist rose from the sea in spires, like a graveyard full of ghosts rising at the call of some unseen master.

The Riddle of Riddles

Will shouldered his way through the clammy wetness that pressed tighter and tighter around him. Each breeze chilled him.

Will heard something, something like the distant tinkling of bells. He stopped to listen but all he heard was the soft *swassssssh* as the sea broke up onto the foggy beach.

He looked back to the water's edge where the sea surge wet the sand. The beach twisted its lonely way into the fog like the dark gray pavement of some ancient empty street. The sun, a hazy, white wafer, hung just above the once discriminating, but now barely visible, horizon.

Will continued pushing forward through the damp folds of that sheer, white shroud when he heard it again. This time there could be no mistake; from somewhere back down the beach came the jingle-jangle of bells. He turned back toward the sound.

There, silhouetted by the sea, circled by the circus sands, was a young boy skipping lightly toward him. The sound Will heard was not bells after all, but came from a tambourine the boy carried. He could hear the boy's laughter spinning, swinging madly across the sea.

Will ran down the beach toward the boy. "Hello," he yelled. "Hello there!"

The boy skipped on down the beach paying no heed.

Will ran up alongside the boy. "Hello," he repeated, louder this time.

The boy looked over with a jacknicholson grin but said nothing. He continued on his way, tambourine in hand, and Will turned to follow.

The boy, who looked to be about the same age as Will, had his hair braided in a tight, greasy rat-tail that hung halfway down his back. It whipped back and forth as he skipped along. He wore a pair of bottle-thick glasses that managed to both magnify his eyes and distort them at the same time, so much so that it was impossible to tell where, or on what, the boy was focusing. He was barefoot and bare-chested, dressed only in a pair of multicolored pantaloons gathered tightly at his ankles, but which ballooned

Chapter 3 - Belvidere

wildly about his legs.

"Where are you going?" Will asked in purposely-modulated tones.

Still the boy paid him no mind.

"Perhaps you can help me," Will puffed, side-skipping along, trying to keep pace with the boy. "I'm lost. Can you tell me where I am, please?"

The boy continued skipping on down the beach with one hand waving free, the tambourine jangling in the other. Will hurried after him. At a point where a slight dip in the beach swept the sea inland and had trapped there the rotting remains of some brown-green edgelay, Will caught the boy by an elbow.

The boy stopped abruptly, wrenching free his arm. He spun around and glared at Will from behind his thick green glasses. "Don't *ever* touch me," he snapped.

"I'm…I'm sorry," Will stammered. "It's just that I'm lost. I have no idea where I am. You see, I was in my room where I met this…this…Lou guy who gave me a wish which meant I had to solve this riddle which I looked for in this book which, which next thing I know—I'm here, wherever here is, though not exactly here, more over there," and Will pointed, his breath having quite given out.

"I'll say you're lost." The boy threw back his head, looking down his nose at Will.

"So where am I?"

"You are at the beginning of the sea and the end of the land as any fool can see," the boy sneered.

"Or at the end of the sea and the beginning of the land as any fool can likewise see." Will glared back at the boy.

The boy stared at Will, his face devoid of emotion, his eyes impenetrable behind the myopic glasses.

"My name is Will," he offered, holding out his hand. "What's yours?"

"My name is Belvidere," the boy answered, quite ignoring Will's outstretched hand.

The Riddle of Riddles

"Horrid fog, huh?" Will added, dropping his hand, quickly wiping it against the leg of his trousers.

Belvidere smiled. "I kind of like it," he said.

"Horrid odor, too," Will added.

The boy stared at Will. "The tide is out," he said.

"Don't it smell awful?" Will asked, wrinkling up his nose in revulsion, "like something…"

"Where did you say you were going?" Belvidere interrupted.

"I told you. I am looking for the answer to The Riddle of Riddles," Will replied. "You see, I made this bargain that I would solve it before sundown and…"

"Well, don't look so unhappy." Belvidere broke in. "Sundown is a long way off. Why, it's barely past sunrise."

"Where are you going?" Will asked.

"There is no place I am going to," Belvidere replied. "I have no one to meet. Come follow me."

"But I can't." Will shook his head. "I told you. I must find the answer to the riddle I'm looking for."

"Aw, you've plenty of time. It's early." The corners of Belvidere's lips curled upward slightly. "Come on and follow me. We'll have great fun. I promise. We'll make our own parade. Here, you can play my harmonica." He thrust his hand toward Will. In it was a shiny harmonica.

"I can't," Will repeated. "I need to find the answer to The Riddle of Riddles. Do you have any idea what the answer might be or where I can find it?"

"Why do you keep on asking useless question on top of useless question?'

And with that Belvidere began singing and twirling.

"Come disappear with me, inside a smoky theater, welcoming the shrill glee of broken karaoke meter, come far passed any frozen emotions, and haunted, frightened unchosen notions, out to this windy beach."

"Stop singing!" Will snapped. "Please stop. Can't you see

Chapter 3 - Belvidere

I need your help?"

"Help? Why, certainly Will. I'll help you, but first you must promise to come wandering with me.

"I'll take you in my car, far out beyond the stars, your mind unlatched, ajar, your fingertips all scarred, your soles too dead to tread."

Belvidere sing-songed, circling Will.

"Your course is a charade, come join in my parade. Dancing spells in dark shades. You need not be dismayed. To my ways I will persuade."

Belvidere sang seductively, banging his tambourine in time.

"Stop!" Will yelled clapping his hands over his ears. "Can't you see I need your help? Stop! Please stop."

"Stop?" Belvidere laughed. "We are stopped. We have yet to begin,."

He paused a moment before picking up the melody again.

"And to begin your fate must lose its weight, you must welcome all new sorrows, and forget about today until tomorrow."

"No! No!" Will cried. "I don't have until tomorrow. Today is all I have!" And without thought, he spun and ran away from Belvidere as fast as he could, away from the jingle-jangle of the tambourine, away from the horrid odor of rotting life at Belvidere's feet, its stink in his brain forever.

Will ran as hard and as fast as he could across the soft, slow sands, never once looking back. He ran until he could run no more. Still he pushed himself forward until, without warning, his legs gave out from under him, and he collapsed face down onto the sand, gasping raggedly for air.

CHAPTER 4 – KNORBERT

Will rolled to his back, his breath returning slowly.

The heat of the morning sun had begun to burn away the thick fog. The breeze, too, carried it out to sea until only the palest of white veils hung over the seascape.

Will sat up and looked around. The view blew away in the direction of reach grass and distant clouds, in the direction of crashing surf and sheer cliffs. No one was in sight. He was, once again, all alone on the beach.

Before him was the headland. Rocks and boulders met the soft sand there like high cliff ambassadors. The cliffs, beginning rather gradually in low outcroppings, ascended rapidly. In the near distance they rose precipitously, straight above the sea which slashed at them as if trying to reclaim what it considered was once rightfully its own. Overhead, jonathanlivingston seagulls checked the sky.

"If only there was some kind of sign to show me the way," Will mused.

A sign? He instantly snorted at his own foolishness.

Yet…suppose there was a sign.

Nah.

But suppose there was. Where would it be?

"If I was to tempt the fates, whatever sign I'm looking for should be right smack-dab in front of me." Will shook his head, but this very ambivalence moved him to raise his eyes, almost half-afraid that there would be no sign, more than half-afraid that there would be.

Will's heart very-nearly-stopped. Then it thumped so loudly Will thought he actually heard it.

There it was!

A sign—or something that he could, perhaps, take as a sign.

Chapter 4 - Knorbert

Directly above the high cliffs glowed a star, a star still quite bright despite the rising sun, a star encircled by a ring which expanded and contracted with detectable rhythm. Directly below it, like the point of an arrow, was the sharp *"V"* of a fissure in the cliff wall.

Will blinked—and then blinked again. Then he shook his head violently.

The pulsating star remained.

Will giggled. He remembered a story he had read about a young boy who had drawn a picture to scare people, but when he showed it no one was afraid of a picture of a hat. So the boy drew the picture of what the grown-ups failed to see, the picture of an elephant that had been swallowed by a boa constrictor, a picture that looked like a hat until you looked inside.

Will remembered that lesson. Sometimes there was more to what you were seeing than first perceived.

As he watched, his star began to sink slowly into that *"V"*, beckoning him, daring him to follow, leading him as it grew fainter and fainter until, finally, it disappeared behind the headland.

Will jumped to his feet and hurried toward the cliffs, keeping his pace rhythmic, his breathing steady until, finally, he reached their base. Rock by rock he pulled himself up the steep cliff face—up, over and between sharp-edged stones and large boulders until he reached the fissure that split the moody cliffs. By the time Will reached the top of the promontory, however, his star was gone .

The sea was far below and behind him now. Ahead was a wash of reeds higher than Will was tall, and beyond the reeds was a dense wood of twisted witch spine and scut choak. Will followed a winding break in the reeds but a short distance before he came upon a taller stand of stout lollygags and set seedar. Sassyfracas and scrabble crowded together there too, overgrown with scatbriar, grope vines and poison soonact, creating a veritable fortress, or hideout.

The Riddle of Riddles

Wwwooo...

Will heard something. At first he thought it was the wind, so softly did the sound float above the murmur of the washing waves and rustling reeds.

But no... there it was again, louder this time.

Will listened closely. He heard something like the sound made by blowing across the top of an empty bottle, ebbing and flowing. It was a broken, plaintive sound—a hint of a sad, sad song. It sounded like no music Will had ever heard before.

That sad song was coming from deep within the thick growth up ahead.

With memories of Belvidere so fresh in mind, Will's first impulse was to ignore the sounds and move on, but something in their resonance piqued his curiosity. Whoever, or whatever, was creating such a melancholy sound certainly did not seem threatening.

Quietly, Will stole along the edge of the dense wood until he came to where the sounds were originating. He found an opening in the brush and, pushing aside the leaves and branches, picked his way toward those sounds.

Just ahead he could make out a clearing. He edged forward and was just about to peek out into that clearing when he stepped on a twig.

      S   P
    N   A

The music stopped instantly, followed by a long empty...

    S
    I
    L
    E
    N
     c
      E

Will held his breath, listening, but could hear nothing but the wind in the wallows. Carefully separating the leafy growth in

Chapter 4 - Knorbert

front of him, he peered out into the clearing.

There, surrounded on all sides by the heavy growth of the thicket, stood a small wooden shack about the size of Will's room back home. It had a small porch out front with an overhang to keep off the rain and, in back, a stone chimney from which trailed a thin wisp of smoke. The windows wore bright curtains for make-up, lending a friendly air to the ramshackle structure.

But no one was visible, and all was quiet.

Whoever had been there was not there now.

Will's heart beat rapidly. He did not enjoy sneaking around like this, and, besides, whoever had been here must have heard him and was now as wary of Will as Will was of him, or her, or it or whatever.

He took a deep breath, pushed aside the branches, and took one small step out into the clearing.

"Hello," he called out softly. "Is anyone here?"

There was no reply.

He took a second, smaller step.

"Hello there..." He had meant to speak louder, but the words came out as a half-whisper.

Still there was no reply.

A third step. "HELLO..." he said louder this time.

Silence.

Will took a nervous step backwards when

WHAM!

He bumped into something and was sent sprawling.

Will scrambled to his feet and turned.

The silliest looking creature Will had ever seen was slumped on the ground staring up at him.

The creature had an enormous egg-shaped head, bald on top, with a frizzy fringe of hair sticking out all around. Its big head sat atop a round, pudgy body that strained against a threadbare, gray tunic. The creature sat startled, blinking round, blue eyes, so pale in color they could scarcely be called blue.

"Oh me, oh my, oh no!" The creature pushed against the

ground until it was sitting upright.

Its eyes were deep-set behind a carrot-like nose that stuck straight out, as did the large wrinkled ears on either side of its big head. On the ends of its muscular arms, almost as though an afterthought, were a pair of enormous hands, rough with calluses. Its short legs ended in bare feet, as large for their size as were the hands, or for that matter, the head.

"Hi there! I'm sorry I bumped into you," said Will. "Here, let me help you up." He approached the creature and stuck out his hand.

"Oh me, oh my, oh no!" the creature wailed. "Stay away from me. It is a wonder I am still all right after that bump you gave me."

With one last mighty shove from its brawny arms, the creature clumsily righted itself.

"Why, pray tell, were you spying on me?" the creature asked with a clipped, staccato rhythm. It brushed its hands together and then dusted off its gray tunic.

"I wasn't spying on you. Honest. I came here looking for help."

"Just who," the creature demanded, looking Will up and down, "or I should say, just *what* are you?"

"My name is Will. I'm lost. When I heard someone trying to play music…"

"Oh me, oh my!" The creature's face grew quite red. "Trying to play music? Trying to play indeed!"

"Actually it sounded quite lovely," Will added-quick-as-he-could.

The creature leaned forward nervously wringing its large hands, its pale blue eyes searching Will's eyes. "Oh me, oh my, you will not tell anyone you heard me play, will you?"

"It wasn't *that* bad." Will laughed.

"Oh me, oh my, please do not make fun of me. Please promise me that you will not tell anyone."

"Of course not, not if you don't want me to. But everyone

Chapter 4 - Knorbert

has to practice to learn how to play."

"Learn? Learn how to play?" The creature howled at Will. "I will have you know that I am the inventor of music. Yes, that is right. Me! I have invented music and-you-need-not-look-so skeptical."

"What's your name?" Will asked, not the slightest bit afraid of this big awkward creature.

"Oh me, oh my. Where *are* my manners? I am so sorry. My name is Knorbert, Master Knorbert Knothead." And with that, he flourished a deep bow.

"Pleased to meet you, Norbert. My name is William Woodew, but everyone calls me Will."

"That is Knorbert with a *'K'*, of course," Knorbert explained.

"OK Knorbert."

"No, no, no," Knorbert snorted. "Not *O-K* Knorbert. Just Knorbert with a *'K'*. No *'O'*!"

"OK, I see."

"No! No! No!" Knorbert fumed. "No *'O-s'*. No *'I-s'*. No *'C-s'*. Just *'K'*. One *'K'*. Knorbert. Got it?"

"Yes, of course," Knorbert with a *'K'*." Will pressed a finger to his lips to help keep from laughing. "How interesting…and most unusual too."

"Why, thank you, Will. I am named after my great-great-great uncle, thrice removed."

"You're welcome, Knorbert. Great, great, great, thrice removed, you say. I don't understand all this second and third uncle or cousin thing, once or twice removed. I find it confusing. It's all a bit beyond me."

"Beyond, indeed," Knorbert shook his head slowly side to side as he looked Will up and down again. "You do look like you are from beyond somewhere, but from beyond where?"

"Exactly. I *am* from beyond somewhere, beyond here. I don't know where I am. That's what I was hoping you could help me with. Where am I, Knorbert?"

The Riddle of Riddles

"You are," Knorbert replied with the briefest of shrugs and a single arched eyebrow, "here. Where did you think you were? You are certainly not *there*," and Knorbert giggled out loud.

"But, what I mean is, where is here? What place is this?"

"You are in the Realm of Reflection."

"In the Realm of Reflection? I don't understand. Just where, exactly, is this Realm of Reflection that you're talking about?"

"The Realm of Reflection is exactly on the interface between Inner Space and Outer Space."

"Whoa. Not so fast. Where is my room? Uh… that is, where is Earth? I mean…uh…where is Reality?" Will stumbled over his ideas as well as his words.

"Reality is the very next dimension in the direction of Outer space. Do you know it?"

"Know it? I'm from Reality. I'm real. I mean, I think I am…therefore I am…I think."

"*Tsssk, tsssk, tsssk*. Such logic…but what should I expect from a mere figment of my actualization."

"Me, a figment of your…" Will laughed out loud, "your…your what?"

"A figment of my actualization. Why?"

"This is absurd," Will threw up his hands. "You are the *figment*—the figment of my imagination."

"Imagination? Do you know it too?"

"Of course I know imagination. You're part of my imagination. This whole thing is imagination."

"Not quite. This is the Realm of Reflection, as I mentioned. Imagination is the next dimension in the direction of Inner Space. But why do you look so perplexed?"

"Well, you must admit that this is kind of strange."

"Oh me, oh my, yes. I do agree with you about that."

"Look, Knorbert, maybe you can help me. I'm here because I am on a quest. I am looking for the answer to a riddle, The Riddle of Riddles to be exact, and I was wondering if,

Chapter 4 - Knorbert

perhaps—just maybe—you might be able to help me. Maybe you have some idea as to what the answer to The Riddle of Riddles might be, or where I might find it, or what direction I should go, or . . ."

Knorbert went wide-eyed. "UAMIMAU! You must tell me more! Please. I just love riddles. In fact, I consider myself to be something of an expert on the matter, a riddle master if you will. A quest. Riddles. How exciting! Come along. Let us go inside. I will fix us some bits and bytes to eat, and you can tell me all about this riddle of yours." Knorbert turned and wobbled off toward his cabin.

That was when Will noticed that Knorbert had no knees. He walked with a stiff-legged gait, wagging from side to side like a metronome.

It was not at all like Will to laugh at anyone, ever, but this was just too much. In all fairness, Will tried not to laugh. It was just that the more he tried not to laugh, the more the pressure built up until—finally—with a most unkind snort, and then with great booms, the laughter poured out of him like an avalanche of boulders on a hollow mountain.

Knorbert looked about, confused. "What? What?" he asked, drawing his chin down to his chest. "Why do you laugh?"

"I'm sorry," Will explained between laughs and gasps for breath. "I'm sorry, Knorbert. I didn't mean to laugh. It's just that, well, you must admit that you *are* a most unusual looking character."

"Me? Me unusual looking? How about you? I mean, I have been extremely polite until now. I have maintained *all* my Knothead manners but...but how about you...*pinhead*! You, with a head so tiny it could not possibly hold enough brains to possess a modicum of good manners, to say nothing of logic; you with ears so tinny they *obviously* cannot appreciate good music; you...you with those...collapsible legs!" Knorbert pointed at Will's knees.

Will chuckled. He watched as Knorbert huffed and puffed, and slowly regained his composure.

The Riddle of Riddles

"Oh me, oh my, I am so sorry, Will. I hope I have not offended you. I did not mean to lose my temper. Usually I am quite unflappable and most polite. All Knotheads are, all the time. I did not mean to call you names or make fun of you like that. I suppose it must be hard being a keek. Believe me, I know. I have been called a keek myself."

"I'm sorry too, Knorbert. I didn't mean to insult you either, but I'm not really a freak or a geek, or…keek, as you called us. Where I come from, we all have these. We call them knees," and he demonstrated with a deep knee bend.

"Knees. Yes, quite, but what makes you think that I was referring to your knees?'

Will looked at Knorbert, and Knorbert at Will.

Simultaneously, both burst out laughing, and then, surprised by their coincidental laughter, both stopped just as quickly to eye one another suspiciously.

That only caused another round of spontaneous laughter.

A warm feeling flooded Will's body. He felt like he knew Knorbert, had known him his whole life.

"Well, come along now." Knorbert waddled off toward his cabin. "I will fix us something to eat while you tell me all about yourself and this riddle of yours." With that he wobbled up the steps and disappeared inside.

CHAPTER 5 – RIDDLES FOR BREAKFAST

Outside the front door, leaning against the side of the cabin, Will noticed a long hollow reed with holes let into its side. "Is that your musical instrument?"

"Oh my, yes. I have named her Forlorn. Does she not have lovely voice?"

"Uh…yeah, she does…yes, she does, a lovely voice."

While Knorbert was busy fixing breakfast, Will told him about his human world as best he could, finding the subject more difficult to explain than to live.

"But what brings you *here*, and what is all this about a riddle?"

And so it was that Will told Knorbert all about his greedy wish, about his task of answering The Riddle of Riddles, including the consequences if he did not succeed.

Knorbert gasped. "You mean you will…will…*die*?"

"It's even worse than that, Knorbert. I am immortal. If I fail to solve the Riddle, I lose my immortality and die."

"Kockypop! No one is immortal."

"I am."

"And what makes you think so?"

"I was born that way."

"If you were born, that means you must also die."

"Not me."

"Does everyone from your Reality believe that they are immortal?" asked Knorbert.

"I suppose a lot do, but I'm the only one who really is…immortal I mean."

"I do not believe that you are immortal, Will. I think you are just knaive and eggotistical because you are young."

"I'm what?"

The Riddle of Riddles

"You are eggotistical, an eggotistical being from the Realm of Reality, or I should say, the realm of unreality."

Will sighed. "I know what I know."

"And what I know, or rather deduce, is that your presence here verifies Doctor Kneinstein's Theory of Realativity."

"Doctor whose theory of what?" Will squinted his eyes.

"Doctor Kneinstein's Theory of Realativity. He is one of our greatest thinkers." Knorbert raised a finger into the air. "He hypothesized that $i = rt^2$, where imagination (i) equals reality (r) times the speed of thought (t) times itself—that is, 't' squared. Imagining you being here, Will, requires multiplying my speed of thought times my speed of thought again, and then multiplying that against what is real. How else could I have an actualization from Realm of Reality being here in the Realm of Reflection?"

"And what about me?" Will asked, laughing. "Am I actualizing you from my imagination as well?"

"Hmm," said Knorbert. "I will have to ponder that. Could actualization require a negative 't' squared? Hmmm, a negative times a negative becomes a positive. Why, that is positively brilliant, Will. Well done. Perhaps your kind does have some brains packed into those little heads after all. I must learn more about your kind. Please tell me more."

Will snorted, paused, and then resumed his story. He told Knorbert about looking in this book for help before finding himself alone at the edge of a crimson sea at dawn, and all about his encounter with the strange boy who called himself Belvidere.

"Oh me, oh my!" Knorbert's eyes were as wide as a child's astride its first ride. "What an exciting adventure. I do love adventure! That is...I just love *hearing* about adventure. I must admit, though, that the real thing makes me quite nervous."

"Me too." Will slumped back in his chair. "I'm afraid I'm a weakling at heart as well as in body, although if I were as big and strong as you are, I might feel a whole lot more confident about my task."

"Big and strong? You think I am big and strong?"

Chapter 5 – Riddles for Breakfast

"Of course. Why, look at those arms and those hands. How did you ever get such big muscles?"

"It must come from turning over rocks and boulders looking for eggs to eat. These eggs in fact." Knorbert nodded toward the platter he'd set down in front of Will. "Seminal eggs."

Knorbert followed with another platter heaped over with long multicolored strips he called raw factors and then with a basket filled with warm sweetbrains. He poured their cups brim-full with a hot liquid he called synapsecha.

Since Will could not speak very well with his mouth full, it was quite some time before the conversation resumed. Eventually, he pushed his chair back with a contented sigh. "That was delicious. Thank you."

"Oh me, oh my, but you are welcome. I am glad you enjoy Knothead food."

"Just what is a Knothead anyway?" Will asked, wiping his mouth.

"Why I am a Knothead, of course. My kind are called Knotheads."

"And where is the rest of your kind?"

"Well most, except for a few outcasts like me, live in and around the capital city of Sapientiopolis. I do not really like it there though. It is too well organized for my taste, too regulated. Everything always has to be perfect, perfectly geometric, perfectly straight or perfectly square. Everyone in the city marches to the beat of the daily rhythm, always in straight lines, executing perfect right angle turns. I do believe they even think in straight lines, and that is why I live out here."

Knorbert hesitated. He threw a quick furtive glimpse in Will's direction. "To be perfectly honest, Will, I have been banished from Sapientiopolis."

Knorbert got very red in the face. "They…they call me names. They call me egg…**eggcentric**! All my life I have been laughed at by other Knotheads because I was not like them. Eggcentric indeed! So I took to associating with those who were

The Riddle of Riddles

also rejects from society for one reason or another, other keeks, if you will. These associates of mine also live on the fringes of society. Some of them preach the most radical ideas...even..." and he whispered, "Kapitalism."

Knorbert let out a loud sigh. Then he threw back his shoulders. "If they can preach—" he whispered the word again "—Kapitalism, then why can I not invent music? Do you think that makes me eggcentric, Will?"

"No, of course not. Music is cool."

"Kool as in kold?" Knorbert arched an eyebrow. "Is 'kool' bad?"

"No way. Cool is good, excellent, hot."

"How can kool be hot? I do not understand."

"What I mean is that music is magical. Cool is an expression coined by musicians to mean fresh and breezy and, yes, hot, so hot you scarcely dare touch it."

"As hard as I try to understand you, Will, you continue to confuse me. Music *is* magical, but *kool* and *hot*? Dare to touch? I gather that music is not forbidden in Reality."

"Forbidden? Of course not. Music is celebrated where I come from. Why in the world would music be forbidden?"

"It is here. That is one of the reasons I was banished."

"Why would you be banished for playing music?"

"The BGK strictly forbids any experimentation with sound combinations. They fear it will interfere with the normal Knothead thinking process, a process so revered that any variation from the dictated norm is against the law. The BGK considers music an ASCAPist plot to subvert the citizenry by making them tap their toes. Imaging the chaos that could occur should citizens begin swaying and bumping into one another! Catastrophe!"

"Yeah, they might even start dancing."

"Dancing? What is dancing?"

"Dancing is moving in time with the music. It's a lot of fun. We usually dance *together*."

"Fun? Dancing in time with music...and...dancing

Chapter 5 – Riddles for Breakfast

together?" Knorbert said the last word breathlessly. "Those might be the very reasons why music is forbidden."

Knorbert began cleaning up the remains of their breakfast. "Besides," he continued, "most Knotheads are frightened by music, afraid it appeals to a most base part of their nature. It all goes back to the Willi-Nilli legends I suppose."

"Willi-what-i?"

"Not Willi-what-i. Willi-Nilli. Have you never heard of the Willi-Nillies?"

"No, never. What are Willi-Nillies?"

"Willi-Nillies are...well, we have all kinds of legends about the Willi-Nillies. Supposedly a long, long time ago, deep in the Interior, far beyond the safe walls of Sapientiopolis I should add, there lived a brood of simply horrid creatures called Willi-Nillies. There are numerous descriptions of them in our legends. Some say they looked like dragons, some say big cats, while others say they were some kind of enormous bird. They were supposed to have two heads, each on the end of a long neck. They have been variously described as long or short, fat or sleek, colorful or drab, sweet or vicious. One legend even has it that they could change color, that they cried when they were happy, and that they took pleasure in pain. As you can see, contradictions abound."

"Why are you shaking, Knorbert?"

"Am I? Oh me, oh my, I see I am. I am so silly sometimes. As children, we were often told scary stories about Willi-Nillies. I guess I must be remembering how scared I was back then."

"Are these Willi-Nillies really that frightening?"

"No, of course not. They are not even real. They are just a silly stupidstition. It is an involved hoax that has been elaborated with many details. What the legends all do seem to agree on is that Willi-Nillies could fly, fly through the sky at fantastic speeds, totally out of control, of course. By some accounts they had four wings, a set of two on each side. These wings allowed them to hover, fly backwards and upside-down, to spin in place and then

The Riddle of Riddles

dart off in any direction. Did I mention that they were supposed to be blind?"

"No, you didn't," Will replied, eager that the story continue, loving Knorbert's intensity, watching his hands speak with him, enormous butterflies floating on the breaths of his ideas.

"Yes, quite blind. Can you imagine careening through the air at fantastic speeds without being able to see where they were going? I guess that is why there are so many stories of them crashing into one another. When they crashed, it is said, they would ricochet about like so many squarks after a synchronicity collision. Sometimes, however, it is said that they collided with such force that they would actually destroy one another, never to be seen again. There would be a bright flash of light and a thunderous boom. The remaining Willi-Nillies would all cry, their tears falling from the sky. One legend talks of a time when two Willi-Nillies collided with such force that even their next of kin were annihilated. Another story tells of a time to come when an uncontrollable chain reaction of Willi-Nilli collisions will destroy the whole world unless they are tamed in time."

"Where are these Willi-Nillies?" Will asked.

"There are no such things as Willi-Nillies. I told you, Will, this is all just legend, just a silly stupidstition, a fairy tale for our children."

"But what does all this have to do with music?"

"Well, while rocketing around in the skies, a Willi-Nilli was supposed to have emitted a wide array of sounds, sounds capable of driving inane any Knothead who heard them. Some of those sounds were said to be very eerie, while others were said to be very beautiful. I think one reason music is forbidden is that it barkens back to those Willi-Nilli sounds. Their sounds never had any order to them, however, so they could hardly be classified as music, not, at least, in the same sense as the music that I have invented."

Knorbert hesitated. "Since I invented music, does that make me a musician?"

Chapter 5 – Riddles for Breakfast

"Absolutely."

"Does that mean I am 'kool'?"

"You bet, Knorbert. You're one cool cat."

"A kool kat. I like the sound of that." Knorbert smiled. "We have kats here too, Will. They chase glitches."

Will folded his arms. "Do you think you could help me find the answer to The Riddle of Riddles, Knorbert? I'm at a complete loss as to where to even begin looking."

Knorbert finished the dishes and sat back down. "Do not be discouraged, Will. I am sure you will find the answer you are looking for. In fact, I envy such a quest. Riddles are such fun. Would you like to hear one of my favorites?"

"Sure," Will shrugged. "Why not?"

"What number, other than zero and infinity, yields the same result when it is either added to itself or multiplied by itself?"

There was a long silence

"Well," Knorbert asked, "what is the answer?"

"One?"

"Oh me, oh my, oh no. Of course not." Knorbert sounded absolutely gleeful, clapping his big hands together. "One plus one equals two, whereas one times one equals one. Here, try another:

The begetter of alpha and the end of omega.
Seen not in any mirror, though I'm seen in every face.
Begetter of allusions, end of every enigma.
I cannot be found in here, though I'm found in every place."

Will shrugged his shoulders. "I have no idea,"

"Not even a guess?" Knorbert drew his chin in to his chest.

"The alphabet?"

"Close but again incorrect. Here, try one more:

Not every riddle is solved by clues.
Some are solved quite simply by spelling.
Tabulate numbers, each line a cue,

The Riddle of Riddles

> *For letters thus found therein dwelling.*
> *To see what you will find so dignified."*

Will puzzled over this last riddle a long while before finally admitting, "You've got me again."

"I told you," Knorbert shouted, clapping his hands rapidly together, louder this time. "I told you. I am a Riddle Master."

"Well, aren't you going to tell me the answers?"

"Oh me, oh my, oh no. Certainly not. They would not then be riddles, would they?"

"Of course they would. They'd still be riddles, but I'd know the answers, too."

"But you do not, do you?"

"No, I do not, and you're not going to tell me are you?"

"Absolutely not. You must solve them by yourself."

"How about The Riddle of Riddles? Would you like to try to solve that one?"

"Sure, Will. Why not? How hard can it be? What is this riddle of yours, this Riddle of Riddles?

"When is the riddle the answer?"

"I have no idea, but I must know the riddle if I am to help you."

"That is the Riddle."

"What is the riddle?"

"When is the riddle the answer?" Will repeated

Knorbert wrinkled his brow.

"The Riddle of Riddles is the question, *'When is the riddle the answer?'*" Will laughed. "I made the same mistake myself, Knorbert. I didn't get it at first."

"Uh...oh, of course. I got that part. I got it. I am just, eh...I am just using my reductive reasoning."

"What kind of reasoning?"

"Reductive. That is when you reduce the elements of the problem to their most basic units and examine each one independently looking for selfsight." Knorbert looked over at Will, smiling proudly. "I told you. I love riddles, and I am very smart."

Chapter 5 – Riddles for Breakfast

"So you say, but don't worry about not getting The Riddle at first. I did the same thing."

"I got it, Will. I did"

"Did you?" But Knorbert was no longer listening. He grew silent and then fell off to muttering quietly to himself.

There was a long pause during which Will leaned forward, his arms on his knees, listening and waiting.

Knorbert's eyes were closed, and he kept stroking his chin. Finally, after a deep sigh, he said, "I do not know, Will. That is a very difficult riddle—either that or it is very simple, so simple I am overlooking the obvious. I am sorry, but I do not know the answer."

Will took a deep breath. "That's OK, Knorbert. Do you have any idea where I could begin looking for the answer?"

"That is going to be very difficult for you," Knorbert replied. "You are a stranger in a strange land, and you do not know your way around."

"That's for sure." Will's voice trailed off.

Silence packed the room, each of them absorbed in thought. Then, suddenly, Will lifted his head. "Knorbert, since you *are* a Riddle Master, and since you said that you envy my quest, why don't you come along to help me?"

"Oh me, oh my, oh no! I could not. I am not the one for adventure. I told you that." Knorbert pushed back his chair and stood up. "Ah, but riddles! I do love the challenge of a good riddle."

Knorbert began pacing back and forth. "I do love riddles," he muttered, "and I am very smart, and I would be of immense help since I know my way around. I could be a guide and, maybe, I could even solve The Riddle of Riddles and become as famous as Syllogius."

"It does sounds like a quite a challenge," Will interjected. "I have no idea who or what a Syllogius is or was, but yes, indeed, we would have a much better chance of success by working together. In fact, I would be honored if you would agree to help me. Will you help me, Knorbert? Please!" Will fell into the deep well of Knorbert's eyes, imploring him.

Knorbert looked down, shifting his weight from foot to foot. "I will do it," he blurted out quite suddenly.

"*Fan*-tastic!" Will jumped to his feet and held out his hand.

Knorbert backed away when he saw Will's outstretched hand.

"What's the matter? " Will asked. "Have I offended you again?"

"Oh me, oh my, oh no. Certainly not. But I do not understand what it is you are doing. Why is your hand stuck out like that?"

"I want to shake hands." He shook his hand at Knorbert. "You know, to kind of seal our partnership."

"Oh me, oh my, oh no. We never touch here. It is prohibited."

"*Touching* is prohibited too?" Will dropped his hand. "You mean you never touch one another, ever?"

"Oh my, never. Of course not. It is quite forbidden. That is why I was so upset when you bumped into me, not that I do not do a forbidden thing now and then, like playing music."

Knorbert tilted his head to one side. "Does your kind touch often?"

"Sure. Lots. We shake hands when we say hello and goodbye or when we agree on something, something like joining together on a special mission. But that's not all. We pat each other on the back too, especially if we accomplish something worthwhile. We even have a special kind of touching when we feel really close to someone. We put our arms around one another and squeeze. We call that hugging. It's quite pleasurable."

"Well, I will be a Willi-Nilli!" Knorbert opened his eyes wide and did not blink. "Hugging, you call it. And it is pleasurable you say? I do not think I would like to ever get that close to someone."

Chapter 5 – Riddles for Breakfast

"You might be surprised. You might get to enjoy it. Come on. Let's shake on it," and with that Will again stuck out his hand. "There's nothing to be afraid of. Come on, try it. It will seal our partnership in the search for the answer to The Riddle of Riddles. Come on."

Knorbert looked down. "Oh me! I do not know." He glanced up shyly, blushing.

Will waited patiently, his arm extended, hand open.

Knorbert's arm started up, then retreated, then started up again, then drew back. "Oh me, oh my, I really do not know. It does look harmless enough, but...but touching?" Then, finally with a deep sigh, he held out his hand. It trembled slightly.

Will took it and squeezed gently, his hand lost in Knorbert's enormous fist. Knorbert, unaware of his own strength, squeezed back.

Will winced. "Congratulations. We are now partners." He retrieved his hand, giving it a quick shake. "That wasn't so bad now, was it?" He flexed the hand a couple of times, making sure that everything was working properly.

"Not at all," Knorbert said looking down at his palm. "I kind of liked it. I like what it stands for, intellectually, of course."

"Of course."

Knorbert turned toward the door. "Wait a parsec while I get some things together, and then we can be on our way."

He grabbed a sackpack and began scurrying about the cabin stuffing it with the oddest objects, including different bits of clothing. "Let me boot up," he said, lacing a pair of well-worn, thick-soled boots onto his enormous feet.

After one last look around, he slipped the sackpack over his shoulders, and stepped outside, closing the door firmly behind them. He smiled as he lifted Forlorn and, with a gentle stroke, slung her over his shoulder.

The sun sat low in the sky. It was still early. Time seemed to be advancing as slowly as Will's progress.

Will waited at the edge of the clearing, anxious to begin,

The Riddle of Riddles

but Knorbert stood on the bottom step, hanging back.

"Let's go," Will urged. "We only have until sundown."

"Until what down?"

"Sundown. We only have until sundown."

"What do you mean sun down?"

"The sun," Will said pointing. "Sundown."

"Oh, you mean Luci, till Lucidown."

"You mean you call your sun Luci?"

"Or you mean that you call our Luci your sun."

"Whatever. It's all just basic English," said Will.

"What is basic English?"

"This language we are speaking, of course."

"The language we are speaking is BASIC, not English."

"What?"

"BASIC is our language. I do not understand this English of which you speak."

"Well we are communicating." Will turned his palms upward and raised his shoulders.

"BASICALLY!" Knorbert emphasized. "But then again there is no reason not to suspect that we would not, after all, have different words for the same idea."

"Right, different words for the same ideas."

"Right."

"So what are we waiting for?" Will asked.

"Nothing really. I was just wondering if I might have forgotten something."

"What?"

"I do not know…probably not."

Still Knorbert did not leave the bottom step. "How do we know that we will succeed?"

"We don't, but how do we know that we won't succeed?"

Knorbert remained on the bottom step. "We do not know that, nor do we know that we will…succeed, I mean."

"Right. We have a chance to either do, and possibly succeed, or not do, knowing we never will succeed. Since I

Chapter 5 – Riddles for Breakfast

already know what my outcome will be if I don't succeed, I'll go with the doing. What's your choice? Are you staying or are you coming?"

There was another pause, this one longer.

"Oh me, oh my, Will, I guess I am just using any alibi I can. I am sorry. I guess I will never know everything for sure always."

"I'd be happy just to know anything for sure," said Will.

"I can certainly believe that."

"So *Guide*, are you coming?"

Knorbert took a deep breath. "Of course! Whatever did you think?"

"I was starting to wonder." Will turned, and looked down the mostly indistinct path that led off from Knorbert's cabin. "Where do we start?"

"From where else does one start but from where one is? It certainly is a good thing I decided to come along."

Will shook his head.

"Why do you shake your head? Come along now. Do not dawdle! We have a riddle to answer." With that, he stepped off the bottom tread.

CHAPTER 6 – CHOICES

Knorbert led them out of the clearing, through a small, narrow gate. Those who could find it would certainly be few.

They turned right, out onto an indistinct pathway that was really no pathway at all. Knorbert stepped forward with one leg, and when that foot was firmly planted, he pivoted, stretching his other leg forward until he could plant it firmly. He moved along quite deliberately, but it was a slow go.

Will followed behind as Knorbert wobbled forward side to side. Still, it was not long before they broke out onto a narrow trail fraught with new growths of knoncertainty weeds that disappeared back into the Wild Wood on either side. Thick branches of knignorance trees spread overhead, blocking out most of the light.

Knorbert stopped and rummaged about in his sackpack before turning to Will with a bonnet in his outstretched hand. "Here, put this on." Will noticed that Knorbert had a similar bonnet for himself.

"What's this?"

"A bonnet, of course."

Will took a deep breath. "I can see that."

"Then why did you ask?"

"What I meant was—why must I wear a bonnet? It's much too big for me."

"If that is what you meant, that is what you should have said rather than have me try to guess what is really on your mind. I may be a genius, but I am not a mind reader, Will."

Knorbert placed the bonnet precariously atop his big head. "We must wear bonnets because everyone traveling in this period is required to wear one. It is Knothead law. We must all wear the required gray tunic wherever we go, but hat styles change with each period. We do not want to be caught without them, as we are a strange enough looking pair as it is."

Chapter 6 - Choices

"I'll say." Will tentatively donned the bonnet, which was, in fact, much too big for him. "What did you mean when you said this period? Is a period a time or a place?"

"Both."

"What's that?" Will asked, the bonnet having fallen down over his ears so he could barely hear.

"I said both. A period applies to both time and space."

"I see," said Will who was having a great deal of difficulty seeing as well as hearing, since the bonnet kept falling down over his eyes as well as his ears.

The trail they were following was so narrow that Will was forced to walk behind Knorbert. The Wild Wood there was full of bright pink and blue dollidill flowers and rattle sticks. On either side, the heavy vegetation grew in such abundance that they could scarcely see beyond its surface.

Still the path, though not wide, became clear enough that the going was fairly easy. Here and there they got tripped up by the roots of konfuzion bushes, and occasionally they came upon large knotknowable logs laying across their path, fallen by the passing of some previous storm. Knorbert easily guided them clear of most obstacles.

Before long, they came to a crossroad. Numerous routes led off in a bewildering number of directions. Some were straight and narrow, some wide and meandering. Some led laser-like for as far as the eye could see, before disappearing into the distant future. Others twisted and turned, giving only glimpses, here and there, of what was ahead. Some were so overgrown with disuse that it was near impossible to get even a glimmer of what lay beyond. The newer, well-worn paths were rather featureless.

Without hesitating, Knorbert marched right up to the junction. First, he stared intently down each leg of the numerous forks. Then he looked them all over again, and then a third time. Finally, standing dead center at the junction, he began wobbling back and forth, wobbling faster and faster, back and forth, faster and faster, in smaller and smaller arcs until, finally, he came to a

The Riddle of Riddles

shuddering halt and clicked a turn in the direction of his choice.

He then slipped off the sackpack, rummaged about again and came up offering Will a peaked cap. "Here, change hats."

"Are we entering a different period?"

"Oh me, oh my, yes. Yes, we are. I am happy to see you are using your brain, Will."

Knorbert started off down the path he had chosen. Will caught him in three giant steps, falling in close behind.

"Where are we going?" he asked.

Knorbert turned his head, shook it, and said, "To find the answer to The Riddle of Riddles, right?"

"Uh…right…" Will swallowed the words.

The Wild Wood had receded into the near distance with fields of grasses now flanking their path. Baseball berries thrived here alongside skateboards of skallywaggies.

When they reached the next junction Knorbert stared intently down the length of each of the many legs. He wobbled back and forth, faster and faster, in smaller and smaller oscillations, until he clicked another turn.

Knorbert removed his peaked cap and returned it to the sackpack along with Will's. This time he was undecided, looking at both a helmet and a beanie. Finally, he donned a beanie, gave one to Will, and quickly wobbled off.

"This way, huh," said Will.

Knorbert shot him a look. Will did not say another word.

Ruts soon appeared in the trail, and the heavy growth pressed in on them once again. A stand of taller testing trees, from whose branches hung konfounding koans, leaned in overhead. harvard kumbuyahs grew here alongside berkeley knihilisty kranks, struggling for a share of light with a scrappy undergrowth of kerouack kurrents that wrapped around their trunks, climbing to the highest branches. Sacred kreeds and ancestral kustoms littered the path, trampled by the heavy footfalls of previous common traffic.

They moved on slowly, so slowly that time hung on Will

Chapter 6 - Choices

as thick and heavy as a sodden, woolen overcoat. It took hours and hours to get just this far. Will's only solace was that the sun was moving as slowly as they were.

Will peeked around Knorbert to see where they were going, and Knorbert shot him another look.

"I sure wish we didn't have to go so slowly," Will said more to himself than aloud.

"What was that? Did you say slow? Slow? Did you?" Knorbert's indignity grew like a politician caught in a lie, his face white and still, one cheek ticking.

"I was just talking to myself, Knorbert. Besides, slow go is better than no go."

"Oh me!" Knorbert's voice quavered. "Slow go he says, slow go!" And with that Knorbert began waddling along as fast as his no-kneed legs could wobble him.

It took all Will's power to keep from laughing out loud at this charliechaplinesque spectacle, but he did not have to bite his lip for long because Knorbert was soon sweating profusely and sucking for air. Shortly thereafter, he stopped and made a great show of retying the laces on both of his boots. When they resumed their journey, Knorbert was again back down to his normal speed, suffering no apparent loss of dignity, with Will still trailing behind, impatient but amused.

The trail eventually widened enough for them to walk abreast, and Will stepped up alongside Knorbert. "How far do you think we've come?"

"Oh, I would say about one third of a pardew so far."

"How far's a pardew?"

"A pardew is one third of a pardah." Knorbert paused. "I keep forgetting that our dimensions are so different. Would you like to learn about our system?"

"Oh yes, please."

"A doodah lasts from Lucirise to Lucirest. A pardah is one thirty-third of a doodah, with thirty-three pardews in every pardah and thirty-three parsnips in every pardew. Got that so far?" He

The Riddle of Riddles

looked over at Will.

"Hmm, let's see," Will replied. "Your day is one doodah long and is divided into thirty-three pardahs. That's kind of like our hours, though we have twelve of those. Yes, I'm beginning to understand. And each pardah is made up of thirty-three pardews, which are like our minutes—though we have sixty of those—and each pardew consists of thirty-three parsnips, which are like our seconds, of which we also have sixty."

"Very good," Knorbert exclaimed, and he actually skipped a step. "And I am glad to learn your system as well: seconds, minutes, hours and days—quite an accomplishment for a species of creatures with such small heads."

"You know, Knorbert," Will cocked his head to one side, "you're very insulting when you get so conceited. Did it ever occur to you that maybe, just maybe, I'm just as smart as you are and that my culture is just as good, maybe better, than yours?"

"Oh me, oh, my, of course not. That would be quite impossible. Please understand me, Will. I am not trying to be insulting at all. It is just that it is a proven fact that the larger the head, the more brains, and the more brains, the more intelligence. It is as simple as that. And, once again, not to be insulting, I ask you to note the size of your head. Your head, Will, is infinitesimal compared to mine."

"Infinitesimal…" Will choked. "Infinitesimal?"

"Infinitesimal means tiny, as in…"

"I know what infinitesimal means, Knorbert. It means insignificant, inconsequential and…it's insulting."

"Oh me, oh my, Will. As I said, it is not my intention to insult you. I am merely relating facts to you. If you are insulted, you are insulted by facts—not by me."

"And you're sure about all of this, all of these facts, I mean?"

"Positive."

"Oh yeah, if it's as simple as that, how come when I asked you how far we had come, you answered me in terms of time

Chapter 6 - Choices

rather than distance? Could it be, just maybe, that the reason is because you are so *slow* you *have* to talk in terms of time rather than distance?"

"Oh my." Knorbert frowned. "I see I have offended you. It was quite unintentional. I assure you. But I must tell you that I did answer you in terms of distance. You see, Will, a doodah and all the other smaller increments I have already explained, are measurements of distance as well as time. A doodah is the average distance a Knothead can travel from Lucirise to Lucirest over a clear and level terrain. It is also called a Morae."

"A Morae?"

"Yes, it is quite simple, you see."

"That doesn't seem so simple to me. I mean, using the same word as a measure of both time and distance seems more confusing, not less. What does one have to do with the other? It does not make any sense."

"It makes perfect sense if you think about it. They are related, triplets you might say, along with their third brother, speed. But," and here he sighed, "I do not want to confuse you. That is probably beyond human comprehension."

"Oh yeah!" Will's voice rose. "Well, our system is a lot better than your system, if you ask me. We have days, hours, minutes and seconds for time, and miles or kilometers for distance."

"Miles or kilometers for distance?" Knorbert interrupted. "Which is it?"

"Both."

"Both indeed, just like space and time are related."

"No, no! You don't understand. You see, miles are one system of measuring distance, and kilometers are another system."

"Oh my, systems within systems. *Tsssk, tsssk, tsssk*! That does not seem so simple to me. Quite the opposite. Quite complicated. Can you measure miles by kilometers?"

"Of course, you simply convert one to the other."

"Let me get this straight," Knorbert began. "First, you

The Riddle of Riddles

have two different systems—one for time and one for distance. Now, within your distance system, you have two separate systems—miles and/or kilometers. To use either of these systems requires a conversion from one system to the other system and vice versa, providing, of course, that we are dealing with distance and distance only. If we are dealing with time, we use only the other system. Am I correct so far?"

"Oh never mind," Will snarled. "I know exactly what I mean, but you are confusing me."

"Never mind a mind that does not mind its mind," Knorbert chided. "But please explain. I would like to understand."

"You don't want to understand. You just want to feel superior, and I wouldn't feel so superior if I were you. Any culture that calls their seconds *parsnips*, which, where I come from, are vegetables—and horrid tasting ones at that—can't be all that smart."

"My, oh my! Are we not testy?" Knorbert said, looking down his long nose. "Time, distance, and vegetables, all related. What a strange culture."

"Oh, you make me so mad sometimes, Knorbert," Will growled from between clenched teeth. "You're so...so...so superior!"

"Yes, you mentioned that before, Will. Thank you. I am genuinely honored."

"I didn't mean it as a compliment. At least where I come from a parsnip's a vegetable and amore is love."

"Love?" Knorbert asked. "What is love?"

"That figures." Will barked a short laugh. "You seem to know everything about everything, but when it comes to the most important thing of all, love, you're as dumb as...as a parsnip!"

"Well, if you cannot explain what love is, I do not suppose you really understand that either."

"Oh, I understand love all right, Knorbert. It has a lot to do with touching—touching inside and out—but I don't suppose you'd understand anything about that."

Chapter 6 - Choices

"That is ridiculous!" Knorbert trumpeted, drawing himself up to his full height. "How can you possibly touch someone inside? That is impossible."

"Not as impossible as you, Knorbert. It's really very simple. You begin by touching someone outside—handshakes, pats on the back, hugs. You'll soon discover that there is an inside touching that accompanies these actions. Oh, it's a light touch to begin with—light enough to be overlooked at first. But once it is recognized, it becomes so overwhelming that one wonders how it could ever have gone unnoticed."

"You are just talking nonsense now. Love? Touching inside? It all sounds like mumbo-jumbo to me. Hah! Of course, one of your culture's silly stupidstitions. A touch so light it overwhelms! Bah! That is ridiculous."

"You'd better watch out, Knorbert. You might wind up believing in love."

"Never!"

"Never say never 'cause you never know," Will chided with several wags of his finger.

CHAPTER 7 – DETOURS AND SHORTCUTS

When they arrived at the next crossroads, Knorbert repeated his ritual: the looks, the wobbling, the choice.

"Here," said Knorbert. This time he swapped the beanie for the helmet he had not chosen earlier. "This period requires either a beanie or a helmet. They are interchangeable, but necessary, depending on conditions."

"What conditions?"

"Whether our surroundings are peaceful or might become hostile."

"Hostile?" Will squeaked. He stuffed the helmet onto his head.

Knorbert slipped the sackpack over his shoulders, and took another long look down the path he had selected.

Will looked down the path, and then up at Knorbert. "How do you decide which path to take when you get to each junction," he asked. "Do you recognize familiar paths and take them because you already know where they will take us?"

"Well, I know our goal and the general direction to go to get there, but, no, I have never been down these roads before. They constantly change over time anyway. I weigh many factors in making my decisions such as the direction each path takes, or seems to take, any obstacles I can see, or that may be anticipated in the foreseeable future, whether there are outright dangers or pitfalls. It involves hard, conscious decision-making."

"But if you know the destination, isn't the route already predetermined?"

"Of course not. There are many routes we could take. Some are roundabout and cause unwanted delays. Others may be more direct, but have no end. With some, the risks are greater than with others. Some roads are smooth and scenic, but all roads

Chapter 7 –Detours and Shortcuts

contain obstacles, some more than others."

"So how do you decide?"

"I am not really sure, Will." Knorbert hesitated. "I just have trust."

"Trust in what?"

"Did a kninquery bug just bite you, Will?"

"Nothing bit me, Knorbert. I'm just curious, that's all. I was just wondering what you trust in."

"I trust in myself and my instincts, my inklings." And without further comment, Knorbert hastily waddled off.

His sudden departure caught Will unaware. Will had taken a step down the path that he thought Knorbert had selected, only to realize that Knorbert had decided on an alternate route. Will spun around, and hurried after him.

Will noticed that much of the territory through which they were passing looked vaguely familiar. It was not so much that he knew he had been here before as it was that he recognized, somehow, that he had to pass by these landmarks, landmarks that were vague yet, somehow, anticipated. He glanced over at Knorbert. Perhaps this was the inkling that Knorbert had referred to.

The territory they now travelled through threatened with rifles of blood-red targetwood and explosions of spineapple grenade blossoms. Pungent knuclear ploomes hung overhead.

Will started feeling nervous. He glanced over toward Knorbert again, but Knorbert was no longer beside him. He stopped and turned.

Several steps back Knorbert stood staring at a sign that read *DETOUR* with an arrow indicating the direction.

"We take this detour," Knorbert said. "Detours must be expected, though we can never be sure where they might take us."

"Then why take the detour?"

"Because the sign says we must," Knorbert stated matter-of-factly. "Authority must be making some sort of repairs, needed or not, along this route."

The Riddle of Riddles

He fished around in the sackpack. "Here, put this on." He offered Will a gray fedora, took Will's helmet, and stashed it along with his own.

"We had better wear these. I am not sure through what periods we may be traveling, but these are usually accepted in most of them. They are kind of like a universal uniform that is often, though not necessarily, accompanied by black wing-tip shoes." He snapped his brim in place and tottered off.

"What's all this with hats anyway?" Will asked with a quick hop, step and a jump that brought him up alongside Knorbert.

"I told you. It is the law. If we get caught without the proper attire, we are subject to detainment, and detainment means delay, and we do not want that now, do we?"

"No, of course not, but who is going to stop us? We haven't seen anyone since we set out."

"Any agent of the BGK, that is who."

"The what?"

"The BGK. The Bureau of Government Knoses. We must always be on guard. They are everywhere. Just when you least expect it, there you will find them. They are especially suspicious of anyone or anything that is out of the ordinary. Authority does not allow any variation from the norm greater than twice the root-mean-square deviation. The BGK is tasked with the responsibility of youthanazing all such deviants, and I am afraid we both deviate far beyond their allowable limits. It is best if we blend in the best we can."

"Youthanazing?" Will asked.

"Yes, they erase all memories, reverting your mind to that of a child with no original thoughts."

"Yikes! And what about…" Will stopped himself.

After a moment, Knorbert asked, "Yes, you were saying?"

"Nothing, just a thought," Will replied.

Variation from the norm? Root-mean-square? Will shook his head and then nodded. He continued nodding until he shook

Chapter 7 –Detours and Shortcuts

his head again. Just when he thought that he understood what Knorbert meant, he realized that he did not understand him at all.

"I say, Will. What is wrong with your head? You shake it, then nod it and then shake it again. Are you all right?"

"Yeah, I'm fine." Knorbert continued confusing him. Whether he did it on purpose, or not, Will was unsure, and he certainly was not about to ask.

Soon they came to another detour which led to yet another. The road narrowed, and Will was forced to trail behind Knorbert once again. The landscape no longer looked the slightest bit familiar. Detour after detour shunted them first this way, then that, until Will lost all sense of direction.

"Do you have any idea where we are, Knorbert?"

"Yes, I am familiar with this area, but I am tired of all these detours. I am beginning to wonder if Authority is purposely taking us out of our way. Authority says that they mean well, but Authority's concerns about the public's welfare are too often self-serving, and often wrong. When they insist that they know best, become suspicious. What do you think about taking a shortcut?"

"A shortcut?"

"Yes, I like taking shortcuts if I can."

"I thought there were no such thing as a real shortcut, that shortcuts were lazy attempts to avoid the usual difficulties that lie ahead."

"I have heard that too, Will, but those are the sentiments of the unimaginative or fearful. Knowing when and how to take a shortcut comes with calculated daring, and from past trial and error," Knorbert chuckled, "usually more error. Someday you will realize just how lucky you are that I decided to come along."

Will glanced left and then right. "I don't see any trails."

"Follow me." Knorbert gestured with his head. He led them off the road, over a slight incline, and then down a gentle decline onto a nearby meadow.

The meadow was covered with light skirt grazzes that

The Riddle of Riddles

came up to Will's knees. It was wide, and dotted here and there with gaggles of biddy trees, clumped together as though sharing the daily gossip. The light breeze through their leaves sounded much like whisperings.

Gradually, the skirt grazzes grew higher and higher until Will could no longer see over their tops. Abruptly and without warning, they came up against a heavy growth of scrambles and concintina bushes, thick with sharp, crescent-shaped, purple thorqs. Knorbert led them along the length of the forbidding hedge, searching for a passageway. Eventually, he found a narrow break through which they were able to squeeze without getting scratched.

On the other side was a dense thicket of overgrowth and undersnags. There was no real path—just narrow passageways between the scrub. They followed these twists and turns as best they could, as the growth became thicker and wilder. Soon they could no longer stand upright, and shortly thereafter, they had to crawl, Knorbert on his belly, dragging himself along.

"Ouch!" Knorbert yelled, a large thorq stuck through his tunic, pricking his shoulder. "Will, I'm stuck. Can you help me?"

Will crawled as close as he could, reached over and unhooked Knorbert. Then he rolled to his back. "Whew," he breathed, "some shortcut. We're not making much progress."

"We are all right. Come on. We will push on. This thicket will end sooner or later." Raising himself up on his elbows, Knorbert resumed pulling himself forward.

"Let's hope it's more sooner and less later," Will grunted.

"Trust me, Will. This shortcut might be difficult but it is a lot shorter than bureaucratic meanderings."

"I do admire your determination, Knorbert. Once you commit yourself to an endeavor, you certainly do follow through."

"Thanks," Knorbert breathed. "It takes commitment to be eggcentric."

Will was not sure whether Knorbert snorted or laughed.

Innumerable times they had to free one another from the

Chapter 7 –Detours and Shortcuts

snags that continued impeding their progress. Will lost track of time. Sweat burned both his eyes and the scratches from the thorqs. They seemed to crawl forward for pardahs and pardahs and pardahs.

CHAPTER 8 – BOGS OF DISCOURAGEMENT

Mercifully, their efforts paid off and the thicket ended as abruptly as it had begun. Soon they were pulling themselves beyond the reach of the telling thorqs out into a dark, dank wood.

Too-tall trees pressed in, their intertwining leaves playing peek-a-boo with the sunlight high above. There was little brush, choked off as it was by the heavy fall of leaves that tapestried the sloping terrain. The wood did not look very inviting, but at least it was an improvement over the thicket of snags they had just succeeded in overcoming.

"That was some shortcut!" Will wheezed, breathing deeply.

"Shortcuts are usually difficult."

"I thought shortcuts would be easy."

"Not initially. The first time you take a new shortcut you have to expect a thorq or two. Shortcuts are difficult to find and explore, but once one Knothead discovers a shortcut," Knorbert shrugged, "you can be sure that other Knotheads will soon follow. Then the way becomes well-worn and passage becomes easier."

"Has it saved us any time?"

Knorbert looked up, but the heavy growth of trees prevented any real glimpse of the sky. "I cannot see Luci so it is hard to tell what time it is."

"Does anybody ever really know what time it is?" Will asked.

"Of course." Knorbert jerked back his head, and looked over at Will. "Our clock tower in Sapientiopolis keeps exact time, self-correcting in fact, constantly adjusting kosmic time to the nearest knanoknanoknanoparsnip governed by Syllogius' Percipient Precessional Prognosticator."

"This Syllogius fellow sounds quite remarkable."

Chapter 8 – Bogs of Discouragement

"He most certainly is," Knorbert emphasized with a firm nod of his big head. "Come on," and he set off into the soggy wood.

As they moved down the sloping terrain, the air began to take on the musty odor of rot. Even the trees had trouble standing here as the footing grew softer and moister. Logs had fallen every which way, forcing them to climb up and over, further slowing their progress.

"Oh me!" Knorbert cried, stopping suddenly to grab hold of a nearby branch. "Watch out, Will. It is almost too soft to even stand here."

"I know," Will yelled back. "I almost lost a shoe in the muck."

They had come upon the beginnings of several large bogs. Knorbert picked up a pokey stick and began probing the ground. Will found another and did the same. Like blind men, they probed the bogs' edges, feeling their way.

"Watch out for quicksend," Knorbert warned. "One wrong, wayward step and you are sucked down into anonymity."

"There must be a way across to the other side," said Will. "Perhaps a tree trunk or a fallen log."

There were, in fact, many, but they bypassed them all, Knorbert commenting about this one's lack of length or that one's lack of strength.

Deeper and deeper into the dank wood they moved.

"They will never succeed," a deep, gruff voice said.

"What did you say?" asked Will.

"I did not say anything. I thought you said something."

"Of course not. They cannot possibly prevail," an unfamiliar voice said from somewhere behind them.

Will turned. They were in a grove of ravaged and gnarled old trees. Each tree was twisted and bent as though it had carried some massive weight all its life. Its broken and leafless branches poked crookedly toward the sky like so many accusing fingers, accusing, perhaps, a once friendly environment with betrayal. A cold wind ran over them unconcernedly, whistling as it went. Will shivered.

"Why do they bother?" a hoarse voice asked from the vicinity of one of the cold gray trunks.

"They must enjoy punishment," another chilling voice croaked.

Will peered closer at the surrounding trees and saw that each tree-trunk had etched upon it the long, thin face of some sad old Knothead. They were drawn-out-faces with trapped eyes, their chins resting on the cold, damp earth at their mangled roots, roots that resembled feet stuck in muck.

"They will never succeed," said a guttural voice in a most discouraging tone.

"Who are they trying to fool?" asked another in tones bleak enough to dishearten even the most optimistic.

"How can they hope to prevail where even we have failed?" scoffed a tree bent so far over its back creaked with every word.

Will drew back his head and looked over at them. "Who are you, and why are you all so gloomy?"

The trees completely ignored him, continuing the conversation.

"That thicket of snags delayed them too much," said one of the bigger trees, its chin never leaving the ground as it spoke.

"It is their own fault, thinking they could take a shortcut," jeered another out of its thin, pinched face.

"What's wrong with you?" Will asked. "Why are you all so...so negative?"

"Yes, it was that impatient shortcut that did them in," growled the tree right in front of them, quite ignoring Will. "They are much too sure of themselves."

"There's no such thing as a real shortcut. It's so much easier to just give up," came another throaty, cracked groan.

"Yes, they should just give up," rattled one with blood-shot eyes. "They must know they cannot succeed."

Chapter 8 – Bogs of Discouragement

"*Give up*? Never!" snapped Will. "We will not be so easily discouraged, especially by...by...***deadwood***! We will push on and leave you here...leave you here to rot."

A mocking laugh died in his throat as a herd of grunting and snorting Worry-Wart hogs broke out of the growth between the too-tall trees. The lead boar and several of the other large, hairy beasts spied Will and Knorbert and charged directly at them, their tusked snouts close to the ground, white foam flecking their jowls.

Their large heads, long curved tusks, and beady yellow eyes struck such terror into Knorbert's heart that he took off with a speed that, had he been clocked, would, in all probability, have set a new Knothead land speed record. Will, knees pumping, was by him in a parsnip.

"Here Knorbert, over here!"

Will had found a mighty kismet tree stretched across the bog to a step of land on the other side. It was so overburdened by change-for-change-sake weeds and tradition-strangling creepers that the root system of its once uncompromising stance had given way. It now lay fallen and obsolete, but it provided the bridge they needed.

Will quickly scrambled up its side and turned to help Knorbert, but he need not have bothered, for with surprising agility, Knorbert caught hold of an overhanging branch and swung himself up onto the log next to Will.

Hurriedly, they sidestepped along the fallen log toward the other side of the desolate swamp, leaving the ugly anxiety of their pursuers behind. The Worry-Wart hogs squealed and snorted, their snouts plowing the soggy soil in frustration.

Upon reaching the far side, they found themselves on higher, drier ground.

"What could possibly be next?" Will stepped off the log, shaking his head.

"Oh me, oh my, I...well...I never anticipated that...to be honest, I never calculated on running into..." Knorbert's voice trailed off.

"Do you know where we are?"

"Well...kind of, I mean, not exactly, but I have a good idea of where we are approximately."

"Oh great!" Will barked, plugging his eyes into Knorbert's. "Approximately? What's the matter, no more positives? Does this mean we are going to find an approximate answer to the Riddle too?"

Knorbert looked so unhappy that Will instantly regretted his words. "I'm sorry, Knorbert," he said, his voice softer. "I'm just getting impatient, that's all. Do you have any idea where we are?"

"Well, if I could catch a glimpse of Luci, I think I would be able to get us pointed in the right direction again. I am very good at figuring these things out, as you well know."

"Do I?" Will looked away, afraid that Knorbert would see the doubt in his eyes. Did Knorbert really know what he was doing?

"Let me see. We left the path..." Knorbert talked softly to himself. He looked up now and again. Then he looked off through the trees, first in this direction, then that. Occasionally, he threw back his head and closed his eyes, muttering all the time to himself as though lost in some lengthy calculation.

"According to my reckonings, the likens on that side of that tree and the apparent position of Luci," he squinted his eyes, peering up though the leafy cover, "and computing the length of time and the distance we have come, I would say...I would say that we need to climb that rise over there." He pointed a finger and immediately started up the incline. Will took a deep breath and trudged after him.

The land rose dramatically, and the footing became more and more solid. The too-tall trees began to thin, more light reaching them, and before long they broke through a light cover of brush out onto a paved road.

Knorbert gave no sign of surprise. "See. I knew we were

Chapter 8 – Bogs of Discouragement

on the right path. Perseverance pays, along with a knose for knowing the right way. We have hit upon the main road to our capital city, Sapientiopolis."

"How do you know?"

"The main road is the only road that is marked this far from the city walls."

"Marked? I don't see any markers."

"They are subminimal markers."

"Subliminal?"

"No, subminimal. "

"What do you mean?"

"Sapientiopolis sits atop a high, flat mensa. All its final approaches are uphill. This road looks like it is going uphill, right?"

"Yes."

"So that must be the direction of Sapientiopolis."

"If you say so."

"Take a couple of steps in that direction, Will, and you will see what I mean by subminimal markers."

Will took a few steps up the hill toward Sapientiopolis. Then he took a couple more. "This is amazing. It actually feels like I'm going downhill."

Will walked back and forth several times. "Going downhill feels like going uphill while uphill feels like going downhill. How is this possible?"

"It is because of the intellectro-magknowtic force generated by Authority to attract the entitled and to induce them to stay."

"Even you?"

"Even me." Knorbert laughed. "I am one eggcentric that Sapientiopolis will come to appreciate someday."

Will looked up so see how late it was. Much to his amazement, the sun did not look to be much higher in the sky than when they had left Knorbert's cabin, but that was impossible, after all the roads traveled, all the detours, the thicket, and the bog.

The Riddle of Riddles

Why, it must have taken them pardahs and pardahs and pardahs, yet the sun was only slightly higher in the sky—unless, of course, it was already very late and the sun was on its way *down*.

"Knorbert, which way is north?"

"North? What is north?"

"North is...uh, north is the direction opposite south."

"What is south?"

"South is the direction... Uh, forget about south for now. North is... north is the direction toward the top."

"That is north?" asked Knorbert, pointing a finger straight up into the sky.

"No, no. Look, what I'm trying to figure out is whether or not the sun, that is Luci, is still rising."

"Why did you not just ask? It is my job to figure these things out. Yes, Luci is still rising. She rises in that direction there, Image," he said pointing a large finger in the direction of the sun. Then he swung his arm in a wide arc across the sky until it pointed in the opposite direction, "and she sets over there in that direction, Object."

"If East is called Image and west is called Object, what do you call the other two directions?"

"Why, Cause and Effect, of course, of course, Cause and Effect, of course."

"Cause and Effect, North and South; Image and Object, East and West. I'm learning."

"Oh my, yes, and I am most proud to witness your progress. Why we just might make a Knothead out of you yet."

"No thanks. I like me just the way I am, if you don't mind."

"No mind," Knorbert smirked.

"You think you're so smart, don't you?"

"Oh my, I am the leader here because I am so smart. I have gotten us this far, have I not? How many times must I tell you that I am smart, though I guess I should not be surprised that your infinitesimal head has forgotten. All Knotheads are smart. It is our greatest attribute."

"It is a great tribute to my patience that I'm still listening to you. If *I* was really smart..." Will stopped, and then suddenly exclaimed, "Look, Knorbert, look! People."

CHAPTER 9 – KNOTHEADS

"Knotheads, you mean…" Knorbert commented slowly.

Up ahead, two Knotheads were wobbling determinedly down a side road toward its intersection with the main road to Sapientiopolis.

"That is strange." Knorbert said quietly. "They appear to be dressed rather oddly. Not one of them is wearing the required gray tunic."

"Are they agents from the Bureau of Government Knoses?"

"No, no. The Knoses always wear blue serge suits with tiny flags in their lapels."

The Knotheads had, by this time, reached the main road and, having executed an exact turn, wobbled off in the direction of Sapientiopolis.

"Of course!" Knorbert exclaimed. "Today is a holiday. How could I have forgotten? The roads will be jammed with Knotheads today."

As he spoke another group of Knotheads moved out from another of the side streets onto the main road. Each Knothead was dressed differently, each in a costume adorned with gaudy arrays of colors.

Knorbert clapped his hands together several times, crying out, "UAMIMAU! What luck!"

"You believe in luck, Knorbert?"

"Oh me, oh my, oh no, of course not. It is merely an expression. All Knotheads know luck is merely the fortuitous confluence of unpredictable events in a manner that seems to bode well for the one experiencing said events."

"Whatever that means." Will shook his head.

"What that means, my good human, is that we conduct our mission on a day unlike any other day—a holiday. Please listen

Chapter 9 - Knotheads

closely. Everyone will be going to the city for the festivities. There will be crowds of Knotheads all in costume, the crazier the costume the better. We will never be noticed, and so, we will no longer need these." He returned their fedoras to his pack.

Then he turned to Will, looking him up and down several times. Finally, after a particularly long look, he said, "I think your appearance will have to do just as it is."

"Gee, thanks. I'm glad you approve."

"It is not a matter of approval or disapproval. It is just that you look strange enough to fit right in just the way you are."

"And what about you?" Will asked, sarcasm lolling deliciously on his tongue.

"I know just what to wear," Knorbert crowed, removing several items from his sackpack. First he took off his boots, and packed them away. Then, giggling all the while, he slipped into a motley coat several sizes too large before placing atop his head a tall, bright red conical cap. "How do I look?"

Will looked Knorbert over from his big fat feet to his multicolored coat and that comical conical cap. He chuckled. "Cool."

"Thank you. I do look kool, do I not?" he said, fluffing out the thin fringe of hair that encircled his head.

Knorbert then turned toward Will with a most serious face. "I need to explain some things to you about our culture before we join the crowds so you do not make some disastrous mistake. First you must keep in mind that all Knothead activity is regimented by law. We travel in single file unless the road is multi-laned, in which case we may use all lanes, provided we stay in lane. There are maximum and minimum velocities permitted, depending upon the road. All signs must be scrupulously obeyed. Changes in direction must always be accompanied by the proper signal. There is an elaborate code that we Knotheads use to indicate our intentions while in motion so we do not bump into one another. I will show you as we go along. Whatever happens, do not bump into anyone."

The Riddle of Riddles

"OK."

"This road has two lanes so we can walk abreast. Just let me hide Forlorn, and we can be on our way." Knorbert carefully stashed his instrument, and off they went.

"Today is Korpus Syllogius Day," Knorbert began, "the single most important holiday on the Knothead calendar. I do not know how I could have forgotten. Today we celebrate Syllogius' birthday."

"Who is this Syllogius anyway?"

"Syllogius is the venerable title we have bestowed on the most renowned of all Knotheads. He is the inventor of Logic, our greatest gift. He is also the Father of Extrasupranumerespecialongologologiation."

Will hooted. "Father of what?"

"Extrasupranumerespecialongologologiation, the happy creation of very, very, very long words. It is one of our favorite pastimes."

"That figures." Will bit his lip. "But tell me, didn't you mean to say that Syllogius *discovered* the principles of logic rather than invented them?"

Knorbert's face went ashen. He looked quickly about to see if there were any Knotheads close enough to have heard Will. "Be careful how you speak. What you just said is heresy. I said *invented*, and I meant *invented*, just like I invented music."

"I am glad you brought that up. I'm not trying to take anything away from you or Syllogius, or from any other inventor or discoverer for that matter, but *invent*, to me, means to devise something from nothing, while *discover* means to find something that already existed though no one knew it. Both are creative, I agree, but you cannot claim to have invented music. What you really were doing was composing a song. What Syllogius did was merely to discover the existence of logic and explain its laws."

"Merely? Discover? Composing?" Knorbert sputtuttuttered loud enough to attract the attention of the pair of Knotheads directly in front of them. They both looked back over

Chapter 9 - Knotheads

their shoulders. Knorbert smiled at them and nodded his head. They smiled back.

"Don't get so excited, Knorbert."

"I am not excited. I do not get excited. Knotheads never get excited. I told you that."

"So you did. Still you must admit that there is a certain logic to my argument."

"Logic? What do you know about Logic? Are you saying that Logic existed before Syllogius?"

"Sure. Why not?"

"And where, pray tell, did it exist? In thin air, I suppose, and Syllogius caught it in a flutterby net, I suppose."

"You don't have to get sarcastic, Knorbert. Why couldn't logic have been an ability of the mind whose principles Syllogius discovered through careful study? His feat is no less remarkable."

"This is absurd. Next thing I know you will be telling me that Willi-Nillies are real too, flashing around in thin air with your foolish ideas about Logic."

"I never said logic flashed around in thin air. Those were your words. As for the Willi-Nillies, I haven't seen any, but that doesn't mean they don't exist. Who knows, maybe I'll be the first to discover one, maybe even catch one in a butterfly net."

"A flutterby net. As for discovering Willi-Nillies, inventing is more likely, invent them flying around in that empty cavern you call your mind." Knorbert huffed, tilting back his head. "And mind the traffic signs. We do not want to attract any undue attention."

There were traffic signs limiting behavior spaced all along the road:

"Speed Limit 33 wpp"
"Keep to the Median"
"Limited Head Room"
"Glitch Crossing"
"One Way Only"
"Kno 'U' Turns."

The Riddle of Riddles

And lots of signs that read:

"Kno Stopping. Kno Standing. Kno Knonsense."

The closer they got to the city the more formal and orderly things became. The road was jimmycarter straight here, all intersections at exactly ninety degrees. Even the crowds, which were by now rather large, were more orderly. Gone was the occasional wavering of some shameless Knothead. All stops, starts and turns were executed in the smartest manner possible, each accompanied with its own proper signal.

Will learned that a right turn was signaled by sticking the right arm straight out to the right. A left turn, just as logically, was indicated by extending the left arm out to the left. Stopping was indicated by throwing both arms down, palms to the rear. To signal that one was about to move forward, both arms were bent at the elbows and pistoned back and forth. Will never noticed a Knothead wobbling backward.

He did notice a long line of Knotheads all dressed in dark gray, proceeding slowly in the opposite direction. They were joined together by a length of rope that was looped around each of their waists. The two Knotheads in front carried an oblong box between them, and at the rear, was a Knothead dressed all in black, carrying a large tether-bound book with guilt-edged pages.

"Paul bearers," Knorbert whispered. "A funeral."

"How sad."

"Nothing sad about it," Knorbert said in a hushed tone. "Knotheads expire when proven wrong. The internal repercussions are such that the cranium cracks."

"I'm so sorry."

"There is nothing to be sorry about. This is all for the best. We must not allow illogical or inaccurate information into our culture. The survival of our species depends on it."

"Maybe if you didn't put so much emphasis on being right all the time, the internal pressure would never get high enough to make you crack."

"What, and let radical ideas into our culture? No, never!

Why, we might wind up just as confused as...confused as you humans. No, ne-ver!"

"Radical ideas like the music you *invented*, Knorbert?"

"Oh me, oh my, oh..." Knorbert stammered.

"Who was that fellow dressed in black back there, the one carrying that large book?" Will asked.

"That was one of our High Priests. They read from the Sacred Text at funerals."

"Was that the Sacred Text he was carrying?"

"Yes. The Sacred Text is the definitive history of Knotheads as far back as it can be traced, and then back even further. It is a compilation of the wisdom of the Ancients. It predicts a time in the future when lies will become accepted as truths and ignorance will become accepted as wisdom. Then war will break out."

"Between who?"

"The proper grammar is 'between *whom*.'" Knorbert looked down his nose at Will before continuing, "War will break out between good and evil, of course."

Will shook his head. "Where I come from, Knorbert, everything is all mixed up. There are few true values left. In fact, the latest fad is that nothing is truly good and nothing is ever evil, except, of course, not embracing this latest fad. I call it a fad, but most everyone else considers it cutting-edge fact."

"Do not let them lead you astray, Will. There most definitely is a right and a wrong, a good and evil. To determine whether an action is good or evil, we must merely remember our own place in the scheme of things. I am not a piece of kosmic debris. I am a living, breathing Knothead. As such, I am Knothead-centric."

"Knothead what?"

"Knothead-centric. By that, I mean that my measure for judging an act is whether it is good, or not, for us Knotheads. As a human, your measure should be whether something is good, or not, for humans."

The Riddle of Riddles

"Knothead-centric?" Will laughed. "Isn't that redundant?"

"Are you at all interested in what I am saying, Will or is this all a big joke to you?"

"Yes, of course I am interested, Knorbert. It's just that sometimes you sound like a preacher."

"You asked me a question, Will, and I answered it. Your problem is that you know I am right, and to you that sounds like preaching."

"Well, I must admit that you do make some sense...occasionally."

"Occasionally, indeed! Of course I make sense. I always make sense because I am *sensible*. That is what the word means. I am a Knothead."

"My sensible, logical, genius Knothead friend."

"So, we are still friends?" Knorbert asked.

"Of course. Friends can disagree and still be friends. We just agree to disagree."

"About what are we disagreeing? I thought we were in agreement. Perhaps you find the fact that I am smarter than are you disagreeable." Knorbert raised his chin, and looked off into the distance.

They had not gone far before the gray-matter mensa on which the city of Sapientiopolis was built came into view just over the top of a nearby hill.

Knotheads packed the road. There was such a near press of them that their progress was reduced to a slow wobble. Quite a few Knotheads pointed at Will, commenting about his remarkable costume. Knorbert dismissed them all with a brief nod and a wave of his hand. Not a single Knothead said anything about Knorbert's costume.

In the distance, Will could hear the steady beat of a drum to which all the Knotheads, and Will, marched.

CHAPTER 10 – SAPIENTIOPOLIS

The road wound around the mensa three times before reaching the city walls, which were high and made of some bone-colored material.

"Why is your city surrounded by such high walls? Afraid of Willi-Nillies?"

"Of course not. These walls were not built for protection. They serve as borders. You know how important borders are. I mean, where would things begin or end without borders?"

"Where indeed?"

Up ahead, a gate came into view. It was circular in shape with a camera's diaphragm-like apparatus controlling the size of the opening and the flow of traffic. It was fully open.

"We have arrived at a most opportune time," Knorbert said as they shuffled slowly forward. "There will be no gate checks today because of the crowds. This gate is one of five. We call them 'wits.' This is called the Wit of Optiluminal Lucidation. That one there," he pointed to another gate in the near distance through which streamed more Knotheads, "is called the Wit of Amplitudal Audiation. Each wit is different. One is even a river. It is called the Somatificat Tactilious Wit."

"Oh you Knotheads and your love of very long words! Why do their names have to be so...so...long and complicated?"

"The use of long words indicates an intelligent mind, Will."

"Or maybe, you Knotheads could just be showing off."

"We do not need to show off our intelligence. It shows itself in everything we do."

"Yeah, like giving long and complicated names to things."

"The name of the gates may be a bit long, but they are quite appropriate."

"Why you don't give each gate a nickname?" Will

The Riddle of Riddles

suggested.

"A knick-kname?"

"Sure. You know, like…uh, let's see…we could call the river, uh, Som-tact, yeah, and this here gate we could call the uh, the Opti-luck gate. Get it?"

Knorbert chuckled. "Yes, yes, I see. I must say, Will, I love the way your curious mind works. Curiouser and curiouser."

They came abreast of the gate and its guards, three Knotheads on either side. Each guard was dressed in a button-down uniform of dark gray with shoulder patches embossed with the symbol of an eye of the same pale blue color as Knotheads' eyes. On their heads they wore tall, black, furry hats that looked so top-heavy Will expected them to topple over at any moment. The guards looked bored and gave neither Will nor Knorbert a glance.

"Did you see their weapons?" Knorbert whispered when they were safely past the guards.

"Yes," Will replied. He had noticed the holsters on the guards' hips in which were handguns whose barrels flared out at the ends like suction cups.

"Those are Magnetomatics. One blast and you lose your memory forever. Quite horrid." Knorbert shivered. "Remember *youthanazia*?"

Will nodded. "Yeah, I remember, but that sure beats the alternative."

"What do you mean?"

"Dying unfulfilled," Will sighed.

"You fear death more than loss of memory?" Knorbert's eyebrows arched, almost meeting the ring of frizzy hair around his head.

"Don't you?"

"No, I do not. Once proven wrong, you are dead, buried, and gone anyway. Wandering about with no memory of even who you are, losing your identity, not recognizing friends and family, having to be cared for by others, who may not care…I would say

Chapter 10 - Sapientiopolis

that is worse."

"Good point, but I'd still rather have my immortality."

"Of course it is a good point." harrumphed Knorbert. He turned his head to look straight ahead. "Mind where you are going," he said, and wobbled forward, muttering under his breath, "Immortality, indeed."

Just inside the walls was a bridge over a scarlet river.

"This is the river I mentioned," Knorbert pointed. "It runs through all the lobes of the city."

Beyond the river and parallel to it, was a wide avenue into which the wits emptied, mingling the crowds. The steady beat of a drum filled the air, all Knotheads stepping in time. Everywhere Will looked, everything was immaculately clean and neat, straight and trim, not a curved line anywhere, much less a squiggle.

CHAPTER 11 – THE KORTEXTIUM

Knorbert led them toward the central city. The streets were wide and straight, gray avenues leading directly to the very brain of the city.

The drum drummed.

The avenue became a wide boulevard divided down the center by a deep furrow. Crowds of Knotheads wobbled along in both directions. On either side, kivy-covered ivory towers protruded up into the air like imperial proboscises .

"We are entering the Kampus Kortextium," said Knorbert. "This is where we maintain all accumulated Knothead knowledge."

In the near distance loomed a massive white building. Between them and it stood a high, shiny monolith shaped like a giant's double-edged sword. It shimmered in the light.

"That is our national monument to Truth." Knorbert nodded in its direction. "It is fashioned after a mythological sword of obscure origin."

"It is very beautiful."

"Would you like to see our Clock Tower?" Knorbert asked.

"Do we really have time?" Will smirked.

"No, I suppose we do not," Knorbert answered, oblivious to Will's small joke. "Still you will get to see the Knontientium." He pointed. "It is that building there. It is situated in the very center of the Kampus Kortextium, and is used to keep us aware of all we do, in fact, know. It is a most useful tool and very beautiful as well."

The Knontientium was a massive building, a perfect pure white cube, surrounded all around by square, white columns, with several sets of wide steps layering each side of the building.

"There will be many celebrants paying their respects to

Chapter 11 – The Kortextium

Syllogius today," Knorbert said in explanation of the many Knotheads heading toward the Knontientium, "but we should have little trouble searching for the information we desire. Most will pay their respects, and then leave for the festivities. Few will be studying today."

As they mounted the wide steps, Will could only marvel at this formidable and exquisite work of architecture built in honor of consciousness. The structure's grandeur instilled a silence of awe. Two massive burnished doors stood open to lines of Knotheads slowly shuffling into the building. The doors were flanked on either side by sculpted shaggy-maned beasts with wings.

"Those are flions." Knorbert pointed at the reclining beasts. "One is called Knous and the other Klogos."

Above the doors was an inscription as high as Knorbert was tall. It read: "IN THE BEGINNING WAS THE WORD."

"Do just what I do," Knorbert cautioned slipping Will some small, hard discs.

Just inside the doors, on either side, were rack upon rack of stubby candles, some lit, some not. Knorbert deposited several of the coins in a large black box beneath the candles, took a taper, and lighting it from a lit candle, transferred the flame to an unlit candle. Will repeated the action.

"We light candles today as a symbol of our dedication to keep the flame of knowledge burning," Knorbert whispered.

Most Knotheads, having lit their candles, returned outside just as Knorbert had predicted.

Inside, the Knontientium was brightly lighted by high clerestory windows that ran the full length of each side of the building just below the ceiling. There were row upon row of long tables on either side of a central aisle. Only a few Knotheads were scattered about, some with their long noses buried in books, but most were sitting before keyboards and monitors.

At the far end of the central aisle was an altar covered with a pure white cloth. Upon the cloth sat a large black box with a busy array of tiny blue-white lights blinking randomly about on

The Riddle of Riddles

a pulsing gray-black screen. In front of that black box, stood an unsmiling Knothead robed in dark gray, his bald head bowed forward, his hands lost in the folds of his robe.

When they reached the foot of the altar Knorbert whispered, "Stay here. Only Initiates may approach the High Priest."

Will moved off to one side and stood silently as Knorbert mounted the steps.

"Hail Syllogius, Father of Logic! Hail, Ada, Mother of Analytics!" he chanted, and he bowed.

"Welcome Pilgrim of Knowledge," intoned the High Priest. "May the hunger of your mind be satisfied by bread kneaded from the leaves of the Knontientium. What is it you seek?"

"I come in search of information concerning The Riddle of Riddles," replied Knorbert. "I seek the answer to the Riddle or to accumulate enough information to allow me to humbly discern its solution."

The High Priest shook back the folds of the robe from his hands, turned and bowed three times. With arms upraised in supplication, he addressed the computer. "Hail Ada."

He leaned forward, his forehead touching the altar. His voice grew soft, indistinct and foreign. Knorbert waited patiently.

Presently a loud hum filled the room. Then silence.

"Ada needs data," a female voice intoned, as colors pulsed on the screen of the black box keeping time with the words.

"Do you have any additional data?" the High Priest asked.

"No, Elder," replied Knorbert.

The High Priest turned back to the computer. Again he bowed and muttered softly to himself.

Again, a hum filled the room, then a silence. Then came a clatter like the chatter of a troop of anxious monkeys. For several moments, the machine spewed out information onto a narrow strip of paper.

When it stopped, the High Priest tore off the printout and

Chapter 11 – The Kortextium

handed it to Knorbert. "Here is a complete list of all works that mention The Riddle of Riddles. Most of the references are to obscure Far Imagian texts."

"Hail, Syllogius! Hail, Ada!" Knorbert chanted. He took the printout, bowed, and descended the steps.

Together, he and Will went over the list they had been given. It consisted of row after row of numbers and was quite long. They gave the list to another High Priest sitting in a glass enclosed niche. The cleric placed the list into a feeder that sped it horizontally before his unblinking eyes. After several moments, there was a pause and a whir. Then a partition in the wall slid open revealing several high stacks of books.

"Most of the information you seek has been logarithmed onto a memory bank cloud and is available at any terminal," the High Priest said. "These books, however, have not as yet been collated, so you may need to refer to them as well."

Struggling to balance the high stacks, Knorbert and Will carried the books to a nearby table. Knorbert sat before a console and began typing in the numbers from the printout. They watched as the data flashed onto the screen.

It took quite a while to enter all the numbers and check the results, but eventually Knorbert leaned back and said, "Nothing."

"So let's check the books." Some of the books were very, very old and dusty with dried, fragile pages. Others were new with some pages still stuck together. Some were as large as atlases, while others were as small as breviaries.

Searching through the books, they found Brain teasers, Enigmas, Hints, Epigrams, a literary Rebus, Equations, Numerology, Observations, and What-nots. The Riddle of Riddles was never mentioned by name. It was alluded to a few times but only in the most circumspect of ways. It was never quoted, nor was an answer even mentioned.

"Oh me," Knorbert sounded most distressed.

"What is it Knorbert? Have you found something?"

"Some of these riddles are so hard," Knorbert whispered

The Riddle of Riddles

leaning forward. "Listen to this one."

> *Behold the righteous man, blest with children and substance.*
> *Till he who cometh from going to and fro on the earth,*
> *Taketh away all, leaving him to writhe in the agony of sore boils.*
> *There cameth three friends to comfort him,*
> *But instead they mocked him and accuseth him of wickedness.*
> *But a voice spoketh out of a whirlwind to lay low the proud.*
> *And he repented and was restored much greater than before.*

"Well," asked Knorbert, "What do you think?"

"I don't know. That doesn't even sound like a riddle."

"Ah, but it is," Knorbert asserted louder that he should have.

"*Shhh!*" scowled a Knothead at another table.

"Listen to this one," whispered Knorbert.

> *"Here I am,*
> *What I am,*
> *What am I?"*

"Knorbert!" Will said louder than he should have.

"*Shhh!*" The same Knothead glowered over at them.

"Pay attention," Will hissed. "We are looking for The Riddle of Riddles, remember."

"One more," Knorbert continued, oblivious to Will's admonition. "This one is cute."

> *"Four digits have I,*
> *One 'pposable friend,*
> *Applaud you do I,*
> *Who grasps this pun's end."*

Will and the Knothead at the other table both stared hard at Knorbert. Knorbert sighed and took up one of the few remaining volumes.

Chapter 11 – The Kortextium

They searched them all but found nothing.

Outside, the morning sun was intense, and as their eyes adjusted to that brightness, so did their sense of purpose.

"Do not be discouraged, Knorbert," Will said smiling over at him. "We'll just keep looking."

"What makes you think I am discouraged?" Knorbert asked. "I know exactly where to look next. In fact, we probably should have gone there first."

CHAPTER 12 – CAFÉ AVANT GARDE

Knorbert led them off the boulevard down a narrower avenue and then down one narrower still.

"Where are we going?" Will asked.

"Oh So."

"Oh So?"

"Quite so."

"If you say so."

"I did though."

"I know."

"You know Oh So?"

"No, no"

"No, Oh So."

"Oh So."

"Quite so."

"You said so."

"I did though."

"I know."

"You know Oh So?"

"No, no. Whoa! Whoa!" said Will, falling unwittingly into Knorbert's rhyme scheme. "What are you trying to do? Lead me in circles?"

Knorbert smiled, and then seemed to do exactly that with a quick succession of left turns.

The farther they got from the center of the city, the more the crowds thinned, and the more outrageous the costumes became, none more so than Will's however, for wherever they went, Knotheads would exclaim in delight at Will's marvelous legs and tiny head.

"I just love your costume," one Knothead said. "How did you ever come up with such an original idea?"

"How about my costume?" Knorbert interjected before

Chapter 12 – Café Avant Garde

Will could reply. "Is it not splendid?"

The Knothead looked Knorbert up and down. "It is comically average," he replied with a slight toss of his head.

"AVERAGE?" Knorbert barked. The Knothead quickly stepped back, and then hastily retreated.

"Average, indeed," Knorbert sniffed. "Did you notice that that lout never signaled his intention to go backwards?"

"As a matter of fact, I did. What *is* the signal for going backwards?"

"It is like the signal for stopping. You drop both arms down, palms to the rear while pushing the palms backwards several times. You are also required to sound three loud brays."

"Loud brays like this?" Will asked, about to mimic Knorbert's description.

"Do not dare!" hissed Knorbert looking around. "Remember, we do not want to bring any unwanted attention to ourselves. Behave!"

The streets grew narrower and narrower. They were not so perfectly straight here, nor were the intersections quite so exact. Will felt more at home in this part of the city. It seemed more human; if that was possible in a Knothead city, decadent, even, not to be completely efficient all the time, especially in the face of such perfection.

A big black bug, nearly the size of Will's head, scurried across the street in front of them and disappeared around one of the buildings.

"What was that?" Will shuddered.

"A glitch. There are many of them in this section of the city, but you need not worry. They are ugly and a pest but generally harmless, unless, of course, they carry a nonsurvirus."

Another turn led them across a bridge over the red river, and onto its left bank.

"We are now in Oh So," Knorbert remarked.

"Oh So." Will repeated.

"Quite so."

The Riddle of Riddles

"Whoa!" Will held up a hand. "Please don't start that again. Why is this section of the city called that? Why Oh So?"

"The elite of our social rejects, those who prefer to be called Dissident Inteselectuals, and who are regarded, by many, as the real leaders of Knothead society, often assemble here in Oh So at their favorite watering holes to imbibe in mugs of cheer."

Knorbert wobbled forward at an ever-increasing pace.

"They sit around in cafes drinking and arguing the most radical, taboo subjects. The term *'Oh So,'*" Knorbert drew quotation marks in the air with his fingers, "was by coined by a kounter kulture journalist named Konzo. "Ohso literally means boneheaded," he laughed, "with obvious derogatory overtones, and the name just stuck."

Knorbert smiled over at Will. He then made several more left turns down narrower and narrower alleyways.

"They especially enjoy arguing about politics, their favorite targets being President Klinton's scandalous affair with the ingénue Is It Truth, President Knebbush, he of the tumbling tongue, and President Knobama, champion of Kommunocialism. They even argue about how many warheads can fit on the head of a pin and whether Knotheads are very, very, very smart or very, very, very ignorant. No conclusions are ever drawn, but that never stops their arguments."

"Maybe that's why boneheads argue," said Will.

Knorbert laughed aloud. "That could be it. Personally, I think they love to argue. It makes them feel inteselectually superior."

Another turn brought them in front of a sidewalk café.

It was a rough-hewn structure, pressed tightly between the other buildings on this very narrow street. It was set back a bit from the others, however, which gave it an intimate appeal. It had tables with brightly colored knumbrellas clustered tightly together, crowding to the very edge of the walk. Jutting out over the front door hung a large sign that read, *CAFÉ AVANT GARDE* in bright purple letters, and on which was painted the picture of a hookah-

Chapter 12 – Café Avant Garde

smoking blue caterpillar, sitting atop a mushroom.

The café was crowded. All the tables were full, and the guests were making a terrible din.

Off in one corner, toward the back of the courtyard, were a number of tables all pushed together around which a large group of Knotheads were gathered, some sitting, some standing. Most had large, frothy mugs in their hands that they swung from side to side as they chanted in a monotone:

"OH
Syllogius was a fine man, a fine man indeed,
In deeds well done, straight thoughts begun,
Syllogius was a fine man, a fine man indeed.
HO
One day he went a-wanderin',
O-ver the meadows green,
And came upon a fair maiden.
Quite far from home it seems.

Fair maid, says he, reason with me,
Great riches yours shall be.
Be-gone, says she, before I scream,
And keep your pause off me.
OH
Syllogius was a fine man, a fine man indeed,
In deeds well done, straight thoughts begun,
Syllogius was a fine man, a fine man indeed.
HO
One day he was a-wanderin',
Foot loose and fancy free,
And came upon some software men,
But not a byte had he.

Waremen, says he, memory's empty,
I beg some bytes from thee.
The waremen laughed aloud with glee,

The Riddle of Riddles

    I guess you must go hun-gr-y.
        OH
  Syllogius was a fine man, a fine man indeed,
  In deeds well done, straight thoughts begun,
  Syllogius was a fine man, a fine man indeed.
        HO
    One day he was a-wanderin',
     One foot after the first,
    And came upon a ta-ve-rn,
     With quite a mighty thirst.

   Barman, says he, I'll reason free,
    Deductions yours shall be.
  See all my kids, the barman pleads,
     I have no need of thee.
        OH
  Syllogius was a fine man, a fine man indeed,
  In deeds well done, straight thoughts begun,
  Syllogius was a fine man, a fine man indeed.
        HO
   I premise this before all men,
    Logic my gift shall be,
   The gift that keeps on givin',
    Conclusions all for free.

  Be-gone Old Man, we're shut of thee,
     Willi-Nillies are near,
  You premise this, then premise that,
    We'd rather have our cheer!
        OH
  Syllogius was a fine man, a fine man indeed,
  In deeds well done, straight thoughts begun,
  Syllogius was a fine man, a fine man indeed!
        HO!"
Hurrahs and laughter spilled across the café as the group

Chapter 12 – Café Avant Garde

ended their chant and, raising their mugs on high, quaffed their cheers with evident satisfaction.

The group had just begun settling itself when one of them cried out, "Well, well! Look what the glitch dragged in."

"Hello everyone," Knorbert said. "Hi, Knorm. Hi, Knihil. Hello there, Knickwit. Hello, Knipper." He greeted each by name. "Greetings, Knumnul. Hi, Knosey, Knonplus." He waved at a Knothead slouched in his seat with his arms crossed across his chest, "Hello there, Kneerdo and look, if it's not the Knobsy twins, Knervy and Kneuro," and he waved. "Hi, Knatty, Kneedle, Knerd. Quite a party you have here. Please allow me to introduce my friend Will."

"Hello," Will said with a smile and a slight wave of his hand. "Pleased to meet you all."

"Where are *you* from?" asked Knosey.

"*What* are you?" asked Kneedle, wiping some froth from his lips.

"Where did you find him?" Knonplus elbowed his companion.

"And why did you bring him here?" asked Knerd.

"Slow down everyone," Knorm interjected. "Would you like a mug of cheer?" He pointed to a tray full of mugs sitting on the table.

"I would love to," said Knorbert, "but we are on a most serious mission, and we need all of our senses about us. Another time perhaps."

"Well, that's all the more for me," said the one introduced as Knipper, a Knothead with a nose as red as a rose. The others all laughed. Someone pulled up two more chairs. Knorbert sat in one, indicating Will should take the other.

"So," said Knorm when everyone was comfortably arranged, "where are you from, Will?"

Before Will could speak, Knorbert began telling them all about Will. He explained where Will was from (or said he was from), about his humankind (who all looked more or less like

The Riddle of Riddles

Will), how he happened to be here (not that Knorbert completely understood himself), about how they had met (leaving out the bump), about Will's quest (the Riddle), and how they had decided to strike out together (leaving out the handshake, of course). Most of the story was met with glints of skepticism or sneers of ridicule until the very end when it was left in silence.

Will looked about at the others and then broke the uncomfortable silence. "I know my story sounds kind of strange, but what Knorbert has told you is all true."

"Well, if Will is from Reality, as you say Knorbert," said Knorm, "that would mean Doctor Kneinstein's Theory of Realativity equation is correct."

There were murmurs all around the table as the assembled Knothead's nodded their heads in agreement.

"That's glitchbish!" Knonplus spouted. "That theory is non-falsifiable. It can be neither proven nor disproven. His much more important theory explains how time seems to accelerate as we get older."

Knorbert dropped his arms to his sides and sat upright, frowning.

"What do you mean?" Will asked.

"Time is relative. Doctor Kneinstein figured out that $T_r = N/n$ where T_r is the relative speed of time, "N" is the number of years alive and "n" is the number of years in question."

Will cocked his head slightly. "Does time *really* accelerate as we get older?"

"Time never accelerates—we only imagine it does," said Knumnul.

"But..." Will stumbled over his thoughts, trying to make sense of what he was hearing. "If I imagine that time is accelerating, doesn't that mean that it really is? At least for me, I mean."

"That is correct," nodded Knonplus. "Each of us experiences relative time, each according to his own respective age. So in that regard, yes, time is relative as each of us

Chapter 12 – Café Avant Garde

experiences it."

"So each of us lives in his own different time zone, so to speak," snickered Knickwit.

"So then, is it any wonder that we each see things so differently at any given time?" asked Knatty, throwing up his hands.

"Wow!" Will's eyes opened wide. "I'm not sure I understand exactly what it is that you are telling me, but I guess I better start paying attention to how I spend my time since it's going to go by faster and faster each day."

"That is a wise idea, Will, very wise." Knorm nodded.

"Do not worry, Will," said Knickwit. "We say we understand, but we continue to go on wasting time anyway."

"Enough of this inteselectual stuff, already," interjected Knipper. "Pass me another mug of cheer, please."

Kneedle turned to Knorbert. "Besides this special mission you are on, Knorbert, what else brings you here?" he asked. "Was it only indecision, or did you have a bad case of indigestion too?"

A few Knotheads laughed.

"Neither, probably. Most likely he just forgot his point…again," said Kneuro (or was it Knervy?) to more laughter.

"No, no. I'll bet he lost his place—in life—again. Right, Knorbert? Right?" said Knervy (or was it Kneuro?)

Again the Knotheads laughed. Their laughter was harsh and metallic.

Will looked over at Knorbert, who wore a silly smirk, apparently not the slightest bit embarrassed by their ridicule.

"So," said Knosey, "I guess what with all of today's excitement you two must have had little trouble slipping passed the gate-guards, eh?"

"They never so much as gave us a glance," Knorbert replied.

"Cannot blame them for that," Knumnul interjected to another round of laughter.

"Yeah," yelled Knickwit, "what do you think, Knumnul?

The Riddle of Riddles

Is Knorbert uglier than he is dumb or dumber than he is ugly?"

All the Knotheads fell to laughing uproariously. Some of the other patrons were beginning to look on smiling, some laughing, caught up in the fun. Will looked over, but Knorbert just sat there grinning, as though he was privy to an understanding that they did not possess. Perhaps Knorbert really was smarter than his so-called friends.

"I cannot really say," replied the one called Knumnul. "That is kind of like trying to figure out the essence of quiddity."

That only caused louder laughter.

"Yes, yes, Knorbert," Knorm broke in waving his hands for silence. "Tell us, Knorbert, have you figured out the essence of quiddity yet?"

"As a matter of fact I have." Knorbert nodded.

The laughter, which had subsided during Knorm's question, burst like a water balloon, spraying them all. Even the others in the café laughed openly now, as though they too were privy to the joke. Everyone was laughing, everyone, that is, except Kneerdo, who remained slouched in his chair, arms crossed, an angry scowl on his face.

"*Shhh!*" Knorm called for silence. "This I have to hear."

Slowly, the laughter ebbed, and a semblance of calm returned to the tables. Some of the Knotheads took this opportunity to wash down the last of their laughs with more frothy quaffs of cheer.

Knorbert waited for silence.

"Well," Knorm said, "let's hear it. As I recall, last time you visited you said you were going to get to the bottom of this problem. So tell us. What is the essence of quiddity?"

"Well, I cannot answer that question directly," Knorbert began.

"I knew it," scowled Kneerdo.

"But," Knorbert continued, "I can tell you this. The essence of quiddity can only be understood in relation to its opposite, quoddity, and with an equal understanding of that

Chapter 12 – Café Avant Garde

opposition."

"Whaaat?" drawled Knihil.

"Yeah, let's have that again," said Knonplus.

"Before you forget," Kneedle snickered, looking around at the others.

"Certainly," said Knorbert. "Quiddity can only be understood in terms of quoddity, its opposite, and with an equal understanding of what it is that makes quid differ from quod. You cannot even talk about one without talking about the other two. Any understanding requires this trinity of understandings; namely—itself, its opposite and the concept of opposition. In fact, it may well be that we will never be able to understand anything simpler than this."

"Or to put it more simply," Kneedle said, leaning back in his chair, his eyes closed halfway. "The essence of the essence is the essence, which, of course, can only be understood in terms of that essence."

"Oh yes, of course. Simply put, simple Knorbert has simply simplified his simple simplicity," Knihil mocked.

Everyone laughed openly, including those at other tables.

"And Knorbert is simply out of his simple mind," Knatty added with a slow shake of his large head.

"Sounds like prattle-rattle to me," said Knipper, reaching for yet another mug.

"Here's to you, Knorbert," Knonplus said, raising his mug on high. "Forever a source of wonder. Forever a wonderful source."

"Of humor," Knickwit added.

And they all raised their mugs and drank.

"You two seem to get on well together," said Knorm. "I must say that's quite an accomplishment for creatures coming from such different dimensions. Are you constantly misunderstanding one another?"

"We were," Knorbert nodded, looking over at Will.

"At first," Will agreed, "until we defined our dimensions."

The Riddle of Riddles

"And now?"

They looked at each other, stopped, and then said in unison:

"Knope/Nope."

"I envy you," said Knorm. "Conflict too often arises from misunderstandings. One Knothead says one thing while another hears something entirely different. Take this group for example. We misunderstand one another all the time."

"Glitchbish!" said Kneedle. "We understand each other just fine."

"Yeah," said Knatty. "That's why I never understand any of your trains of thought."

"You mean strains of thought, don't you?" Kneuro (or was it Knervy) smirked.

"Yeah," added Knervy (or was it Kneuro). "I know I get a headache trying to make some sense out of your knonsensical knonsenses."

"Well, I knever!" Kneedle crossed his arms and sat back in his chair, his nose in the air.

The table grew quiet for a bit and then Knosey said, "So, tell us about this riddle you are looking to answer, Will."

"This is not just any riddle," Will answered. "We are looking for the answer to The Riddle of Riddles."

"What is The Riddle of Riddles?" Knorm asked.

"The Riddle of Riddles is 'When is the riddle the answer?'"

"Huh?" said Knumnul. "Would you please repeat that?"

"When is the riddle the answer?"

Knerd rubbed his chin in thought. "Sounds like some more quiddity-quoddity, prattle-rattle to me"

"When is the riddle the answer? How can anyone answer such a riddle?" asked Knatty.

Knorm shook his head slowly. "Such a riddle cannot have an answer."

"That is ridiculous!" sneered Knumnul. "If there is such a

riddle, it must have an answer."

"Who says?" asked Kneuro (or was it Knervy?)

"I do," said Knervy looking at Kneuro (or was it Kneuro looking at Knervy?).

Will's head turned from side to side to side as each spoke.

"Just the fact that we are discussing it proves that it must have an answer," said Knickwit.

"There you go again!" Knonplus shook his head. "That seems to be your favorite argument for proving everything."

"I never did understand that argument," Knumnul added. "It has no logical basis."

"What would you know about logic?" asked Knihil.

"Logic?" laughed Knerd. "What's logic?"

"Who cares?" asked Knihil.

"Are there any more mugs of cheer?" interrupted Knipper.

"So does anyone have any idea what the answer to the Riddle might be?" Will asked.

"I told you. There is no answer."

"Knonsense. There must be."

"Knonsense yourself."

And with that they fell to arguing among themselves.

They argued about the answer to the Riddle, then about the Riddle itself. Will thought they had their priorities reversed, but he knew better than to enter into a discussion where everyone thought they were the experts on everyone else's business.

"Arguing is fun," smiled Knihil.

"It is only fun," sneered Kneedle, "when the subject is so vague. That way you cannot be wrong."

Since no one could be proven right or wrong, the debate waxed fiercely for a long while. Finally, however, the table grew quiet, each Knothead absorbed in Knothead thoughts.

"Any ideas, Knorbert?" Will asked.

"I think we will have to look elsewhere," Knorbert replied.

"Why bother?" asked Knickwit. "You really don't expect

The Riddle of Riddles

to succeed where we have failed, do you? We are the bohemians of thought, the politburo of argument."

"I know just where to look." Knorbert pursed his lips.

"Sure," Knorm laughed. "Just like you were going to figure out the essence of quiddity and just like you were going to invent music."

"As a matter of fact I have invented music, is that not right, Will?"

All heads turned toward Will. "Uh…well, yeah. When I first met Knorbert, he was playing music. He was composing a song."

"I told you!" Knorbert smiled broadly. "I will even write a tune for Syllogius' Song if you would like. That way you could actually sing it."

"Sing?" asked Knumnul.

"What is a tune?" asked Knosey.

"A tune is a melody," Knorbert responded, "a linear succession of pitches and rhythms that sound pleasing to the ear."

"Oh," snickered Knerd, "is that is why your ears are so big and floppy?"

"This brings us back to the dumber or uglier question." Kneedle grinned, poking Knihil with his elbow.

Knickwit laughed, but most of the humor had gone out of the group.

"You should all be ashamed of yourselves." Will swept his finger back and forth across the group. "All of you! Ashamed! At least Knorbert is pursuing something worthwhile while you sit here…sit here drinking your cheer." He looked around the table, but the Knotheads all looked down or away.

"You're all embarrassed because you accomplish nothing. All you do is argue. Come on, Knorbert. Let's get out of here."

"Kool," Knorbert said, placing his hand on Will's shoulder.

The Knotheads all gasped as one. Will's lips twitched, and then a wide grin creased his face.

Chapter 12 – Café Avant Garde

"This is a true friend," Knorbert said, patting Will on his back. "He takes me as I am."

"Thank you, Knorbert. Shall we go?"

Arm in arm, they strolled down the narrow alleyway, away from the gaping jaws of the inteselectual bohemians.

"That's against the law," one of the group remarked.

"And indecent," another faint voice was heard to say.

When they were out of sight of those in the café, Will impulsively threw an arm around Knorbert's shoulder and gave a big squeeze. "You're brilliant, Knorbert! No kidding. I mean it. I have to admit that you Knotheads *are* very smart. Doctor Kneinstein's equations are astonishing. But you, you truly were the genius back there. I've never heard anything like your explanation of quiddity, I think you called it, never heard anything like it before."

"Oh my." Knorbert blushed, glowing as bright as a three hundred watt bulb. "I know I should be modest, but the truth is, after all, the truth. I am rather brilliant, am I not?"

Knorbert stopped and looked directly at Will. "And you know something else, Will? You were right. I did enjoy patting you on the back."

"Then you felt the touch that overwhelms."

"Do not be so hasty. I merely said I enjoyed it. I enjoyed it intellectually because it shocked the others. I did not feel this touch of which you speak."

"You will, Knorbert. You will. So…where to now?"

"Well, we tried the old and we tried the new, so I guess we move on to the now."

A glitch, surprised by their presence, scurried away.

CHAPTER 13 – THE TOO-GOODERS

They had not gone far, when, after squaring a corner, they came upon a large crowd of Knotheads gathered around a raised platform from which a female Knothead with long, unkempt hair was ranting in a loud screeching voice. Stretched behind the speaker was a long banner upon which the letters "A-R-E" stood out in bold red print. Some of the crowd carried placards with the same lettering, which they waved on high, at times, cheering the words of the speaker.

"These are the Too-Gooders," Knorbert whispered to Will as they skirted the rear of the crowd. "They are the supporters of the Annually Resurrected Emendment,"

Will spotted one Knothead dressed in coarse brown cloth, the Sacred Text in one hand, carrying a sign, tilted back over his shoulder, in the other. The sign read, "REPENT! THE END IS NEAR. THE WILLI-NILLIES ARE COMING."

The speaker's words pierced the air. "We must stamp out these subversives. Their end is chaos. They are challenging the concept of equality, the very foundation of our social order. They would have us believe that male Knotheads and female Knotheads are not the same, are, somehow, different. They would have us believe that male behavior differs from female behavior because of biology, because of nature. That is the old double standard dressed up in new clothing." She continued speaking through her nose. "But it is not new. It is hand-me-down clothing. Are we going to stand for this? Are we going to permit this heresy?"

"**No!**" the crowd roared.

"Sameness in the guise of equality is all the rage now," Knorbert whispered.

Again the speaker's voice rose. "Chaos is coming, I tell you, if we allow them to pollute the minds of our children, trying to turn such fantasy into reality." Her tone was venomous. "The

Chapter 13 – The Too-Gooders

next thing you know, they will be telling us that Willi-Nillies are real too."

The crowd laughed.

"This is no laughing matter. The time for double standards is over, and our time is now. Equality is sameness, and sameness is equality. Equality now!"

A murmur ran through the crowd like a wave, and they began chanting in unison:

"A-R-E
A-R-E
A-R-E"

Only after Will and Knorbert had drawn away from the crowd and turned another corner did the noise subside.

"I thought Knotheads never got excited, Knorbert. They certainly seemed excited to me."

"Too-Gooders do tend to get a bit excited. The more excited they get, the more sure they are that their cause is right. They preach the political correctness of being politically correct. It all sounds like sloppy, self-serving solipsism to me."

"Sloppy sloppyism?"

"They are hopeless." Knorbert shook his head. "They cannot even save themselves from their eggocentric self-satisfaction. I would like to believe that their sentiments were held only by the radical fringe, but I am afraid that this cult has managed to infect most of Sapientiopolis, including even, some of the inteselectuals." Knorbert took a deep breath and slowly exhaled. "It is those fundamentalist sociosilliologists! They continue to preach that the environment alone dictates who we become, that there are no such things as instincts, that male and female natures are the same." Knorbert's voice began to rise.

"I thought you didn't get excited, Knorbert."

"It is obvious that male and female natures differ," Knorbert continued, purposely ignoring Will's taunt, "that we Knotheads are driven by something basic, something resembling instincts, something biologically built-in upon which the

The Riddle of Riddles

environment acts to mold our individual personalities."

"Are you talking about feelings?" Will ventured.

"I do not know what to call them."

"How about Willi-Nillies?"

"Can you never be serious?"

"I was only joking, Knorbert. Are you sure you're not a Too-Gooder too? You sure can't take a joke."

"No, I am not a Too-Gooder, Will. Nor do I believe that you were just joking."

"OK, I was half-joking."

"If you were only half-joking that means you were half-serious, does it not?"

"Uh…yes, I guess so."

"I knew it. That means that you do equate instincts, feelings and Willi-Nillies. No wonder your kind is so often confused."

Abruptly, and with no signs or signals, Knorbert turned on his heel and started toward a narrow road that led off toward the city walls.

"This way, huh?" Will hurried after Knorbert.

Knorbert never even looked in Will's direction.

"Are we leaving the city?" Will asked.

Knorbert issued a loud sigh. "Yes, since we have had no luck finding the answer to the Riddle in either the new or the old, we must search the unknown now. We must dare to explore deep into the Interior, all the way to the Heartland."

"OK." Will took a deep breath. He was uncertain about Knorbert's certain certainty. He was nervous but he did not want Knorbert to know. "Let's do it."

"I computed that coming into the city would be easy because we would blend right in with the heavy crowds, but going out this early in the day might arouse suspicion. So I conclude that the most inconspicuous way out of the city would be best."

"That makes sense."

"And so," Knorbert continued, "we will immerse

Chapter 13 – The Too-Gooders

ourselves in the blood-red waters of the Som-tact River, as you have knick-knamed it. The river flows out beneath the city walls, runs through the Interior, into the Heartland. That is it there," and he pointed.

Will hesitated.

"What is the matter, Will?"

"I'm afraid I'm rather a poor swimmer. I can probably float some though—maybe even tread water if I really had to."

"All you have to do is float, Will. We will go with the flow. Come on."

"Cool," Will said, even though he was so unsure.

"Yes," Knorbert smiled over at Will. "The water will be kool and refreshing."

CHAPTER 14 – THE INTERIOR

A sign at the edge of the road read:
>Kno diving
>Kno swimming
>Kno wading
>Kno kidding

Knorbert led them as close to the river's edge as was permitted. Then when there were no other Knotheads in sight, he wobbled quickly off the road into a thick clump of trees.

Once in the trees they could not be seen. Knorbert stopped and dropped the sackpack onto the ground.

"I will not need these anymore," Knorbert said, removing the conical cap from his head and returning it to the sackpack along with the motley coat. He rummaged about and took out his boots, tied the laces of each to each other, and draped them around his neck. "I will need my boots once we reach the shores of the Interior. I would prefer to go barefoot but who knows how rough the journey might become." Then he slung the sackpack over one shoulder, Forlorn over the other. "Follow me, and try not to splash too much."

Before Will had time to protest, Knorbert had slipped quietly into the river, only his head showing above the water.

Will followed, paddling slowly out toward Knorbert as best he could. The current pulled at them easily, growing stronger the farther they got from shore. Soon they were being drawn swiftly down the center of the river and had only to concentrate on staying afloat. The city walls loomed closer overhead.

Will heard a gurgling sound, but before he could determine its origin, he and Knorbert were gurgled up and spewed out of the city through a spillway in the city wall. They fell, fell with the water, fell down…down…down into a deep, deep, deep cool pool.

Chapter 14 – The Interior

Will came up gasping for air, his hands slapping at the water like a frightened child. In a near state of panic, he stroked frantically for the shore. Though it was but a short swim, he was exhausted when he finally dragged himself from the pool, his lungs half-full of water, his arms and legs aching from his efforts.

Knorbert slogged ashore behind him and flopped down next to Will, Forlorn clutched firmly in hand, his boots hanging around his neck. The sackpack was missing.

"What...happened...to...your...sackpack?" Will coughed up a mouthful of water.

"I lost it." Knorbert wiped his face with his hands, and then shook off the beads of water. "I almost lost Forlorn, too. It was a choice of one or the other. Actually, I am kind of glad to be rid of all that baggage."

"But what about the hats? Won't we need them to pass through the different periods?"

"We are heading into the Interior now, Will. The periods through which we will be passing are, for the most part, little traveled. There are relatively few Knotheads and seldom any authorities where we are going, so we should have little trouble. Once we get to the Heartland...well...we will really be on our own then."

Knorbert issued a deep sigh. "I sound so calm and matter-of-fact. I should be terrified. You know how I feel about adventure and," he added looking around furtively, "it looks like our adventure really begins here."

As they rested, Will noticed that his muscles were actually taking on a roundness and firmness they had never before had. A sense of his own power, a confidence in his own abilities, suddenly swept over him with a magnitude that was at once both exhilarating and frightening. He was beginning to feel a genuine righteousness about his efforts and a confidence in his abilities he never had before.

As soon as Knorbert finished putting on his boots, he tottered to his feet. "It is time to go," he said, and he turned from

The Riddle of Riddles

the river. They had to push their way through the encircling brush, dense enough to cause some minor anxiety, but so brightly colored as to be alluring.

They broke out into a small clearing from which a number of pathways—not nearly as numerous as before, nor as well tended—led away in various directions.

Knorbert made his wobble-click choice and moved off down one of the narrower but relatively well-kept paths.

As they hiked up one of the low hills on this latest path, Will noticed that going uphill was no longer as easy as going down. "Knorbert, what happened to that electro-whatever force you told me about, the one that made going uphill so easy? It's not working now."

"That is korrect. Authority does not want to encourage travel in these parts, so there is no intellectro-magknowtic force field here. Authority is suspect of any areas beyond their control, so they discourage traveling to those regions."

"That's fine with me. I don't like help that I never asked for, especially when it's kept secret."

As they approached the next junction, a band of Knotheads emerged from one of the side roads, a group quite unlike any Will had ever seen.

Members of the group wobbled about haphazardly, changing places as they went. There was no order to the group and no apparent leader. They were arguing among themselves, their arms gesticulating wildly.

Each individual was dressed differently in what could easily pass for rags, yet that ragamuffin look united them in a common fashion. Almost all wore color-faded shirts with no sleeves over broad, sloop-shouldered backs. Several wore suspenders holding up baggy, thread-worn pants. Their long hair was tousled, and their eyes bulged from their sockets, eyeballs moving slyly side to side.

It was not until the mob reached the intersection that one of them noticed Knorbert and Will. He immediately elbowed his

Chapter 14 – The Interior

nearest cohort and pointed. The Knothead who had been prodded threw a wild-eyed look at his tormenter, but then, following the outstretched finger, he also spied Knorbert and Will.

He grunted so loudly that the rest of the gang stopped arguing to look around. Once they noticed Will and Knorbert, they dropped their heads and started muttering, throwing crazed looks in all directions from beneath their furrowed brows. The muttering grew louder, and they began arguing more loudly, pointing first down one trail and then up another, each time glancing uneasily over at Knorbert and Will.

The spaces between them collapsed, creating a jostling, incoherent mass that resumed moving in their original direction. The grunts grew louder, the pushing and shoving more forceful. Those in front were shaking their heads aggressively back and forth. Slowly, the mass curved toward the nearest path, down which it slowly shuffled until it disappeared behind the first bend in the trail.

Knorbert looked over at Will. "Knowmads," he said.

"Nomads?"

"Yes, I had never seen any before, but they fit the descriptions I have heard. Knowmads live in the hills and hollows deep in the Interior. Their experiences, isolated out here on the fringes of the Heartland, have, reportedly, affected their behavior."

"Yeah, and scrambled their brains," Will added. "It's almost like they have been frightened by something, something that has confused them. Maybe they've seen some Willi-Nillies out here."

"I know you are teasing me, Will, but there must be some explanation as to why they act so crazy."

"Don't crazy people choose to live in isolated places?"

"Or do they get crazy because they live in isolated places?" Knorbert asked. "Now you understand why Authority has no intellectro-magknowtic force field in these areas. They do not want to attract such undesirables."

The next path Knorbert selected was in the opposite

direction to the one taken by the Knowmads. The terrain became more and more wild, the yellow wood crowding right up to the edge of the long and winding road that stretched out before them, its dark gloom hanging too familiarly, too close by.

At the next junction even fewer ways led off in varying directions, all in differing degrees of disrepair. The better-kept roads led back toward Sapientiopolis, while the most ill-defined and unkempt led deeper into the Interior. Knorbert studied them all, staring nervously down each leg.

Before Knorbert had a chance to select their next path, Will suddenly exclaimed, "Look, Knorbert! Look! A star! My star! There's the star I told you about, the one with the pulsating ring around it. There. Right there." He pointed. "Do you see it?"

Knorbert squinted. "I see nothing, Will. Are you sure you are not imagining it? Stars cannot usually be seen during the day."

"I'm not imagining. I'm not dreaming. I..." he stopped. "Then again, maybe I am dreaming. I see my star right there." He pointed again. "Uh...that is, I did see it."

His eyes swept the sky again. "I'm pretty sure I did, right over there." He gestured with his thumb. "And that's the direction I want to go. Come on, Knorbert. Let's follow my star, second to the right and then straight on 'til morning."

"Oh my, I do not know."

"That's the road that leads deeper into the Interior, toward the Heartland, isn't it, Knorbert?"

"Yes, yes it is. Why?"

"Isn't that where the Willi-Nillies live? You wouldn't be afraid of the Willi-Nillies, would you?"

"There you go again. Of course, I am not afraid. What is there to be afraid of? Story book monsters? Do not be ridiculous."

Will started down his road, his eyes searching for his star, and this time Knorbert was forced to catch up. He looked over at Will but said nothing.

Will was drawn in this direction, even if he had not actually seen his star. He could not put his finger on exactly what

Chapter 14 – The Interior

it was that drew him this way, just that there was a peace, a lack of inner conflict about it.

When they arrived at the next junction, there were even fewer choices. This time Knorbert was quick in making his decision. He wobbled back and forth in smaller and smaller oscillations like he always did when deciding, but this time he selected the road that curved back toward the city and quickly waddled off. Will looked helplessly for his star but saw nothing, and was, once again, forced to follow Knorbert.

Way led to way, each junction offering fewer and fewer possible choices. At each intersection Knorbert selected the road that led away from the Interior, but each time that road wound back, back in the very direction Knorbert was intent on avoiding, deeper into the Interior.

It did not take long before their latest road withered to a path and the path to a trail. Disquietry trees overgrew the trail in some places, hanging down in front of them, partially blocking their way, further slowing them and causing Will a growing sense of uneasiness.

Suddenly, a shriek, fleet and deep, rent the shuddering keep.

Will was so startled that he stumbled, his face pale and slack.

"Beware, Will," Knorbert whispered in a quivering voice. "Danger is near, and it makes me feel queer. Where the Jubjub resides the Bandersnatch is nigh, two birds of a feather who flock frequently together."

Will could not reply. He merely nodded.

"Stay alert. We must be wary of the Jubjub, which lives its life in perpetual passion, and avoid the frumious jaws of the Bandersnatch at all costs."

Will shivered. He peered into the heart of darkness that pressed in at him but could discern nothing.

And then without warning, he started to cry, all sense of recent wellbeing completely deserting him.

The Riddle of Riddles

"What is the matter, Will? What is the matter with your eyes? Water is dripping from your eyes."

"What's the matter?" Will sniffled. "Haven't you ever seen anyone cry before?"

"Oh my! Crying?" Knorbert repeated in a hushed tone. "Why are you crying?"

"Because...because...I'm scared, that's why," said Will, choking on his sobs.

"Oh my, Will. Please do not cry."

"I'm sorry." Will wiped away some tears. "It's just that I'm afraid. Here we are in the middle of nowhere, with no real direction and time running out, and then that scream from that Jubjub or whatever it was." He shuddered. "I just got scared, that's all."

"That *was* the shriek of the Jubjub. I can understand why you were frightened."

Knorbert was fidgeting. His hands trembled. One hand reached up, shaking like a butterfly in a windstorm. Gently, Knorbert touched the back of his hand to Will's cheek. A tear clung to his knuckle.

Knorbert looked at the tear, his eyes like saucers. "Oh my. I wish you would not cry. Please, do not cry. We Knotheads never cry."

"You never cry?" Will snorted. "That figures."

"Oh me, oh my, oh no. Never. Crying attracts Willi-Nillies."

Will choked out a laugh as he wiped away an itchy tear drying on his cheek.

"Not that I really believe all that nonsense."

"And here I thought you were concerned about me."

"Oh my, but I was, Will. Honest."

"You don't cry. You don't touch. You don't even know what love is. Don't you Knotheads have any emotions?"

"Emotions? What are emotions?"

"Emotions, you know feelings, those things that are

inside, those things that make us scared or happy, angry and upset, warm and loving. Feelings. You remember the feeling inside I told you about."

"I do not know what you are talking about."

"Emotions, Knorbert. They are also called feelings. They come from your heart. You have to pay attention to your feelings. It takes practice. You have to pay attention to subtle sensations running through you. You feel them, and then you have to make sense of what it is you are feeling."

"Paying attention is costly, Will. The price is high. That is why it is called 'paying' attention. I lose a part of the awareness of my surroundings when I pay attention to something specific. The more intensely I pay attention, the more fixed my mind becomes, the more of my surroundings I lose. Maybe that is why I am not sensitive to those sensations that you are talking about."

"Do you remember those 'inklings' you mentioned. Remember? You said you had an 'inkling' that determined what road you selected. Those inklings are called feelings, Knorbert, emotions."

"Those inklings I mentioned are intellectual in nature, Will. Nothing comes from the heart. It all comes from the head."

"You think it comes from your head, but if you pay attention you just might discover that those inklings really come from your heart. Try to be receptive—at least a little. Try to be sensitive to what is going on inside of you. You might actually like it."

"Sure, Will. I can try, but what good are emotions if they make you cry?"

"Crying is not a bad thing. There is such a thing as a good cry." Will wiped each eye. "And don't forget, I was crying. You had better watch out." Will watched Knorbert out of the corner of an eye. "I might have attracted a Willi-Nilli. You never can tell."

CHAPTER 15 – CAUSE OR EFFECT

They continued on and had gone but a short distance, when suddenly Will blurted out, "Look, Knorbert, another Knothead!"

Sure enough, directly ahead of them on the same trail was another Knothead. He was dressed rather oddly, as though he was in costume for Syllogius' celebration, but he was heading in the opposite direction, toward the Interior.

He was tall and slim by Knothead standards, wearing a soft, white, form-fitting shirt with bloused sleeves and a high collar, open wide at the neck. His pants fit snugly, girded with a wide black belt that was fastened by a large, ornate silver buckle. The pant legs disappeared into a pair of sturdy, black boots that sported silver buckles with designs similar to those on his belt buckle. On his head he wore a deep red beret pulled down over one eye.

He was standing at a junction of two paths wobbling back and forth.

"Hello there," Knorbert said when they reached the Knothead's side.

The Knothead did not reply. He just kept wobbling back and forth repeating, "Cause or Effect? Effect or Cause?"

"What are you doing?" Will asked.

"Cause or Effect? Effect or Cause?" the Knothead kept repeating, completely ignoring their presence as he continued to wobble back and forth. "Cause or Effect? Effect or Cause?"

Knorbert became incensed. "Unless you are a complete glitch, it is a serious breach of etiquette not to answer a direct question—to say nothing of totally ignoring my greeting. You will, please, answer me. Who are you and what you are doing?"

"Cause or Eff…" The Knothead abruptly stopped wobbling back and forth. "Who… what… uh… what?" asked the

Chapter 15 – Cause or Effect

Knothead.

"I asked you who you are and what you are doing," Knorbert repeated.

"Oh, I am so sorry. You must forgive me," said the Knothead. "I seem to have lost my senses completely. How stuffy of me not to introduce myself. My name, of course. My name is…my name is…How can this be? I cannot even remember my own name! Impossible! My name is…my name is *WHAT*?"

"Pleased to meet you, What," Will said, trying to diffuse the awkwardness of the moment. "My name is…"

"Why are you standing out here wobbling back and forth like this, going nowhere?" Knorbert asked.

"Wobbling back and forth, you say? Wobbling back and forth? Oh yes. I had completely forgotten. Yes, I was wobbling back and forth because…because…"

"Because?"

"Why because…" the Knothead began, "because…oh yes, because I am going…"

"Going?" Knorbert asked.

"Going to…going to…Oh dear me! I cannot remember anything. What *is* wrong with me?"

"You're going nowhere, What, I'd say," said Will.

"What is that?" The Knothead turned and glared at Will. "Who are you? No, no. *What* are you?" he asked, looking Will up and down.

"Will is the name. Pleased to meet you, What." Will's hand started up, but he stuck it in his pocket instead.

"And my name is Knorbert, and my friend is quite correct. You are, in fact, going nowhere."

"Going nowhere, you say. Of course, I am going somewhere. I am going to…going to…" The Knothead blushed and looked down. "I am so sorry. I just cannot remember anything, it seems."

"Sure you can," Will urged. "Think about it. You are going to…where?"

The Riddle of Riddles

"Going to...going to...Of course! Not going to *where* but going to *decide*. Of course! I am going to decide."

"Decide what, What?" Will asked.

"Not what-what," the Knothead said. "Which! I am going to decide which way to go. Yes, of course. That is it. I am going to decide whether I should go Cause or Effect at this crossroad." He exhaled deeply.

"So which way are you going?" Knorbert asked.

"Cause or Effect, of course, of course! Effect or Cause, of course. Cause, of course, or Effect, of course. Effect or Cause, of course, of course." He stopped. "I just do not know. Oh, I give up!" And with that, he plopped down on the ground with a loud thump.

"Oh, what a knunce I am," the Knothead said. "My name is Knumerator. How could I ever have forgotten my own name? I grew so confused by being unable to decide which direction to go that I forgot everything, even my own name."

"Knumerator?" Will sounded surprised. "I thought you said your name was What."

"What? Whatever made you think my name was What?" Knumerator asked.

"You said..." Will began. "Oh, never mind. Sorry for the mistake, Knumerator."

"What are you doing way out here?" Knorbert asked.

"I am on a special mission."

"A special mission?" Knorbert drew back his head. "What kind of special mission?"

"I am searching for the Kommon Denominator," Knumerator replied. "But I am afraid I just cannot go on."

"Why... why...that's one of the Noble Tasks!" Will exclaimed. "We are on a special mission too, a Noble Task. We are looking for answer to The Riddle of Riddles."

"The Riddle of Riddles?" Knumerator shook his head side to side. "I cannot say I ever heard of it, but I am glad to hear of your...your quest. I am so pleased to meet you. It is reassuring to

110

Chapter 15 – Cause or Effect

know that there are other adventurers pursuing their goals." Then he sighed. "But I am afraid I just cannot go on. I cannot go any further."

"Why not?" Will asked.

"I just cannot make another decision," said Knumerator. "That is why I was stuck. I could not, *cannot*, decide which way to go, Cause or Effect, Effect or Cause. I became so confused I could not even remember my own name. It is hard to make it on your own. You two at least have each other. I have to do everything myself, make every decision without the help of any backfeed. It gets very tiring until it gets to be too much. I cannot go on. I am surprised I made it this far."

Will looked to the sky. Then he looked over at Knorbert, and then back at Knumerator. "You can do it," Will said. "You can go on."

"No, I cannot. I was forewarned. I was told that I would need another, need someone like you, Will, to help me, but I did not listen. I thought I could do it all by myself."

"Look how far you have come already. You are a rare individual, brave, strong, independent, and, if I may, even your clothes indicate a dash of self."

"Perhaps too independent, too much self." And Knumerator sighed again. "But I thank you for the compliments. I have indeed come far, but I cannot go on alone."

"Why don't you come with us?" Will suggested.

Knumerator smiled. "I wish I could, but I cannot. I must pursue my own goal. You have your mission. I have mine. We are on separate journeys. You two go on. Go ahead. I will wait here for the rest of the day. Maybe I will be lucky enough that someone I need will come along to help me, a Will of my own." He looked at Will, and smiled. "Then we will continue on together in pursuit of the Kommon Denominator. Until then I must wait here."

"But you cannot stay here all by yourself," said Knorbert.

"Of course I can. I await my fate. You need not worry."

"Come on, come with us," Will urged.

Knumerator looked at Will. "Thank you for the offer, but I know what I must do just as you know what you must do. And right now what you must do is to be on your way. So be off with you now, before you waste any more time. And good luck in the pursuit of the solution to The Riddle of Riddles."

Will did not want to leave him behind, but Knumerator refused their offers. Knumerator knew what his mission was, and he now knew what was needed to complete it. Knumerator fully embraced his fate, whatever that fate might come to be.

Several times Knorbert started to say something but kept coughing instead. Then he just stuck out his hand. The hand trembled but the arm was steady.

"Knorbert wants to shake hands with you," Will explained. "He wants you to clasp hands with him. It is a gesture of friendship and trust, even admiration."

Knorbert held the arm out.

"You mean *touch*?" Knumerator said the last word breathlessly.

"Sure," Knorbert said with a half-smile.

"I do not know."

"Go on," said Will. "It won't hurt. You might even like it—intellectually speaking, that is."

"Sure. Why not?" Knumerator laughed aloud and stuck out his hand. The next thing they knew Knorbert and Knumerator had clasped hands. Knorbert pulled Knumerator to his feet, and the two of them engaged in a hearty handshake, much to Knorbert's red-faced embarrassment even though it was he who had initiated the event.

Then Knumerator shook Will's hand. Then Knorbert's once again. Then Will's once more, all the while giggling at his own impertinence.

"Be off with you now," he said with a wide smile. "I will wait for a Will of my own to come along. Who knows, maybe we will meet again someday, maybe even soon. Go on. I will be fine and…good luck." His smile creased both cheeks. "And thanks for

Chapter 15 – Cause or Effect

getting me out of my rut."

"We did nothing," Will shook his head.

"You are welcome," said Knorbert.

Will and Knorbert did not go far before they turned to wave. Knumerator was again sitting, waiting, still smiling beneath his bright red beret. He waved back. Next time they turned, however, Knumerator was lost from view.

CHAPTER 16 – WHAT BIRD IS THIS?

They tramped on, the trail becoming more and more indistinct with each step.

Deep in a gully, they came upon a stream and stopped briefly to refresh themselves. The cold water was good to drink and cool on the brow. Knorbert lay back on the soft grasses, the fingers of both hands interlaced behind his big head. Will sat on a large, gray boulder beside the stream, his knees drawn up to his chin.

"It looks like the Heartland truly begins here," said Knorbert. "We have run out of trail."

"We ran out of trail quite a while ago."

"What do you mean?"

"You've been making trail for quite some time now, Knorbert. I thought you knew that. We are actually leaving a trail behind us for others to follow."

"I have been making trail?" Knorbert opened his eyes wide. "Oh me, oh my, that is a responsibility for which I am not sure I am prepared."

"It's a little late for that. You assumed that duty when you first agreed to be our guide, and now you are the trail blazer."

"I never realized that others might someday follow me, follow us. It is daunting to know that I am leading anyone. I have enough trouble getting out of my own way."

"You sell yourself short, Knorbert. Think how smart you are and, I must add, brave too. You did not have to choose to help me. You could have let me fend for myself."

"Not really." Knorbert looked down at the ground. Then, with his chin still on his chest, he looked up with just his eyes. "I could not let you venture off into the Wild Wood all alone, not knowing anything about our dimension. Think of Knumerator. Besides, you gave me a sense of being needed. I could show off

Chapter 16 – What Bird is This?

how logical I am. I like that." A small smile lifted the corners of his lips.

"Please, don't remind me of Knumerator. I feel so bad, leaving him behind."

"Do not trouble yourself, Will. You know he would not come with us. He was intent on completing his mission, his way."

"I know, but still…"

Knorbert raised his head and then turned to look off into the trees. "Let me apply some syllogistic logic to our present situation. If we have no more trails to follow, what do we use to guide us?"

"You are our guide, remember."

"I am, but…I mean, am I supposed to know every *place* as well as every *thing*, even places I have never been before, understand even things I have never even thought about before?"

"Yes, Knorbert, even ideas you have never even thought about before. We cannot turn back. We must push on using whatever resources we possess and whatever the universe provides. We must learn to make our own way."

Suddenly, a trill of words rang out sharp and clear:

"Oh you who wish to learn about these things,
Have followed thus far in your skiff-like-boats,
The wake of my great ship that sails and sings,

Turn back and make your way to your own coast.
Do not commit yourself to the main deep,
For losing me all may perhaps be lost."

Will sprang to his feet. Knorbert sat up.

They both looked around, but no one was in sight. Then they heard again:

"We do not travel this world all alone.
Others here help us to not go amiss.
Will show what they can, what needs to be shown.

So come follow me but be not remiss,

The Riddle of Riddles

> *A riddle's answer must still be brought home,*
> *Your task incomplete until it is finished."*

The trill came from a large bird that was perched on a branch high overhead. It had a green head, wreathed in entwined green sprigs. Its body was pure white and its tail a bright red. Its eyes were bright and alert.

"Is that a Jubjub?" Will whispered.

"Of course not. That bird is beautiful."

"How about a Bandersnatch?"

"No, no," Knorbert shook his head.

"Then what bird is this?"

"I do not know." Knorbert turned toward the bird and asked, "What kind of bird are you?"

> *"I come from that land enclosed by the sea,*
> *Boot heel dug into its center deep,*
> *The city where Blacks and Whites disagreed.*
>
> *As I was led from a dark wood so deep,*
> *By that great poet I value dearly,*
> *So I help others to pay for my keep."*

"Are you here to guide us?" Will's words left his lips breathlessly.

> *"As morning manna arrives from heaven,*
> *So it is with all those who chose the way,*
> *To all who dare so choose, a guide is given.*
>
> *I have been chosen as your guide today,*
> *To show you the way that you have chosen.*
> *So come follow me and do not delay."*

With that, the bird flew off across the stream into the trees.

The stream was spotted with round flat rocks much like enormous checkers. Will and Knorbert quickly hop-scotched their way across, following the bird which could barely be seen, fluttering between the trees, leading them deeper and deeper into

Chapter 16 – What Bird is This?

the Heartland.

The trees grew taller, the foliage overhead playing hide and seek with the sun. They pushed on, necks craned, eyes ever on the ever-elusive bird. Occasionally, they would lose sight but invariably the bird would sing out.

"No need for hurrying toward your goal,
Moving steadily forward will suffice,
But tarry not or you will pay the toll.

As fearsome as ever was such a price,
The gain or the loss of your very soul,
More sure than any random cast of dice."

They caught up to the bird at a singularity tree in which it had perched, waiting. In the near distance loomed a towering, jagged peak. It stabbed into the sky, high above the surrounding peaks like some gigantic broadsword. Between them and it, the forest had given way to a wide savannah, as if it too stood in awe of this cloud-enshrouded monument.

"As a drowning man treading water deep,
Spies from afar some lovely island home,
So on this far peak your eyes you must keep.

It is there you will see what is to be shown,
Rememb'ring that to find you must first seek,
Before you continue on your way home."

The bird ruffled its feathers and flew off directly into the glare of the sun, where they could no longer follow its progress.

CHAPTER 17 – MORE RIDDLES

"At least we now have a direction." Will nodded toward the distant peak.

"Mount Kneverest," said Knorbert.

"You know it?"

"It must be. Nothing else approaches its grandeur. It is charted as being at the very center of the Heartland."

Knorbert looked up at Luci. She was still rising, though by now it was late morning. "Come on," he said. "Our goal is in sight, but we have pardahs to go and a riddle to answer."

They started off across the plain, side by side. The going was rather easy now since they no longer had to follow the bends in the trails nor fight the overgrowth.

A slight smile crept its way onto Knorbert's lips, and his wobble took on a sway, swinging him along in a jaunty manner. "Would you like to hear a riddle, Will?"

"Sure, why not. It will help pass the miles, uh, the pardahs, I mean."

Knorbert cleared his throat.

"Questions are pleaded,
The replies come nigh.
Solutions needed?
The response comes by.
Process completed,
By me. Who am I?"

Will pondered the riddle for several minutes and then guessed, "A question mark?"

"Oh me, oh my, no, no. Close, but incorrect."

"Here is another. Try this one:

Out of the eater came forth meat
Out of the strong came something sweet
For love of nectar I labor long

Chapter 17 – More Riddles

Stinging's dances to buzzing's songs."

Will was again lost in thought for quite some time. "How about a hint?"

"Of course not," Knorbert snorted. "Why not just ask me for the answer?"

"OK, what's the answer?"

"Oh no, no way. Think about it."

"Come on. How about a hint?"

"I told you, no."

"Hmmm, strong…and meat…Is it a lion?'

"You are on the right track for the first part of the riddle. Try again." Knorbert's smile widened but then disappeared as he tightened his lips. Then it widened again.

Will's face grew red. "Don't you dare start snickering, It's obvious that I'm not very good at riddles. I give up. What's the answer?"

"I am not snickering, but I hope you do not give up so easily when it comes to solving The Riddle of Riddles."

"That's what I've got you for, right?" Will's inability to solve Knorbert's simple riddles unsettled him.

"Right, and it certainly is a good thing I decided to come along."

"So you keep reminding me. Well, at least these riddles are helping to pass the…parsnips."

"How about another one?" Knorbert asked.

Will shrugged. "If you must. Even if I said no, I don't suppose that would stop you, so, sure. Go ahead."

"Great. Here you go.

Ob - la - di, ob - la - da
What goes on, brah?
La-la what goes on?"

"That's a riddle?" Will asked. "It sounds more like gibberish to me."

"Gibberish? Really?"

Will puzzled over this latest riddle for quite some time.

"Well?" Knorbert asked after a lengthy pause. "Come now, that one is particularly easy."

"To listen to you, you'd think all your riddles are easy." Will glowered.

"Not all, just some. So what is the answer?"

"Oh, I don't know. What does go on?"

"Exactly, Will. Once more you are on the right track. I'll tell you what, Will. I will give you a hint, OK?"

"No, thank you. I don't want any hints. Never mind you and your riddles!"

"Oh, of course, your *never* mind again, in its never-never-never land."

Will stormed off. Knorbert, wobbling along behind him, was soon panting and sweating, struggling to keep up and no longer had breath for riddles or laughter or scorn.

Knorbert was good at riddles, and, obviously, Will was not. Will began wondering about their chances of completing their mission, hating the empty hollow in his stomach for even thinking this way. He walked faster.

The gently rolling terrain soon turned into low foothills, but still their journey was relatively easy. Will continued to push the pace.

The more determined Will remained, the less he was aware of his surroundings. It did not help that the environment around them was so endlessly ordinary as to be unmemorable. The soft grasses, low bushes, and occasional tree caused barely a ripple across his consciousness.

Finally, they put the last of the foothills behind them and stood at the base of Mount Kneverest. Knorbert leaned back against a large boulder, trying to catch his breath, glowering over at Will for hurrying them. He wiped the sweat from his brow with the sleeve of his tunic.

Will was too busy staring up the mountain to notice, trying to peer through the misty clouds that obscured its summit.

It was a high, high, high mountain.

CHAPTER 18 – AN OLD MAN

"Well, hurry up! Don't just stand there gaping. Time is running out. Come on now. Come on!"

Will's head snapped around. Knorbert pushed himself forcefully off the rock face, gaping.

There, standing before them, hanging with both hands on a stout wooden staff higher than he was tall, stood an old man, staring at them out of eyes white on white. A white tunic hung loosely on the short, thin old man, but it could not hide a plump belly that protruded slightly over his short bowed legs. He wore a beard as long and as white as his hair.

"You were expecting us?" Will asked, quite taken aback.

"Yes, of course. I expected you with the same expectation that brought you here. I am a bit surprised you didn't expect me as well." The Old Man's eyes creased in a warm smile, the gap between his two front teeth grinning out at them.

"So you chose to complete a Noble Task," he continued, looking Will over carefully as he circled him. He blinked his eyes repeatedly, as though tuning some mental selector switch. "You certainly don't look like a Noble Warrior capable of completing a Noble Task, but I suppose I must make do."

"Who are you?" Will asked.

"I could be Rumpelstiltskin, but I'm not. The riddle of my name is but a small part of this whole game," the Old Man cackled. "Tear not yourselves in two in the pursuit of the who. The riddle's answer is the goal we must pursue. It is not names, but deeds alone that count. Come, it is precious time we waste no doubt."

Leaning on his staff, the Old Man hobbled toward the mountain. In its side was the mouth of a cave, small and smoke-blackened. Will had to bow his head slightly to enter.

"Watch your head, Knorbert. The entrance is kind of…"

The Riddle of Riddles

"*Owww!*" Knorbert yelped, rubbing the crown of his head.
"Be aware!" said the Old Man.

Inside, a narrow rock passageway led off at an angle, then doubled and then tripled back on itself. Will's sense of direction was soon left behind with the light, his only reference points in the inky blackness being the vague outline of the Old Man's back ahead of him and the solid rock floor beneath his feet. But for that footing, Will felt tethered to nothing.

Slowly, they wound their way down deeper into the bowels of the mountain through a maze of damp, narrow, rock passageways. Down they went, deeper and deeper until, suddenly, the cave expanded dramatically.

The cavern was tremense. The further into it they progressed, the larger it became. Will heard their footfalls echoing,

                         echoing,

echoing

          off

                  into

                           the

                                      distance.

Echoes echoed echoes until Will lost all sense of size in the enormity of the cavern, lost touch with its edges in a darkness so black that the blackness had a weight, a weight he struggled to carry.

Still the Old Man hobbled on with Will and Knorbert close behind until, somewhere in the immensity of this seemingly limitless black void, they came upon a large circle of flat stones. In its center, a low fire flickered, its dull, red glow barely illuminating the surrounding rocks.

"Please, sit down." The Old Man gestured toward the circle of stones. His voice was as hollow as the cavern was empty. Will seated himself on a convenient rock, glad for the fire's warmth and light in this damp, forbidding place. Knorbert looked around nervously, and then sat down right next to Will.

The Old Man disappeared into the darkness but soon

Chapter 18 – An Old Man

returned with an armful of dry sticks that he dumped onto the fire. The lighter branches caught quickly and began to sizzle and pop in the dead of that cold, damp dark. Next, the Old Man added several heavy logs that he pushed about with his staff, assembling the fire to his own particular satisfaction.

Soon the heavy logs caught fire. A purple haze of smoke drifted up lazily into the empty blackness above. For a brief moment, Will welcomed the reassurance of the added heat and light, but in the next instant a cold draft blew away the smoke, and his wellbeing, into the obscure darkness. Will shivered, though by now a hot and roaring fire blazed before them.

The resultant light, bright as it was, lit but a small portion of the mammoth cavern. Will made out some stout, stone columns reaching high overhead, only to be lost in the empty blackness. Short, squat stalagmites ringed the circle, sitting quietly like so many becloaked and bewigged judges. Large, chalk-white stalactites pointed down at them from above like thunderbolts threatening extinction, while across the fire the Old Man's white eyes burned into Will's with an intensity that rivaled the roaring flames.

"The time is now," the Old Man intoned. "A chain of events has transpired to create this moment, a confluence of events creating this opportunity. This event and that event have so moved the digits in the matrix of time that an empty space has been created, a space to be filled now, for good or for nil, as circumstances shall soon dictate."

The ensuing silence was broken only by the crackling of the fire.

"Let it be," the Old Man's hoarse voice startled them as he continued stirring the fire with the point of this staff. Bright sparks jumped, dying as they arced through the blackness.

"You called Will, stand and take three steps forward."

Will's heart dropped into the pit of his stomach where it suddenly began pounding loudly. He pushed himself to his feet. Slowly, he took three steps forward. He shivered, chilled to his

The Riddle of Riddles

very bones though his palms were damp with sweat. His stomach was throbbing fire, and his knees shook.

"You have been called by the Voiceless Voice, summoned here today to be shown what is to be shown, to see what is to be seen." The Old Man churned the fire with his staff, his eyes never once leaving Will's. A thin veil of smoke hung between them, but even so, Will trembled beneath the intensity of those piercing eyes.

"You have chosen to attempt to complete a Noble Task, have you not?" the Old Man hissed across the fire.

"Yes, sir," Will answered softly.

"Speak up," roared the Old Man. "Fill the void."

"**YES, SIR**," Will repeated in a voice so loud he surprised himself.

"Your Noble Task is to solve The Riddle of Riddles, is it not?"

"**YES, SIR**," Will boomed.

"And so far you have had no success?"

"No, sir," Will replied, looking down at the fire.

"**Louder**," the Old Man demanded. "Look at me! I'm looking through you."

Will looked up. "**NO, SIR**," he bellowed.

The Old Man transfixed him with trinocular eyes, an old man no longer so small. He seemed to have grown larger, seemed to, now, loom over Will. Will felt so small, so insignificant, so frightened.

"Are you ready to prove yourself worthy to pursue your goal? Are you ready to become a Noble Warrior?"

"Ready?" Will asked. "Here and now?"

"**BE HERE NOW!**" The Old Man's voice boomed, pointing his staff menacingly at Will, its tip glowing a fiery red.

"Uh… can Knorbert help me? Can he…"

"**SILENCE!**" roared the Old Man. "You leave all behind. You enter upon the battlefield alone and unarmed. I repeat. Are you ready to be tested?"

Chapter 18 – An Old Man

The engulfing silence that lived on after the Old Man's words had died screamed in Will's ears. He could hear the swirling of the smoke as it disappeared up into that deep silence. Will threw back his shoulders, took a deep breath and said, "I am as ready as I'll ever be."

"**YES OR NO?**" roared the Old Man.

"**YES!**" Will yelled as loud as he could.

A slow smile crept across the Old Man's face. He reached into the small leather pouch at his side and sprinkled a few fingertips of its contents onto the fire.

The fire flared. Flames of fuchsia, ecru, amber and red painted the blackness as billows of smoke mushroomed high overhead.

"What are you most afraid of?" the Old Man asked in an even tone.

Will searched his heart for the answer. "Nothing in particular." He gulped.

Yet his mind began to conjure up a shape, a contour, an ugliness of that which he feared most but could not identify. The smoke, as if in response to that conjuring, began to take on that shape, those contours, that extreme ugliness.

"Really?" The Old Man asked, stirring the fire.

Will's mind began giving substance to the smoke, conjuring up the image of that creature he now half-saw, half-felt, crouching in his soul, that creature of his deepest dread.

The image grew.

It rose overpoweringly, black, hideous, threatening. It stared at him out of eyes coal-black with fire-red pinpoints at their very centers. It took on a form Will had never before seen, yet a form that he somehow knew, the form of all the unspeakable horrors that he had buried deep in the darkest recesses of his soul. These slippery repulsive horrors that he dared not face, now reared up over him with a wide fanged mouth drooling slimy strings of anticipation.

Will fought to forget, to clear his mind of this hideous

monster of his own creation, but he could not. It was as if he and the smoke were one, were together seeking out and revealing this ghastly specter he dared not imagine but could not escape.

But still it came.

And grew.

Larger and larger.

Looming over him. Staring down at him.

He tried to dispel its malevolence, but his mind seemed fascinated by its own terror. It was as if he desired to be consumed by this growing evil. The more he tried to turn away from the monster, the more clearly did the smoke define it.

It was an insidious smoke, a smoke which wafted lightly into his nostrils as he breathed. Its stench ran up his nose. The monster's fetid breath filled his lungs. That reek seeped out into his bloodstream where a thousand ragged mouths began to eat at him from within. Will could feel their cancerous jaws gnawing at his entrails, slowly devouring his guts, eating him alive inside out, even as the slimy specter readied, mouth agape, to pounce on him from without.

Will had never been so afraid, as if all his fears had become one, had become this one monstrous, hideous, ugliness ready to devour him outside, already devouring him inside. His body shook. He could no longer control himself. There was nowhere to turn. It was too late to run.

Will howled, leaping forward, fingers clawing. "*Cthulhu!*"

He clutched frantically for the monster's throat, coughing and spitting to rid himself of the evil stench of that slimy, drooling beast. His hands clawed through the smoke, the empty smoke, the thinning smoke, until Will saw no monster at all, saw, merely, clouds of multi-colored smoke, smoke sent skywards by his futile, empty clawing, by the stirring of the Old Man's staff.

Never once did the Old Man's eyes leave Will.

Will's arms fell back against his sides. Tears ran from his eyes. His breath was stuck in this throat. He shook all over. He wished he could get sick, could vomit the ugly bile from his

Chapter 18 – An Old Man

churning stomach, but even that relief evaded him.

A deep silence overflowed the circle of stones.

"What...what happened?" Will coughed. "What was that? What happened? Was...was that the test?" Will coughed again, with equal measures of hope that it both was and was not.

The Old Man laughed softly. "No, no, of course not," he replied. "That would not have been much of a test now, would it? I mean, monsters made of smoke don't really pose much of a threat do they?"

"No...I...I guess not, not really." Will swallowed.

"Not nearly the test necessary for one so brave as to attempt a Noble Task, eh?" the Old Man asked, still stirring the fire. "That was merely the smoke before the fire as they say," and he chuckled. "Indeed, you must face the Monster of Monsters if you are to solve The Riddle of Riddles."

Will breathed deeply in an attempt to regain control of himself. Fear ran through him like quicksilver. The metallic taste of aluminum and ash coated his mouth, his tongue, a putrid taste caused by a monster made only of smoke. What real monster would the Old Man send after him now? What Monster of Monsters to really devour him?

"Are you afraid?" the Old Man asked.

Will's mind stumbled. Of course, he was afraid, but he could not let the Old man know. He must be brave. He must be a Noble Warrior.

No words left Will's lips.

The Old Man asked again, louder this time, "Are you afraid?"

Still, Will could not reply.

The Old Man's eyes branded Will, scalding his very soul.

"ARE YOU AFRAID?"

"**YES!** Yes, yes." Will's voice, first loud, trailed off. "Yes, I'm afraid. I don't want to be afraid, but I am, terribly afraid," he blurted out, unable to check himself.

A deep sigh issued from the Old Man's lips. He stepped

The Riddle of Riddles

back from the fire. "You may return to your seat," he said quite simply.

Will dropped his gaze. He was afraid. He had failed. Only the truly brave deserve to become Noble Warriors, and he was not one. The only thing he had succeeded in doing was to fan away a few puffs of smoke he had envisioned looked like some half-remembered, half-forgotten monster of his imagination. He was empty inside, as empty as the cavern. He dragged himself back to his seat and sat.

Failed!

Knorbert was busy with a lengthy and detailed study of the cavern's rock floor as though he were preparing for a doctoral dissertation on "Hard Places."

CHAPTER 19 – THE REAL TEST

For a few moments there was a deep silence, which even the sounds of the fire could not penetrate. Will took a deep breath and raised his eyes. The Old Man's eyes stuck Will, wiggling to escape, sprawled on that pin. But…but the Old man was smiling?

"Congratulations," he said. "You passed the test. You are now a Noble Warrior."

Will swallowed hard. "What do you mean? You didn't even give me the test yet, just that silly smoke thing which you said was not the test. I don't understand. I admitted I was afraid. I failed."

Knorbert sat with his head cocked to one side, looking at the Old Man.

"The test," the Old Man spoke softly, "was simply to see if you would tell the truth under trying circumstances. The test was the question *'Are you afraid?'* You readily admitted to your fear. The creature of smoke you and I conjured up together, coupled with the threat of a real menace far greater than the one already presented, made your fear quite visible. I knew you were afraid. Your test was to admit to that fear."

"But…but I was *afraid*! I really was terribly afraid. How can a brave and Noble Warrior be afraid?"

"We have all been afraid, every one of us. Fear is a necessary, healthy emotion. It can save our lives by alerting us to flee from danger or fight back against it. How did you feel when you were afraid?"

"Nervous." Will swallowed. The Old Man nodded.

"Uh, I was shaking. I remember that, my hands especially. I couldn't keep them still and my palms got sweaty. My heart was pounding and my stomach…my stomach turned over."

"Make note of those signs. Note the fact that you are afraid. Admit to your fear and face it, but do not be afraid of fear.

The Riddle of Riddles

It is the fear of fear that is crippling, the anticipation of that fear."

The Old Man stirred the fire. It flared high into the blackness but still Will shivered.

"Fear is like wind in a vacuum," said the Old Man. "It has no substance. Deep, deep within us, in the farthest reaches of our hearts, fears breathe quietly, stealthily, ever ready to pounce—or so we fear. We think we can hear it breathing, feel its breath, but if we listen really closely all we hear is silence."

Knorbert held his breath. He cast a quick, furtive glance at Will.

"It is only when we turn to face our fears that we find nothing there, find it *gone*, vanished like some monster made of smoke at the coming of a hand-fanned breeze, *gone* like blackness at the coming of light," the Old Man counseled. "Wherever we shine that light, however quickly, the blackness is gone like it was never there. In the surrounding dark we still seem to hear fear breathing, waiting to devour us. It is only when we illuminate all of the darkest corners of our hearts that we find that, while that deadly beast seems to be everywhere, it abides nowhere. It has no substance."

The Old Man's voice trailed off. The features on his face softened.

"The fear you felt was real. That was the Monster of Monster of which I spoke. You were afraid but faced that fear by admitting to it. You told the truth in spite of your fear. You have passed the test. Yesterday, you were an apprentice. Today, you are a Noble Warrior."

Will was dumbfounded. He did not know what to say. He began to blush. He could not look up or down. Somehow this seemed harder than facing his fears.

But Knorbert was absolutely ecstatic. "UAMIMAU!" he yelled. "You did it, Will. You did it! You passed the test. You are now a Noble Warrior." He jumped up and down, running, as best he could, round and round the circle of stones.

The Old Man stood quietly, hanging on his staff, a warm

Chapter 19 – The Real Test

smile radiant on his face, watching Knorbert's exuberant display.

Slowly, the realization overcame Will. He *had* done it. He felt good. He felt confident. He felt strong.

"The truth shall set you free." The Old Man leaned forward out of the darkness. "Let it be both your offense and your defense, quite like some formidable broadsword, sharp on both edges with a fearsome tip. When tempted by deceit, brandish Truth and deceit will flee, flee the highly polished blade that mirrors only substance, flee knowing full well it has no substance to reflect. That, above all, is what deceit itself fears. Deceit fears facing itself because it has no substance to reflect."

As the Old Man spoke, Will could almost feel that broadsword in his hand, feel its heft. He could see its blade shimmering in the firelight, the light from the fire magnified and reflected, sending multi-colored rays to the most distant corners of the cavern. He visualized it flashing through the air. He heard its whistle — ***SNICKER-SNACK***!

CHAPTER 20 – BELVIDERE – AGAIN

The fire crackled softly, burning low. The flickering shadows on the cavern walls, smaller and quieter, seemed friendlier now.

"We waste precious time." The Old Man's voice broke the silence. "I charge you to listen and learn, for what you hear now could well be the difference between your success or failure. I need not remind you what hangs in the balance." He cast a stern look at Will. "Time is of the essence."

Abruptly, Will's sense of wellbeing left him. He saw his success in the Truth Test just for what it was—one test—only that and nothing more. His real task still lay before him, and if the past was any indication, he still had a long way to go, miles to go before he could sleep. He leaned forward, his elbows on his knees, listening.

The Old Man took a deep breath. "All of us are born with a special purpose. Deep, deep down inside each of us, we are aware, however vaguely, of having our own special purpose, though we may not fully understand what that purpose is. You are fortunate. You know yours. There are others, however, who have chosen through laziness, mischief or design, to overlook theirs. They do not want to hear about such matters. Their purposes sit like so many unopened books under layers of dust in some forgotten corner in the attics of their minds. Some know that their purpose is there. Some even know how thick the dust is on the book's jacket, but still they refuse to pick it up, dust it off, and flip through its pages to see what it is about. They are the ones who will ignore you, hate you, or conspire against you because you pursue your purpose so diligently. Of all of these, the one to beware of most is called Belvidere."

"Belvidere!" Will choked on the word. "Belvidere who?"

"Belvidere of Many Names. Belvidere the Master of

Chapter 20 – Belvidere Again

Disguise. Belvidere the Amorphous One."

"Is he..." Will hesitated. "Is he a boy about my age?"

"That's possible," the Old Man replied. "Belvidere can assume almost any form, from the most hideous to the almost beautiful. That is why he is called the Master of Disguise, and 'He Who Must Not Be Named,' among his many, many identities. But why do you ask?"

"I met this strange boy on the beach who told me that his name was Belvidere. He was singing and dancing around on the sand, all the while shaking his tambourine. He even offered to let me play his harmonica, but, for some reason, I didn't trust him. He wouldn't answer any of my questions directly, wouldn't even tell me where I was. He tried to get me to follow him, to forget about today until tomorrow, but I don't *have* until tomorrow."

"A tambourine, huh?" The Old Man leaned forward. "So, already he has come to test you. That is a good sign. He must be very concerned about the possibility of your success."

"But if he is testing me why would he use his real name?"

"You were innocent then, innocent and unaware. It did not matter. Now you know."

"So you think that really was *the* Belvidere?" Knorbert asked.

"He certainly has all the necessary characteristics."

"What do you mean?" asked Will. "What makes you think that was the same Belvidere?"

"Oh, that's him alright." The Old Man pursed his lower lip. "Belvidere has certain tell-tale signs that give him away."

The Old man paused, and then took another deep breath. "You see, Belvidere exhibited remarkable abilities early on, and he quickly became a favorite of some nefarious higher-ups who encouraged his self-centered behavior. It did not take long before Belvidere began abusing his enormous talents, assuming one disguise or another in order to lead astray the unwary. Oh, at first he was merely full of pranks and mischief, but that soon gave way to meanness and cruelty. Finally, after leading one hapless soul to a particularly ignominious doom, Belvidere was brought to trial before the Grand Triumvirate and found guilty."

"Grand Triumvirate?" Will asked.

"Yes, the Grand Triumvirate of Over-Lords. It consists of the White Lord who rules over the Forces of Life and the Black Lord who rules over the Forces of Death. The third member is the Gray Lord who settles conflicts that arise between the White and Black Lords. He sides with one or the other to settle their disputes. Usually, no sooner is one argument settled, however, before another erupts."

The Old Man let go of his staff with one hand, and shifted his weight to the opposite leg.

"Consequently, there is almost perpetual war between the forces of the White Lord and the forces of the Black Lord, neither side winning a decisive victory, the tide flowing first in one direction, then the other, the Gray Lord as arbitrator."

Will shook his head slowly side to side. "That sounds just like my Reality," he whispered in a hollow voice. "Where I come from, it's war after war after war."

The Old Man nodded slowly. "Such *are* the wars between Good and Evil, between Black and White. The Black Lord has many, many more forces than the White Lord, but he needs them all, because the Forces of Evil fight among themselves, such being their nature. The Forces of Good, similarly, must wait for their enemies to attack before they can act, such being their nature."

"But why," Will asked, "would anyone choose evil?"

"You use the correct word, Will. They purposely *choose* evil, purposely *choose* death. The worst of the worst salivate in the corruption of innocence, gleefully dragging down the virtuous."

"Do they choose evil of their own free will?" Knorbert asked.

The Old Man nodded. "Indeed they do. They choose to do evil even as they deny that they have the free will to choose to do otherwise. That way they do not have to take responsibility for their actions. It's ludicrous, I know. It could be humorous if it

Chapter 20 – Belvidere Again

were not so deadly"

The fire flared momentarily, fed by a sudden gust of air. The Old Man's lips crossed in an enigmatic smile. Then, suddenly, he leaped high over the fire in a single bound, landing between Will and the fire. Will fell back, stopping his fall with back-stretched arms.

He began turning round and round in front of Will, spinning his staff above his head, and he began chanting. "The wicked will try to confuse you, confuse you with confusion. Confusion is chaos. Chaos confusion. Confusion piled on confusion, piled on confusion creates delusion. A lie piled on a lie, piled on a lie that white is black and black is white, and that two plus two equals five."

Knorbert snorted.

Instantly, the Old Man stopped, his staff held above his head, arms spread wide. He took a step toward Knorbert.

"Are you so naïve?" The Old Man squinted down at Knorbert. "If everyone believed two plus two equaled five, would that make it true?"

"Of…of course not." Knorbert drew back his head, looking up at the Old Man. "Everyone knows that two plus two equals four. Calling a tail a leg or a leg a tail does not make it so."

"Unless, of course," and the Old Man's voice became whispery. He turned to look at Will. "Unless, of course, they can convince you that you have the power to hold two contradictory beliefs in your mind simultaneously, and accept that both are true."

"Is that…is that even possible?" Will asked.

"See," said the Old Man, pointing his staff first at one and then the other, "both of you are already wondering. Such is their power of suggestion. You must always think for yourselves. Listen but remain skeptical."

The Old Man breathed in deeply, standing fiercely erect. "Question authority. Assume authority has not been legitimately earned until proven otherwise. Authority can never be owned.

The Riddle of Riddles

Authority can only be loaned."

A still silence overflowed the circle of stones.

"But what about Belvidere?" Knorbert asked. "Was he ever punished for what he did?"

The Old Man smiled. He stepped forward, turned slowly and sat down between Will and Knorbert. He placed his staff across his knees and leaned forward, staring into the flames.

"Yes, yes he did. The Grand Triumvirate had to judge whether Belvidere's actions to that poor, doomed soul were even punishable. The White Lord accused Belvidere of Culpable Cruelty while the Black Lord said that it was an act of Consensual Cruelty, and was, consequently, exempt from all punishment."

The Old Man turned his staff and roused the fire. "Belvidere is one of the Black Lord's favorites, and he pleaded that Belvidere was merely misguided, that he had, unknowingly, deceived even himself.

"But the Gray Lord was unconvinced and cast the deciding vote finding Belvidere guilty. So adamant was the Black Lord's defense, however, that Belvidere's punishment was reduced from Permanent Banishment in Boredom to forfeiture of privileges at his favorite eighteen knoll Flogging Club for six glooms."

"It sounds like he got off easy," said Knorbert.

"Not completely," said the Old Man. "The White Lord demanded and prevailed on one point in particular. In order to warn the unwary, Belvidere was never again permitted to travel in silence. He was required, from that day forth, to announce his presence by a sound not unlike the jingling of a bell around the neck of a cat."

"That explains the tambourine the boy on the beach carried," said Will.

"Yes, it does." The Old Man continued, "Furthermore, over the years Belvidere has become filled with such self-loathing that his heart has died. He is dead *inside*. That stench of death engulfs him wherever he goes, a stench that has been variously

Chapter 20 – Belvidere Again

described as decaying flesh, or burning air."

"Or like the low tide you smelled, Will," Knorbert interjected. "Remember?"

"Like the low tide that *he* said I smelled, you mean."

The Old Man leaned back. He draped an arm over each of their shoulders and squeezed gently. Knorbert twitched slightly.

"Mark it well because you will be able to recognize him by that sound and by that odor. He lies in wait to ensnare those who would do good, those who would improve their own situation or the situations of others, those who, like yourselves, would attempt the difficult. If he cannot ensnare you, he will attempt to delay, in hope that eventually it will be too late for you to complete your task.

"Beware of Belvidere. He is wily and full of tricks. Beware and be reviled by Belvidere the Bedeviler!" The Old Man pulled the two close. "And remember, you must not pursue Belvidere, for if you do, he will lead you on a wildly loose chase until you run out of time. Instead, pursue your goal, and Belvidere will have to come to you."

"Just like he came to you on the beach." Knorbert smiled over at Will.

"Thanks for the advice. Now I know what to look out for," said Will.

"Yes, yes, you do..." the Old Man nodded. He stretched his legs straight out in front of him. "But beside these outside threats, we all also possess within us the germs of our own failures, our own destruction—this lazy reaction here, that backslide into a bad habit there, this or that unfinished task, the work of our own hands or the lack thereof. Those germs begin the gnaw of death long before we are even aware of any pain. Then, suddenly, it is too late. The patient becomes so sick that any effort for revival becomes futile. You, too, are so infected. Do not let your own lacks help Belvidere. Be constant to your purpose, and you cannot fail. In fact, if you pursue your quest unwaveringly, you may even catch some Waves of Grace."

The Riddle of Riddles

"Waves of Grace?" Will asked. "What are Waves of Grace?"

"You need not wonder. You will recognize them if they come." The Old Man rubbed their shoulders. "Look into your heart for the obvious as well as the subtle. But do not speak about what you find there prematurely because the simple act of speaking can dispel the energy of what you have so delicately discovered."

The Old Man let go of their shoulders, grasped his staff and leaned forward to stir the last of the glowing coals. He sat silently for a bit, but then, as though roused from a deep reverie, he stood. He looked directly at Will and said, "And always remember that there are no such things as coincidences. If something appears to be coincidental, look for meaning in that coincidence."

The Old Man twirled the staff between his fingers, stopped suddenly, and pointed it at Knorbert. "What did I just say?"

"Uh...that there are no such things as coincidences?" Knorbert's voice squeaked.

"Correct, but don't ask me. Tell me!"

"**THERE ARE NO SUCH THINGS AS COINCIDENCES**," Knorbert yelled.

"**AND LOOK FOR MEANING IN THAT COINCIDENCE!**" Will added loudly.

The Old Man snorted a short and quiet laugh.

There was a pause, a deep silence broken only by the quiet sounds of the dying fire. An ember popped. A spark arched, sizzling to its death.

"Come along now," the Old Man said in a louder voice. "Let us return to the light. It continues to advance even as we speak, bringing us ever closer to Lucidown." He looked at Will. "Ever closer to sundown," he repeated. "We know what that means."

He doused the remains of the fire by scattering fingertips

Chapter 20 – Belvidere Again

of an ash-gray dust from his pouch on its coals, and started from the cave. He held his staff high. Its glowing tip cast a dull red light sufficient to illuminate their way back through the narrow, twisting passageways leading out, finally, into a dazzlingly bright daylight.

They stood a moment adjusting—adjusting—adjusting to the brightness of a day no longer young.

"Where do we go from here?" Will asked.

"You must find you own way. I can merely show you a beginning," and the Old Man pointed.

Beyond the Old Man's outstretched finger, a narrow path wound up and around the side of the Mount Kneverest. "There lies the way to the summit. From the summit you will be able to see beyond the Edge. The answer to the Riddle lies out past the Edge, lost somewhere in the mostly unexplored depths of Inner Space. Be on your way. The sun nears its peak."

Will and Knorbert started toward the narrow path, to where it bent around the side of the mountain. They had gone but a short distance before Will turned. The Old Man was seated silent, his back to them. He stared out across the savannah, waiting, perhaps, for the next adventurers. Will thought longingly of Knumerator.

"Goodbye." Knorbert waved.

There was no reply.

CHAPTER 21 – MOUNT KNEVEREST

At first, the apron leading up the mountain was wide enough for them to proceed side by side, and its sweep was so slight that it was little more than a pleasant stroll. It did not take long, however, before the trail grew steeper, even as it narrowed, forcing them to walk single file. Knorbert pushed his way to the front, and Will was forced to fall in behind him.

As the incline stiffened, they were forced to use both hands to help pull themselves up rock to rock, ledge to ledge. Eventually, the mountain became bare of most vegetation. Here and there, a plucky bush might offer a handhold of assistance from between the sharp rocks, but the climb gradually became more and more difficult, and their breathing more labored.

Up, up, up, they climbed; climbing through a ring of light clouds whose cool dampness was a welcome relief. Above the clouds they found a ledge on which to catch their breath. The thin white clouds wreathed the mountain beneath them. Above loomed the summit, its stony face hanging over their heads, watching them.

In the near distance, large masses of dense clouds started moving toward the mountain.

"Look Knorbert. Over there!" Will pointed. "A Willi-Nilli!"

Off in a distant cloud was a shape that looked like a flion, only this one had two heads and a long snake-like tail.

Knorbert shook his head. "It is just the clouds, Will. Why are you trying to spook me like that? Look, over there. Doesn't that look like a giant ice cream cone? And there! That looks like a prancing horse with a long flowing mane."

Knorbert scowled at Will's smile.

After a brief rest, they continued up the side of cascades of ridges. At one point, Knorbert led them out onto an extremely

Chapter 21 Mount Kneverest

narrow ledge that forced them to precede sideways, their backs against the mountain, their arms outstretched, fingertips playing lightly over the cliff's face. The view (if one dared look) was dizzyingly spectacular. All around them sharp, gray peaks poked into the ribs of the darkening clouds. Some pierced the cloud cover as though intent on keeping their bare heads in the sunlight. The bottom was black in the distance far below.

The clouds grew darker and thicker the higher they climbed, a thickness of clouds that competed with the thinness of the air. The clouds crowded tightly against the mountainside as the wind blew steadily with a hollow sound across their ears.

"Will, did you hear that?"

Will listened, but all he could hear was the growing howl of the buffeting wind. "I don't hear anything except the wind. What did you hear?"

"I do not know. Perhaps I was mistaken, but I thought I heard someone or something wailing far off in the distance."

"It's probably just a Willi-Nilli."

"Why do you insist on teasing me? I would prefer that you not speak at all, rather than have to listen to your ticklish tongue."

The ledge disappeared completely, forcing them up, over, and between abutments as the weather continued to worsen. A storm of frightening magnitude was rapidly approaching. As far as an eye could see, the sky was covered with dark, undulating clouds. The wind blew fiercely now, tearing at their balance as they slowly made their way up the side of the mountain.

"We've got to hurry, Knorbert. The storm is almost on us."

"I *cannot* hurry," Knorbert's voice quivered. "You know I cannot hurry. You make me nervous when you rush me."

The mountain cracked and then groaned. Rocks began falling all around them. A large boulder crashed down from overhead right onto the spot on which they had stood just moments before. The storm was shaking boulders from the mountain.

The Riddle of Riddles

"We *must* hurry. We can't stay here. We have to get above the falling rock. We have to reach the summit. Hurry Knorbert. *Hurry!*"

But Knorbert had stopped to grasp hold of the mountain. He stood pressing the mountain to his chest, his strong fingers dug deeply into its cracks. He began muttering, "Cause or Effect? Effect or Cause?"

"What's the matter, Knorbert?"

Knorbert did not seem to hear. He just kept repeating, "Cause or Effect? Effect or Cause? Cause or Effect? Effect or Cause?"

Will stepped around Knorbert, reached out and grabbed him by the wrist, dragging him forcibly up the side of the mountain as more rocks and boulders continued crashing down around them. The devastation chased them. The wind clawed at them. This was no time for mistakes.

Around a sharp bend and up over a narrow ledge they finally found the summit—and none too soon, for the storm was now in its full fury.

The wind screamed. It blew in gusts with such power they turned their faces away from its fury. Then it was briefly calm, which only accentuated the storm's ferocity when it came again. The clouds rushed in from all directions at once, crashing together directly overhead with enormous claps of thunder. Lightning struck at them like asps.

Will watched the storm with a wild fascination.

Knorbert stood next to Will, his head buried in Will's shoulder. The sky was black from horizon to horizon.

"**Knorbert**," Will yelled over the deafening scream of the wind. "What is this? You're not crying are you? I thought Knotheads never cried, couldn't cry lest they attract the dreaded Willi-Nillies."

At that, Knorbert cried even louder, his cries lost beneath the noise of the storm. "Oh me, oh my!" he sobbed. "The Willi-Nillies are coming! The Willi-Nillies are coming!"

Chapter 21 Mount Kneverest

"**I thought you didn't believe in Willi-Nillies**." Will shouted.

Knorbert just wailed all the louder, and the wind wailed back, howling and screeching like hordes of banshees, its gusts like fingers probing for pain.

The wind seemed to come from no direction at all, but spun around them, around and around, tearing at their arms and legs as though to rip them from their bodies. It blew hot. It blew cold.

A brilliant flash of lightning split the sky, followed immediately by a grand-daddy clap of thunder.

They stood on the summit as torrents of rain poured down.

CHAPTER 22 – WILLI-NILLIES?

The darkened sky had already stolen most of the color from the day, and the intense rain smeared a runny coat of dull gray water-paint over the rest.

Mixed with the tumult of the storm, but in even louder pitches, they heard shrieking, screeching—and laughing.

They heard moans like the dead, wails like the frustrated, cries like the lonely, and over it all, mixed with it all, a backdrop of laughter like the crazies. Knorbert clung to Will, crying uncontrollably. Will, too, wanted to close his eyes and turn his back on the storm. The urge was intense, but he forced himself to watch, facing into the howling gale.

And Willi-Nillies were upon them.

They were two-headed creatures with the bodies of big cats equipped with two pairs of powerful Roc-like wings, one pair on each side. On the ends of each of their long curious necks was a dragon's head. Each head was alternately breathing fire or choking on its own smoke.

Some Willi-Nillies were thin and sleek, while others were fat and gross. Fur covered some, with while others were scaly and reptilian. Some were multi-colored, some iridescent, some drab, some patterned. In some, the colors ran through them in waves.

Will's heart pounded in his chest. His throat closed. He, too, was shaking with fear of these terrifying monsters.

The Willi-Nillies flashed through the dark sky, screaming and keening, crying and sighing, moaning and groaning, and laughing—bubbling ripples of laugher, hollering hoots of laughter, jolly tubs of laugher. They had so many different kinds of laughter that Will recognized but a few. Will wished that he could laugh as many laughs as a Willi-Nilli could laugh, until he realized that too many of those laughs were making him shudder.

Will and Knorbert clung to each other, quivering with

Chapter 22 – Willi-Nillies?

terror. Will looked up at the storm of Willi-Nillies wondering if all was now lost. Had they come this far only to lose it all, to be destroyed by these terrifying creatures?

But deep within the chaotic clamor of the storm, the sound of laughter remained. The crying and screeching and moaning were there too, but the laughter was like a distant tickle that could not be ignored.

A Willi-Nilli swooped by, so close they felt its wind in passing. One head was moaning while the other head was hooting. Then came another whooping and groaning. One Willi-Nilli screamed down at them from directly overhead. The mouth of one head gaped wide as though about to swallow them, but at the last moment the other head took control, and with the eeriest of laughs, pulled the Willi-Nilli down and around them. Its tail whizzed by and cracked like a whip. Its eerie laugh faded as the Willi-Nilli disappeared off into the distance.

Then out of nowhere, came the sound of a particularly infectious laugh. It laughed and laughed and laughed laughing at its own laugh, and Will could not help himself—he burst into laughter too.

And the Willi-Nillies flashed out of sight like quicksilver bullets, taking the storm with them.

"Look, Knorbert! One burst of laugher, and the horrid Willi-Nillies run away like frightened children!"

"Willi-Nillies?" Knorbert asked raising his head. "If you saw Willi-Nillies, why are you laughing?"

"I couldn't help myself. They made me laugh. You should have seen them, all of them, sweeping through the air, screaming and moaning and howling. Most of them were terrifying..." Will shuddered, "don't get me wrong, but some of them didn't look so frightening to me. In fact, some of them looked downright silly, like children playing make-believe, children trying to look scary."

"Are you sure they were Willi-Nillies?"

"I would say so. They kind of fit your description."

"Oh me, oh my! Willi-Nillies! Willi-Nillies!" Knorbert

started sobbing again.

"See for yourself," said Will. "It sounds like they're coming back."

The clouds started closing in again, though not nearly as quickly as before. The wind picked up and the wailing and screeching, howling and laughing steadily grew louder.

Knorbert started shaking and whimpering. "Oh me, oh my, oh no! Here they come again. What shall we do?"

"Watch," said Will matter-of-factly. Knorbert huddled behind Will, peeking over his shoulder.

The sky darkened, and the wind began to blow viciously again.

The storm was on them with the chilling shriek of hard chalk screeching on slate. With the storm came the Willi-Nillies.

They were everywhere at once. They flashed through the sky achieving incredible speeds, sometimes flying backwards and upside-down at the same time. The two heads waged a ferocious see-saw battle, each head possessed with an emotion opposite the other. Whichever head was in control took the Willi-Nilli careening off in its direction, as the other head tugged vainly in the opposite direction, smoke and fire billowing from both.

Here and there some Willi-Nillies collided. Sometimes there were multiple crashes, each one accompanied by loud booms, all adding to the pandemonium of the scene.

A Willi-Nilli buzzed close by their heads.

And another.

One after another, they buzzed by, each time getting closer and closer, until, finally, one Willi-Nilli flashed by with one head scowling with a deeply furrowed brow, growling gutturally, while the tongue of the other head lolled from side to side as it laughed sillily.

It was just too much for Will, and he burst out laughing.

S W O O O S H...

The Willi-Nillies were gone like run-through beads on a hard tile floor.

Chapter 22 – Willi-Nillies?

"Did you see that?" Will asked. "Didn't they look ridiculous?"

Knorbert wiped his eyes. "Those dumb old Willi-Nillies, they never fooled me. Haw! What is there to be afraid of in them?" He wrinkled his nose.

Will looked at Knorbert.

"Uh…well, that is…well, maybe they fooled me a little…in the beginning I mean, but afraid?" Knorbert's smile stole into the corners of his lips, slipped away, and slowly stole back. "I was never really afraid. Ne-ver. That is…I was skeptical. I had been told all the stories, but I knew there was nothing to really be afraid of. I mean, fear is like wind in a vacuum, right Will?"

"Right," Will chuckled.

"And besides," Knorbert continued, "all it takes is one look to see how ridiculous they really are."

"Did you see that one with its tongue hanging out?" asked Will.

"Oh my, yes," Knorbert answered, laughing a bit more easily now. "He sure did look silly."

Together they watched the sun chase away most of the clouds while it played tag with the rest.

CHAPTER 23 – A LOCOMOBILE

As the storm slowly dissipated, they stood marveling at the spectacular view from the summit.

The summit itself was relatively flat and almost circular, its rim dropping away steeply on all sides. Behind them lay the Wild Wood, Sapientiopolis, and, far off in the distance, the gray cliffs of the headland. All around, a border of white surf crashed against the Edge, and beyond it lay the deep crimson sea. Overhead, Luci radiated a warm, golden glow on the flinty peaks and deep crevasses that lay below.

"Oh my, how beautiful."

"It certainly is," Will agreed, feasting his eyes on the beauty of the scene, "and so vast."

"Oh me, yes. So vast and so distant," Knorbert said with such melancholy that it drew a surprised look from Will.

"What we need is a vehicle," Knorbert suggested. "A locomobile."

"A what?"

"A locomobile. Knothead engineers have been working on the designs of a flying machine for as long as I can remember. They have developed several prototypes but, unfortunately, none have ever gotten off the ground."

"No such thing?" Will pursed his lips.

"Not yet."

Will looked around. The Edge was as far away as the distance it had taken them all morning to cross.

"The Old Man said that the answer to the Riddle lay out beyond the Edge," Will recalled, "but the Edge completely encircles us. Which way do we go?"

"And how do we get there from here?" Knorbert added, glancing uneasily off the summit and then out toward the distant, white-shouldered surf.

Chapter 23 – A Locomobile

"That's what's bothering me. It is rapidly approaching noon. We have no end in sight, and no way to get there. Maybe now you can understand why I'm worried." He shot an unsmiling glance at Knorbert.

"The Old Man sent us up here. He must have had a reason," said Knorbert. Abruptly, he plopped down on the ground, unslung Forlorn from around his shoulder and began to play. Gone was any determined effort to create music. Instead he paid little attention to his playing, lost—completely unaware he even was playing.

And he had never sounded better.

As the notes rang out clear and crisp in the cool, thin air, Will became stilled inside, listening, anticipating the next note and the next and the next.

As he listened there came notes between notes, notes and tones filling spaces no longer empty, creating music as sweet as ever was played by a cricket's leg on a cat's whisker. The music entered Will and seized him. He found himself actually expecting the music, knowing what notes were coming next. So entranced was he that he nearly missed the movement.

It was a Willi-Nilli.

As Will watched, the Willi-Nilli slowly glided toward them, and it was singing! It was singing along with Knorbert's playing, filling in those empty spaces between the notes.

From each of its mouths came rich, colorful melodies, each head in harmony with the other. Knorbert and the Willi-Nilli together were creating the beautiful music.

Knorbert stopped playing. "UAMIAMU! Oh my, did I ever get so carried away. I cannot remember when I ever played so well. Now *that* was music! Even you cannot argue with me about that!"

Will's eyes never once left the Willi-Nilli. It had stopped singing when Knorbert stopped playing, but it had not dashed away. It hovered quietly nearby, its wings slowly rotating. While it was singing colors had passed through it, each note a different

The Riddle of Riddles

color. But now all color had drained from its body and it had become a neutral gray, one head white, and the other black.

"That truly was beautiful music, Knorbert, and look. Turn around and see who else has been enjoying your music."

Knorbert stiffened, and then slowly turned.

"Your playing attracted her," Will whispered. "She was singing with you. The two of you together were creating that beautiful music. Play some more, Knorbert. See if you can draw her closer."

"Closer?" Knorbert sat straight up. "Are you crazy?"

"Relax, Knorbert. See how small she is compared to the others. She looks young, and she seems tame enough. Come on. Play some more. If she becomes the slightest bit aggressive, we can always scare her off with laughter."

Knorbert closed his eyes. A flutter of emotions ran across his face. Then he opened his eyes, got to his feet and resumed playing. At first he was so intent on his playing, trying to recapture the previous mood, that he interfered with himself. But as soon as the Willi-Nilli began singing again, Knorbert found his center, and the enchantment resumed. His big fingers became magic wands, producing musical sounds that overflowed his limits, filtering out into unknown realms. Each note was so perfect that it added a colder crispness to the air.

The Willi-Nilli danced slowly toward them, singing all the while, its wings fluttering in time with the music, music that was better than either of them could have produced alone, better, even, than the sum total of their combined talents.

And the Willi-Nilli drew closer still, so close she now seemed to be dancing with Knorbert.

Knorbert fed off the Willi-Nilli's music, feeding his own in return. They played and fed, fed and played, ascending, ascending in beauty, ascending in power, higher and higher until Knorbert feared he would pop off to heaven, or to wherever it is that Willi-Nillies disappear.

He stopped—had to stop—from the sheer exhaustion of

Chapter 23 – A Locomobile

the entire experience.

"How could I have *ever* been afraid of Willi-Nillies?" Knorbert shook his head, staring at the Willi-Nilli. "That is what comes from listening to gossip."

"Oh, but I cannot remember when last I had such fun," said the white Willi-Nilli head, a few licks of flames flickering about.

"But now that I miss it, I wish I had never begun," said the black Willi-Nilli head, a hint of smoke escaping from its mouth.

Will and Knorbert stared at each other, mouths gaping.

"The music was such," one head said.

"We remained in touch," said the other head.

"I'm glad you enjoyed it as much as we did." Will jumped into the conversation as quickly as he could, not wanting to lose the opportunity to engage such a beguiling creature in conversation. "My name is Will, and this is my friend, Knorbert Knothead, the fellow you've been singing with."

"You play so well, I will never forget," the white head said with a smile instead of a frown..

"But let's not forget he's a Knothead yet," the black head added, its smile curling down.

"And you are an irresponsible Willi-Nilli!" Knorbert shot back.

"Quite right, quite right, but we need not fight," the pleasant white head on the right said, stretching its long neck, its head moving high and wide

"Just wait, just wait, he will soon show his spite," the unpleasant black head on the left said as its neck undulated, its head moving side to side.

"Now, now," Will spoke in tones as soothing as he could muster. "Let's not fight. We have been getting along just fine. Let's not spoil it. Just remember the music you created. Wasn't it beautiful?"

"As dear as ever I did hear," sighed the happy white head.

"Sweet as a treat, though not complete," decried the

grouchy black head.

"Oh my, yes," Knorbert enthused. "The music was beautiful."

"Well then," Will said, "let's all be friends. Friendship is a rare and beautiful thing, as rare and beautiful as your music. To listen to your music is to listen to your hearts."

Each of the Willi-Nilli's necks stretched up and around, and then she settled herself slowly on the summit with a brief fluffing of her wings.

"Friendship is a dream we have never seen," confessed the white head.

"Friendship is belonging instead of longing," professed the black head.

"Friendship is need-feed without greed-feed," the left head said.

"Friendship is heart-smart sharing-caring," said the right head.

With that, the Willi-Nilli insinuated herself between Will and Knorbert, and like a big kitten began rubbing herself warmly against them. Knorbert, at first taken aback at such intimacy, soon found himself stroking the neck nearest him, a goofy smile on his face. Will began scratching the other neck, and the Willi-Nilli started purring.

"Just think, Knorbert. Not that long ago you didn't even believe that Willi-Nillies existed."

"Perceive and believe," said the white head most optimistically, this time from the left.

"Persist to exist," the black head, now on the right, said quite pessimistically.

"Who is who here?" Will asked.

Each head answered alternately:

"Just us."

"Trust us."

"What I mean is, who do I talk to?"

"Why to me, of course, you should discourse," both heads

Chapter 23 – A Locomobile

answered in unison.

"Whoa," said Will. "Not so fast. What do you call yourselves? Do you have a name or names?"

Each head replied in turn:

"No name have I."

"Nor know one to go by."

"But that cannot be," said Knorbert. 'Everything must have a name. "I mean, how could we even begin to discuss a thing, anything, if it did not have a name? No, no. You must have a name. Things would just be too confusing otherwise."

"Why don't we give you a name? Would you like that?" Will asked.

"A game name," one Willi-Nilli head exclaimed after the other, "not the same name?"

"No, of course not," Will answered. "Wouldn't each of you like to have your own name?"

Each head turned toward the other.

"Will I?"

"Nil I!"

Both heads stretched their necks skyward.

"Shill I?"

"Shall I?"

"That's it! Of course!" Will clapped his hands. "Shilli and Shalli!"

"Perfect!" Knorbert beamed. "Shilli-Shalli, our Willi-Nilli!"

"Well then, Shilli and Shalli," Will said, looking first at one head and then at the other. "What do you think of your names?"

"Who is who?" each head faced the other. "Who do I call you?"

"Well…" Will looked at both, "how about if we call you Shilli," he said, stroking the white head, "and then you'll be Shalli," and he turned toward the black head, and rubbed her neck.

"I'm Shilli and you're Shalli."

The Riddle of Riddles

"I'm Shalli and you're Shilli."

"Together we are Shilli-Shalli," the heads sang in concert.

"Well then, Shilli-Shalli," Will cleared his throat. "Now that we are friends, I wonder if I could ask you for a favor. You see...that is...well, Knorbert and I are searching for the answer to a riddle, The Riddle of Riddles to be exact."

"Are you that smart?" asked the right head now known as Shilli.

"So strong of heart?" asked the left head now known as Shalli.

"I am a genius," said Knorbert, "and what I do not know I can always figure out."

"To know a thing," sighed Shilli.

"To know anything!" cried Shalli.

"You see," Knorbert continued, "my mind operates in comprehensively and logically oriented linguistic units conveying the intellectualization of any event as experientially sensed by one subject to another in that form most expressive of the experience to be transmitted, and..." He paused to clear his throat.

"Yes, indeed," Will interrupted. Shilli looked like she was about ready to fall asleep, and Shalli looked ready to flee. "Knorbert is very smart. He is the essence of logic."

"Logic? What's that?" asked Shalli.

"Logic? Is what?" Shilli then asked.

Knorbert grimaced. "How can you function without logic?"

"We go with the flow."

"Soar without law."

"And you go so fast," said Will.

"And so recklessly," added Knorbert.

"We've been informed that the answer to the Riddle lies out beyond the Edge, lost somewhere in Inner Space," Will ignored Knorbert's comment, "and, well, it's such a long way off, that I was wondering, that is, we were wondering, if, perhaps, just maybe, you might give us a ride."

Chapter 23 – A Locomobile

"**WHAT?**" exclaimed Knorbert.

Will shot Knorbert a look. "Knorbert, please! Listen to me." He held his hands outstretched his palms up. "It's almost midday, and we've got such a long way to go. Look. Go ahead, look. See how far away the Edge is. Do you want to walk there? And then what? Can you walk on water?"

"I knew it," Knorbert folded his arms across his chest. "I just knew it. Go ahead. Blame me. Blame me for our slow going."

"I'm not blaming you, Knorbert. You've done a great job getting us this far, but we have a long way to go, and no way to get there."

"And you propose hitching a ride on a Willi-Nilli?" Knorbert drew back, and looked down his long nose at Will.

"Of course. Actually, it was your idea, and a grand idea it was at that." He stood facing Knorbert and started speaking rapidly. "You said it yourself. We need a vehicle, a locomobile, a Willi-Nilli." He pointed at Shilli-Shalli.

"I *never* said a Willi-Nilli," Knorbert said loudly. "I said a locomobile, and apparently you are the one who is *loco*."

Will scowled. "Come on, Knorbert. Shilli-Shalli is big and strong enough to carry us, and she sure is fast enough."

"And reckless enough, too," Knorbert huffed. "You do it. Count me out. Ride on a Willi-Nilli? *Ne-ver*! Not me. I mean, they are wild and uncontrollable. How can you trust a Willi-Nilli? They have too many crazy laughs," he paused, "and they are blind to boot!"

"That's cruel, Knorbert."

"There is nothing cruel about the truth. I mean, it is true. They are blind."

"You are right. They are blind, but they must have some other senses that they use to find their way. Whatever those senses are, enabled Shilli-Shalli to find us." Will smiled and reached over to scratch Shalli behind her ear. "And to cuddle herself here between us."

"The absence of eyes does not mean no sight," said Shilli.

"Subtle senses are freed to guide our flight," said Shalli. Both heads smiled at the same time.

"If the eyes are blind, one must look with the heart."

"Insight is foresight, the end seen before the start."

"The thing important is the thing not seen.'"

"Eyes interfere with the heart's foreseen dreams."

"Did you hear that? She sees without eyes. Come on, Knorbert. Start thinking positively. Shill-Shalli is right. We must trust her, and she must trust us. It is the only logical solution to our dilemma. You're the logical one. Think about it. Why, we could be miles and miles, moraes and moraes, out into Inner Space before we even had time to think about it."

"That is exactly what bothers me," Knorbert answered, gazing out over the Edge, "*before* we even have time to think about it."

"It will be perfectly safe." The pitch of Will's voice rose. "We can do it. I know we can. We can do it if we all work together. Shilli-Shalli will do the flying with us up on her back. Knorbert, you are plenty strong enough. You can steer us by controlling Shilli-Shalli's heads, using her fur like reins, just like riding a horse. I will ride behind you, looking over your shoulder like a guide and lookout. I'll even help steer if you need me to."

"As a horse, he said, are we to be led," sputtered Shilli.

"A horse, of course, never given its head," muttered Shalli.

"What do you think?" Will asked, purposely overlooking the uneasy looks Knorbert exchanged with Shilli-Shalli.

"Oh me, oh my! Illogical," Knorbert said half under his breath, "and blind to boot. What chance would we have?"

"A chance! A chance to succeed! That's something we don't have stuck up here. She may be blind and reckless and illogical, but she is also real. She is lightning fast and strong enough to carry us wherever we are brave enough to allow her to go. You can steer us clear of any dangers. We will steer her together. And think, just think where we can go and what we can

Chapter 23 – A Locomobile

do if we all work together."

As Will spoke he noticed that Knorbert grew quiet, and started stroking his chin.

"We need her, Knorbert. I need her. Don't forget what I have to lose."

Will leaned forward. He raised his eyebrows. "And remember the music you made with Shilli-Shalli. Just think what else you two could do together. This is our chance. We have to learn to use what is provided. We have to learn to trust our Willi-Nillies."

Knorbert was frowning. "I do not know about this." He folded his arms across his chest, shifted from one leg to another, and then unfolded his arms. "But…*tsssk…*" He took a deep breath, folded his arms once again, and shifted back to his other foot.

"You know, Will…" He was speaking slowly. "You may be right. We just might be able to do this." Knorbert unfolded his arms once more. "We *could* do it. We can do it. **We will do it!**" He blurted out quite suddenly.

"Excellent!" Will clapped his hands. Then turning toward Shilli-Shalli, he asked softly, "What do you say, Shilli?" He turned and looked at the other head. "Shalli? We need you. Will you give us a ride on your back?"

"Need, indeed," Shilli cried.

"Is friendship's seed," Shalli sighed.

"Mount up, my friends, and let us fly," Shalli trilled.

"Beyond the Edge, across the sky," Shilli thrilled.

"Yes!" Will pumped his arm. "I am going to find the answer to The Riddle of Riddles with a little help from my friends."

Knorbert grabbed hold of Shilli-Shalli's fur and swung himself up onto her back, his legs sticking out from her sides. Will leaped lightly up behind Knorbert. Shilli-Shalli, a bit jumpy from never before having been ridden, gave a jolt and then bolted.

ZZZOOOOOOMMMMMM…

She streaked across the sky faster than a Nimbus

The Riddle of Riddles

Millennium prototype.

    The sun hung for one moment, motionless, at its zenith and then started down.

CHAPTER 24 – INNER SPACE

They flashed upward in a long sweeping arc, and streaked out beyond the Edge. Will looked back over his shoulder, and then looked again unable to believe his eyes.

"Wow, this is fantastic! I can't believe how fast we're going. We've already left the *Edge* far behind, heading for the depths of Inner Space."

Knorbert scowled. His hands were tangled in the fur on each of Shilli and Shalli's necks, but he was confused as to how to control their flight .

Knorbert first pulled back on one head, and then on the other, then back to the first, and then back to the second. "Steering an actual course is impossible, Will," he said. "The best I can do is to try to aim us in the right direction."

Faster and faster, they careened through the sky. Shill-Shalli's front wings drove them forward with an initial thrust, followed by another surge from the second set of wings. Her whole body undulated, and they whipped forward at a confounding speed. They flashed so far out into the Inner Space that even Mount Kneverest was soon lost to view.

"There is such a different view from the back of a Willi-Nilli," Will said breathlessly. "Things take on an entirely different perspective."

"And you can see so far," Knorbert whispered in awe, his eyes as wide as Frisbees.

All around them unfamiliar flying objects flashed into view and then, just as quickly, were gone.

"Watch where you are going!" Knorbert yelled at Shilli-Shalli. "Oops, sorry. I did not really mean that, about watching. I mean…I forgot you are blind." He was starting to sweat from his exertions trying to control her wild gyrations.

"I know where I am, but know not how I got here," Shilli

The Riddle of Riddles

explained, swooping right.

"I know where I should be, though not how to get there," Shalli claimed, sweeping left.

"I can go anywhere there is to go, but know not where to go," Shilli complained, pulling to the right.

"Yet once I get wherever I should be, then where I am I will know," maintained Shalli, sculling to the left.

Knorbert groaned.

At each incantation whichever head was speaking took control, swooping first this way, then that, screeching along in one direction then screaming along another.

Shilli took off, pulling hysterically in one direction, laughing wildly, while Shalli pulled futilely in the opposite direction sobbing desperately. Then Shalli was off, humming contentedly, while Shilli squealed with fear; then Shalli screamed crazily while Shilli babbled incoherently; then Shilli; then Shalli. Shilli-Shalli. Shilli-Shalli. Back and forth, back and forth, the heads fought for control, each billowing smoke and fire as they went, Knorbert fighting to direct their erratic flight.

Each change of control brought with it a change of color, each color indicative of a temper. Shilli was a raging red, while Shalli was a glowering green. Then Shalli turned a yielding yellow, while Shilli became a bassoon blue—then Shalli an indignant indigo, and Shalli a violent violet. Shilli turned a blistering black, before Shalli became a lightning fast blast of whispery white.

The color started in whatever head was in control. It rippled down its neck, and then slowly back through the entire body until the other head took control. At that time, its particular color would begin to fade and another color, another mood, would take over. Back and forth, the colors flowed in varying segments of time. The power flowed back and forth as the colors and the sounds flowed.

Knorbert struggled to maintain some semblance of control.

Chapter 24 – Inner Space

They flashed off, far out into the Deep in no particular direction that Will could discern, farther than they could have traveled without Shilli-Shalli in a year full of such days.

There were no longer any dimensions to their new reality—no ups, no down, no aheads, no behinds, a horizon that no longer had an axis. They were immersed in the ether of Inner Space, surrounded by it, glimpses of certainty flashing by in the mist of speed like planetary way stations.

Out of nowhere, hordes of Willi-Nillies were suddenly flashing all around them. Knorbert pulled first at one head, then the other, trying to aim them through the squall of buzzing Willi-Nillies.

"Shilli," he cried, "not that way. Watch it, Shalli. There is a…there was a Willi-Nilli. Shilli, slow down! Shalli, be careful."

But Shilli-Shalli paid no heed. It was all Knorbert could do to point them in a general direction, to keep them clear of crashes with the surrounding hordes of Willi-Nillies, some of whom seemed intent on crashing into them.

Careening off in one direction, they encountered a sub-culture of Willi-Nillies who were downright savage. They were all black in color and made gnashing sounds with their teeth.

Forced back in the other direction, they found some Willi-Nillies so happy that both heads were laughing and crying at the same time.

They were flying fast—too fast—much too fast.

Knorbert pulled back desperately on Shilli's head, on Shalli's head, sweating heavily, but Shilli-Shalli sped on, oblivious to all his efforts.

"Help me, Will. Help me rein her in. I am getting very tired."

Will reached around Knorbert, and grabbed handfuls of Shilli-Shalli's fur.

"Slow down!" Knorbert yelled, pulling back with all his might on both heads at once but Shilli-Shalli was totally out of control.

"Pull, Will. Pull!"

Together they strained, pulling frantically on Shilli-Shalli as hard as they could, leaning back, their arm muscles popping, and their fingers aching. Gradually, they managed to slow their maddening dash off into the depths of Inner Space.

An asteroid came into view up ahead. It was as nondescript as any one of the many planetary way-stations that rocketed by like missed opportunities

"I need to find someplace to rest," Knorbert yelled, indicating the direction of the prospect up ahead with a nod of his head.

"No way," Will yelled back. "We must keep going. Shilli-Shalli says she knows where she is going."

"But not how to get there, remember?"

Shilli-Shalli spun into a tight corkscrew coil.

"We are out of control. I need a rest. One stop cannot hurt. Just one stop. Just once cannot hurt."

"One stop, two stops, three stops more," Shilli gasped.

"How many stops are in store?" Shalli asked.

"We'll never get where we want to be," Shilli warned.

"We'll never make it, as we all can see," Shalli scorned.

"We're losing control, Knorbert!"

"I know. I know. We should push on, but I am tired. I deserve a rest. I cannot go on"

"Woe is me, I'm all done in," Shilli wailed.

"Can it be? Is resting a sin?" Shalli railed.

"I'm responsible. Beat me black."

"Poor little me. I have such lacks."

Knorbert pointed with his chin. "That place there, Will. Do you see it?"

"I see it, but we don't have time to stop."

Shilli-Shalli's necks were beginning to twine round and round each other, and she began to squeal.

"Guilty as guilty can be."

"Pity, pity, pity poor me."

Chapter 24 – Inner Space

"Guilty for feeling guilty."

"Self pity-loving pity."

"Guilty, guilty! Pity me."

"Pity, pity guilty me."

Round and round, tighter and tighter, faster and faster, more and more out of control they flew, Shilli-Shalli's necks hopelessly tangled.

"Pull, Knorbert!" Will pulled with all his might. "Get a grip! Pull!"

"It is no use, Will. I cannot go on," and before Will could protest any further, they careened off into a death spiral, completely out of control.

CRASH!

They tumbled head over heels over one another and were scattered.

CHAPTER 25 – THE PLEASURE PALACE

Will was the first to regain his bearings. This asteroid or planetary way-station or whatever it was that Knorbert had steered toward turned out to be an enormous desert that stretched unendingly in all directions. Ridge after ridge of dune rippled off into the distance like a crumpled pale-moon-colored carpet.

A light breeze blew. Close to the surface, it lifted the fine particles of sand and blew them along with a soft, soothing song, carrying them up the faces of the dunes only to drop them as it arched over their summits. Will could see the face of the desert changing before his eyes.

Knorbert wobbled clumsily over to Will's side. "We should never have decided to ride on the back of a Willi-Nilli."

"Are you kidding?" Will gushed. "That was fan-TASTIC! We traveled more in that one brief flash than we have all morning." He looked Knorbert up and down. "Are you OK?"

"Yes, I believe I am," Knorbert replied, flexing whatever joints he had. "And I am sorry, Will. I know we have no time to waste, but I really was tired and I did need a rest." He raised his eyes, one-half of this mouth twisted in the semblance of a smile.

"Where do you think we are?" Will squinted his eyes in the dull glare of the desert's sands.

"I have no idea." Knorbert looked around. "And where is Shilli-Shalli?"

"Good question. She is so unpredictable she could be anywhere."

"I saw her moving in that..." Knorbert stopped. "I...I...I smell something, something awfully good. Do you smell it too?"

"Now that you mention it, yeah. I smell something cooking."

"It smells like everything good to eat all rolled up into

Chapter 25 – The Pleasure Palace

one." Knorbert raised his head, sniffing around.

"It sure does." Will swallowed.

"Over there," Knorbert pointed. "Shill-Shalli must have smelled it too, because she disappeared in that direction."

"Let's go see," said Will.

The sand was so soft that each step was an effort, each step but a half step as the sand gave way beneath their feet. They left deep footprints behind as they trudged up the steep face of the high dune in front of them, footprints rapidly filled by the singing sands.

Over the top of the dune, in a slight depression, lay a disneylandperfect oasis. The sudden burst of the brilliant greens of the vegetation and the rippling blues of the waters caused them to blink, fluttering their eyelids.

A spring gurgled up from somewhere deep beneath the desert surface, creating a small, still, azure pool, a living present donated by some unseen benefactor. Crowded tightly against its shores, all manner of bright green vegetation fought for a share of this gift. Tall, stately calm trees curved above the growth below as though aloof to the vulgar struggle.

At the very center of the oasis, shimmering like a magnificent jewel, stood a dazzling white palace, so brilliant the glarings of the sun were like arrows shot into their eyes.

It was as beautiful a palace as any Will could have ever imagined. The entire edifice was made of seamless, white marble, inlaid with precious stones set in floral designs. At its center tall, white columns supported a bulbous dome, pointed on top. Each corner of the palace sported a slender minaret topped by a similar, though smaller, dome. At its feet, like a mirror in which to admire itself, lay a reflecting pool fed by water from the spring.

They stood in awe for several moments before either dared to speak. "Have you ever seen anything so beautiful?" Will asked.

"Never," Knorbert replied. "Even the sands seem to be singing a song to its beauty."

The Riddle of Riddles

The delicious aromas they had smelled were coming from the palace.

"We have not had anything to eat since breakfast." Knorbert licked his lips, and looked over at Will. "Maybe that is where Shill-Shalli went. If not, we can always ask if they have seen her."

They ran down the face of the dune toward the magnificent edifice, and even at a Knothead's pace, it did not take long before they reached a ruby-red, brick road that led from the spring to the palace.

The palace doors, poignantly carved lace marble screens, stood open, and there was Shilli-Shalli, her noses already poked, indelicately, into the open doorway.

"I guess she is as hungry as we are," Knorbert chuckled.

"Hungrier, I'd say."

Inside, torches lighted the large vaulted chamber. All kinds of creatures mobbed the place, eating and drinking with great gusto. There were boys and girls. There were Yahoos, spotted leopards, she-wolves, and lions. There were three-headed dogs, and creatures that looked like fish but with the heads of eagles. There were horse-like creatures with the heads of lions and the tails of snakes. Some creatures were so hideous that the mind forgot what the eye saw the moment they were seen. And there were frogs everywhere—so many, in fact that they had to watch where they stepped.

A large number of beautiful women circulated about, supplying an unending array of delicious-smelling dishes to the throngs reclining on expanses of soft pillows that had been strewn about.

At the far end of the palace, on a high terrace, a well-muscled man, his body glistening with oils, struck a bronze gong.

Chapter 25 – The Pleasure Palace

)))) GGGOOONNNGGG ((((

As the sound reverberated through the palace, the crowd slowly grew quiet.

A woman stepped out of the shadows and stood atop the terrace with the poise of a goddess. Will gasped. Her black hair, worn loosely, glistened in the torch light. Big, dark eyes and high cheekbones set off a pair of voluptuous scarlet lips, parted in a gentle smile that revealed a set of even ivory-white teeth. She was dressed in a purple robe bedizened with jewels and pearls. She wore rings on all her fingers, and on each of her bare arms were numerous gold and silver bracelets.

"Welcome, Seekers of the answer to The Riddle of Riddles." She raised her arms as she spoke. The bracelets jangled softly.

All heads turned toward Will, Knorbert, and Shilli-Shalli standing in the open doorway.

Then applause began, tentative at first, but it grew louder and more forceful until soon the crowd was on its feet giving them a standing ovation.

The woman gestured for the three of them to approach the terrace.

They picked their way through the frogs and the cheering and feasting crowd to ascend a stairway that finally led them up alongside this most beautiful of women.

After several long minutes, during which the enthusiasm of the crowd gave no sign of diminishing, the woman nodded and the muscular man again struck the gong. The audience grew quiet, resuming it various positions, reclining among the soft pillows, feasting anew.

The Riddle of Riddles

"Please allow me to introduce myself," said the beautiful woman. "I am Lilith, your hostess. Welcome to Cocagne, Oasis of the spring Thele. Welcome to her temple, Thal Ajam."

Lilith's beauty took Will's breath away. He could scarcely hear her words. He longed to gaze on her and nothing else. Even the perfume she wore intoxicated him with its exquisiteness, the scent of Must with just a hint of Longing, and something Will recognized but could not identify.

Before Will could speak, Lilith silenced him with an upraised hand, her bracelets clinking softly. "Welcome, Seekers of the answer to The Riddle of Riddles. We have long awaited your arrival."

"Wow!" Knorbert smiled. "What a greeting."

Will did not reply, his eyes locked on Lilith.

"Please be seated." She motioned toward two large, well-cushioned reclining chairs and a nest of pillows.

They were no sooner settled before other beautiful women came forward with cool, damp towels. The women wiped their brows, taking pains to clean their hands. Others began slowly fanning them with oversized green leaves.

Again the gong silenced the noisy crowd busy at their feast.

"As you all know, we are gathered here today to pay homage to the Seekers of the answer to The Riddle of Riddles," Lilith began. The crowd clapped and cheered, some with their mouths full of food.

"For this special occasion I have prepared a surprise. We are about to witness the exploits of our adventurers, their deeds exhibited here before our very eyes."

She clapped her hands and one by one the torches in the hall were extinguished until only the dimmest of lights remained. Gentle refrains of music began filling the chamber, music not unlike the singing of the sands, played on subtle slutes by the beautiful handmaidens.

A dull cloud of light in which ghostlike shadows began

Chapter 25 – The Pleasure Palace

condensing into recognizable forms appeared before them.

First, Will appeared, and as soon as some of his features could be distinguished in that fog of light, the applause began. It continued growing until the entire audience was applauding loudly. As the background coalesced into a semblance of Knorbert's shack, the audience quieted.

As they watched, the mirage of Will began to move, depicting the scene when Will and Knorbert first met.

When Knorbert appeared, backing into the clearing, he received an ovation second to none—though it was cut short by the loud guffaws that quickly followed when Will and Knorbert backed into each other and were sent sprawling.

"Again! Again!" several member of the audience shouted. "Show us that part again." Soon the entire audience took up the chant.

Lilith provided an instant replay of the scene, over and over, even as the audience clamored to see it again and again, laughing and pointing as they did. The scene was repeated so many times Will could find nothing new in it to retain his interest. Even Knorbert looked bored. Shilli-Shalli was snoring loudly, each head in tandem.

Slower that a Knothead's pace, the mirage replayed the tale of their adventures. Now and again the audience would ask to see this or that scene repeated. Sometimes there would be wild whoops of laughter, but mostly there were cheers and applause. The whole time Lilith never once took her eyes off her guests.

Will started to fidget. Knorbert was now beginning to nod off also, and they had not yet even reached the Thicket of Snags.

Will started to rise but one of the maidens pushed him gently back down into his chair. Immediately, Lilith was at his side.

"What is it?" she asked. Will was about to speak, but another round of cheering interrupted him as the audience applauded their decision to take the shortcut. It was several minutes more before the noise subsided enough for Will to be

The Riddle of Riddles

heard. "I want to thank you for your kind hospitality, but we are on a mission we have yet to complete. You praise us for a task we have not finished."

"Of course, I understand. But you can't leave now. Why, your story has barely begun."

"That's the problem," Will nodded. "At this rate it will take us longer to relive the past than it took to live it. Time *is* being wasted."

"I will advance the story more quickly if you'd like. I'll even show only the highlights if you so desire."

"That would be nice."

When Lilith informed the audience about skipping some scenes, there were moans, groans, and even a few catcalls, but true to her word, Lilith advanced the story to introduce Knumerator. The audience cheered. Shilli-Shalli snored on, light wisps of smoke escaping from each of her six nostrils.

And the story dragged on, the mirage playing to a most receptive audience who still demanded, and sometimes got, replays. By now, Knorbert was snoring as loudly as Shilli-Shalli, and between the two of them, they threatened to drown out the soundtrack.

At the first sign of Will's stirring, Lilith was again at his side.

"Please," she whispered, "do not be so impatient. Think of others. Think of the audience. They are your fans. They love this so. You do not want to deprive them of their little pleasures, do you?"

"No, of course not, but we must get on with our mission. It is already late. We cannot afford to waste anymore time."

"Of course, of course! I understand. In fact, I am actually here to help you. Just let me finish this presentation, and I will be able to send you on your way with some updated intelligence that should help you in your quest. Let me advance the story to Mount Kneverest. That was your last adventure."

Before Will could respond, the scene shifted. The few

Chapter 25 – The Pleasure Palace

protests that were heard were quickly drowned out by new applause at the sight of the Old Man.

It was all Will could do to sit through this three dimensional, holographic representation of their tale. It seemed to progress in strobe-like slow motion with each and every movement freeze-framed for emphasis.

The crowd went wild when the three of them flew from the summit of Mount Kneverest. At that point the audience got to its feet for another standing ovation.

On and on the applause went. The audience called for their heroes and each was required to take a bow, Shilli-Shalli and Knorbert trying not to look too foolish as they rubbed the sleep from their eyes. Then another bow was required, encore after encore, with no signs that the audience's enthusiasm would diminish. But when the crowd started chanting about seeing the parts they had missed, Will shook his head, and turned to Lilith.

"We must be on our way. Thanks again for your hospitality, but we must go." Will paused, and then added, "You did say that you had some fresh intelligence that would help us in our quest. We welcome any help you can provide."

Lilith looked at Will, silently, for a moment. She clapped her hands in the direction of the handmaidens and then turned to Will. "Yes, yes, yes, of course, the new data I promised, of course, all in due time. I understand your concern, but, please before you go at least allow us to refresh you for the arduous journey ahead. We will provide you with nourishment, supply you with some drink, and you can be on your way—with new intelligence," she added. "How does that sound?"

"Great." Will grinned.

A handmaiden pushed back the heavy brocade curtains that separated the terrace from the room behind it. Immediately, the delicious-smelling aromas that had drawn them to the palace in the first place filled their nostrils and set their jaws to juicing.

Knorbert, who had felt a bit cheated not having been offered anything while the crowd feasted all around them, looked

The Riddle of Riddles

beseechingly at Will.

"To eat we must fill our dinner plates," said Shilli.

"To eat before we plumb Inner Space," said Shalli.

"Well..." Will hesitated.

Lilith chimed right in. "Right this way, please. Brief repasts to refresh you before you go." She turned and glided into the back room. Knorbert almost tripped over the hem of her garment in his haste to follow, and Shilli-Shalli bumped into Knorbert's back. Will took a deep breath of the aromas, tasting them by their odors, before following. He could hear the cries from the crowd as they left. Loud shouts of disappointment faded away behind the heavy curtains.

This room was much smaller than the arena they had just left, creating a sense of intimacy. The floor was covered with overlapping rugs of all different sizes and colors. Beautiful tapestries hung from the walls. Big, soft pillows were strewn about with low tables spotted here and there. Incense burned in braziers in the corners, sending up gentle curves of smoke. In the center of the room, a three-tiered, finely polished fountain spilled water gently from one level down to the next.

With a sweep of her hand, Lilith bade them to make themselves comfortable among the downy pillows. One clap from her hands brought forth handmaidens bearing bowls of exotic foods, the odors of which quickly overflowed the chamber.

"Welcome to our Pleasure Palace. Allow us to refresh you after all your exploits. There is plenty, and of such great variety of food and drink that I doubt you will ever tire of their tastes. Eat and drink until you are full. But how many mouths are we really feeding here?" Lilith laughed. "Four, I guess, since Shilli-Shalli has two mouths."

The three of them immediately fell to eating and drinking, surprised by the enormity of their hungers. Will did not feel like he had eaten this morning, but rather like it had been days and days since his last meal.

None of them stopped to use the utensils provided. They

Chapter 25 – The Pleasure Palace

merely scooped out the bowl's contents with their fingers, quite oblivious to the heat, slurping down goblet after goblet of sparkling liquids. No sooner did they finish one delicious dish, one tasty drink, before it was replaced by another, each one lighter, more exquisite than the one before.

"The food's so light," crooned Shilli, nosing into another bowl.

"The taste a delight," swooned Shalli, a nearby dish her next goal.

"Oh my," sighed Knorbert. "This food is wonderful, delicious, but not filling."

Towels were ever at hand, provided by the beautiful, smiling women. The towels were warm and moist and smelled like lemon and cloves.

Will lay back on the pillows. One of the handmaidens removed the empty bowls and drained glasses, while another brought fresh bowls and new glasses, each tempting in its own way.

"Who are you?" Will asked the woman as she set the food down on the low table next to him.

"I have no name, Sire. I am merely a Whouri. We are all Whouries," she added with a blush. "We are here to serve you and your needs. You are to enjoy yourselves until you feel refreshed enough to depart."

"Who provides all of this?" Will asked, dipping into yet another tasty dish.

"You are not to worry. All is provided here in temple Thal Ajam." She pushed Will gently back into the soft pillows and placed a clean, soft cloth across his forehead. It was warm and moist. She placed chilled dandelion leaves over each eyelid. Will sighed and relaxed his muscles.

"Here, eat this," she said, and she began feeding him while others administered to Knorbert and Shilli-Shalli. "Now drink," and Will's mouth was filled with a drink of such sweetness it made him dizzy.

The Riddle of Riddles

"The more I eat, the hungrier I get." Will belched, a satisfied smile on his face.

"Me too," Knorbert agreed, wiping up the last remains of his latest dish, his pinky extended quite regally.

Will opened wide for another mouthful. "Wow," and he coughed, "that is so sweet it almost closed my throat. What is it?'

"It is called Turkish Delight," replied the Whouri.

Though he never got full, Will noticed that he was eating more and more slowly. He yawned as he reached for another tempting bowl. This one was also sweet, yet just tart enough to tang his tongue to alertness. Just as he was about to tire of one flavor, its perfect complement would be in the next bowl, a never ending stream of appetite-whetting dishes, served up by the always smiling, golden haired Whouries.

The drinks, with their teeth-clicking tartness, were especially delightful, full enough to almost chew, yet light as cotton candy and so wet they were quite dry, so dry Will's tongue tip ached for one more taste to slake his lingering thirsties.

"May I have some water, please?" Will asked, pointing at the fountain.

"Water?" the Whouri drew back her head. "Why do you desire water? We do not drink from the holy spring, Thele. Its waters are most precious."

"It's not necessarily water that I want," Will explained. "I just want something to quench my thirst."

The Whouri smiled. "Certainly, here, drink this." She handed Will another glass. One sip satisfied his thirst. So he took two more.

Lilith walked behind Will, and started rubbing his shoulders, gently squeezing his muscles.

"Oh boy, that feels great!" Will let his shoulders slump, allowing Lilith to massage him more deeply.

A contented moan from Knorbert made Will raise his eyes. Knorbert had his legs up on a golden fleece-upholstered footstool, getting each of his big feet massaged by a Whouri.

Chapter 25 – The Pleasure Palace

Shilli-Shalli lay alongside Knorbert, on a cloud of pillows, wings outspread, with a gaggle of giggling Whouries running up and down her back while she groaned.

"Do you have that new information for me?" Will asked.

"Of course, all in due time," Lilith responded. "But for now, concentrate on the pleasure. You do enjoy getting a massage, don't you?"

"You bet," Will sighed. "Try riding on the back of a Willi-Nilli sometime, and see how difficult it is. You'd appreciate a massage, too."

"Oh, I couldn't ride a Willi-Nilli. That is much too dangerous for me. You are so brave. Knorbert, too." She kneaded Will's muscles with surprisingly strong hands. "Is this pleasurable?" she asked.

"Oh yeah!" Will exhaled. "That feels great."

"Welcome to the Pleasure Palace," Lilith cooed, and she laughed softly.

"You are making me feel most welcome," said Will.

Lilith nodded at a Whouri, who then proceeded to draw a curtain around Will and Lilith, creating a private space just for them.

Lilith leaned forward over Will's shoulder. "Since you appreciate pleasure, I have something very special, just for you," she whispered. "I will provide you with a pleasure reserved for the chosen few." Her perfume embraced him.

"What pleasure?"

"This is so special a treat that you must say *please*."

"Please," Will wheedled with a frail smile.

Lilith leaned back, and clapped her hands. The Whouri returned carrying a large apothecary jar. In the jar was something greenish-black. It was moving.

"What's that?" Will frowned.

"Leeches," Lilith breathed out slowly.

"Leeches? What for?"

"Why, for you of course. You are to be blessed."

The Riddle of Riddles

She removed the glass top, dipped her hand into the jar, and removed one of the slimy creatures.

It was about the size of Will's fist but it had no arms or legs that Will could discern, yet it began crawling up Lilith's arm.

Will watched fascinated, fascinated by the magnitude of his own repugnance as the leech moved slowly onto the soft underside of the woman's elbow. Lilith laughed deep in her throat, plucking the leech from her arm.

"No, no, my Precious, I am not to be the one so honored with your blessing. That pleasure is reserved for our hero."

"Uh... on second thought, I'm not really sure I want to do this." Will cleared his throat.

"Don't be silly, Love. These are the very best leeches, Styxese."

"Huh? Uh... Nah. No thanks. I'm not really into leeches, even Styxese."

"Of course you are," Lilith winked. "You even said please, remember." She drew Will's arm toward her.

It twitched.

"These leeches are messengers of the gods," she said, her voice a barely audible hiss. "They carry with them a special blessing. They will bestow upon you the greatest pleasure, the greatest sense of wellbeing. You will feel yourself go out of yourself, and the vacuum remaining is like the sweetest of pains, a pain that never hurts but is, rather, the mother of pleasures, a pleasure you will feel both within you and without you at the same time."

She stroked Will's arm, then gently dropped the leech in place. Will felt the cold slime; saw the light, sticky trail it left behind as it slowly positioned itself over the center of his arm, inside the elbow.

"Now relax," Lilith whispered. "You will feel a slight pinch that will, at first, seem like pain, but you will immediately recognize that it is not pain at all, but rather the most exquisite of pleasures."

Chapter 25 – The Pleasure Palace

Even as she spoke, Will felt the pinch. Immediately, the flood of pleasure exploded.

Will gasped. The pleasure was intense. It was full, and, furthermore, it was not momentary. It went on and on. Will fell back on the pillows as wave after wave of pleasure spasmed through him.

"It feels so wonderful, doesn't it?" Lilith cooed. "Yesss, ssssooo wonderful. I envy you. Would you like one for the other arm?"

"Yes, yes!"

"Say *please*. You must say *please*."

"Please. Yes, please. May I please have one for the other arm? Please."

Will gasped again as the pleasure exploded deeper within him. Never—never could he have imagined such bliss.

Lilith asked again. With pleasure of this intensity, Will could no longer speak. He merely nodded his head.

Soon leeches were applied to the soles of both feet and then to both temples.

The pleasure swept over him in waves so intense that his whole body undulated slowly with their passing. The pleasure was all Will could focus on.

"Oh, ssssoo wonderful you mussst feeelll," Lilith crooned. "Leeches sucking up your blood, repaid with pleasure beyond description. How very, very special you are. Would you like another?"

Will nodded hopelessly.

"Then you must open your mouth and stick out your tongue. This last leech will drink up the last of your blood from your very own mouth. Mouth sucking from mouth. In return your heart will be emptied of all sorrow, all pain, only to be replaced with happiness and pleasure and that most beautiful of all feeling, the eventuality of nothingness. Stick out your tongue."

Will was so weak, so powerless, totally tired, heart-tired, slowing, slowing.

But the bliss!
Slowing.
Blissfully.
Slowing.
Slowing.
Blissfully.
He stuck out his tongue.

He felt the slimy creature grab hold of his tongue. He felt the slight prick as it begin to suck up his life's blood with the payment of pleasure untold in return, to suck up his life's blood from his very own mouth, to suck up his life, to…

WHAT?

Will spit the slimy creature across the room.

He raked his teeth across the top of his tongue and spit. Spitting, spitting, trying to spit—out—that—ycchhh—taste—of—ycchhh—that ……..SLIMY……leech.

Will opened his eyes and tried to sit up. Lilith pushed him back down, gently. "Now, now," she said, "relax. Everything is fine."

"Sucking up my blood? Sucking up my blood? Never!" Will thought he was screaming, but his voice was but a hoarse whisper. "Never!" He sat up shakily, pushing away Lilith's hands.

"Never!" He slapped at the leeches, sending them flying across the room. Beneath each leech, a needlelike extensor dripped a drop of blood, a drop of *Will's* blood! The leeches were fatter now, bloated to a pink tinge.

Will's pleasure faded. Fighting himself for still wanting that pleasure, he ripped the leeches from his temples, kicked them from his feet. The pleasure diminished as each leech was sent flying against the far wall with a dull splat. Will's blood ran down the wall. The silken cushions beneath showed pink.

Will staggered. His body itched uncontrollably at each point the leeches had attached themselves. He slapped his cheeks and shook his head, trying to restore some vigor, some vitality.

When he recognized his own heartbeat, he sighed. He was

Chapter 25 – The Pleasure Palace

alive.

"Calm down," Lilith said quietly. "You are overreacting. Everything is fine. If you don't want leeches, you don't get leeches."

"Want them?" Will choked out the words. "Not only do I not want them, I can't stand the taste of them!" He spat again and then again, trying to rid himself of the slime that coated his tongue.

"Here," Lilith offered, "drink this." She handed him a glass full of a clear liquid.

"No thank you!" Will growled. "I don't need any more… any more of your… your whatevers." He pushed away her arm.

"It's only water," said Lilith. "I thought you might want to wash out your mouth."

"Water?" Will cocked an eye at Lilith. "I'll bet it's just water."

"It is. I promise you. It's pure water from the spring Thele. Here, wash out your mouth if you find the taste of leech so foul."

"Foul?" Will spit. "Foul is too kind a word." He reached for the glass and took a mouthful, running it over his tongue, around his teeth, trying to rid himself of the horrid taste that lingered. Will spit the water onto the floor in thoughtless anger. "I thought you never drank this precious water."

"Oh, we do not. It is reserved for the very special, the truly special like you," said Lilith.

Will rinsed his mouth again. This time he spit the water into a nearby bowl. Then he took a swallow. "Hmmm, this water is amazingly thirst quenching." He took another swallow. "But what else but the best should I expect here in the Pleasure Palace." He took a deep draught and let out a long, extended breath.

"So do you understand, now, about the leeches?" Lilith asked.

"Leeches?" Will asked. "What leeches?"

"You don't remember the leeches?" Lilith asked.

"What are you talking about?" Will shrugged. He looked

The Riddle of Riddles

at Lilith quizzically, and took another sip of water.

"Nothing," Lilith shook her head. "Nothing at all."

She reached into the top drawer of the low table in front of Will. "I understand that you play chess," she said, retrieving a chessboard and an intricately carved black box from the drawer.

Will smiled. "Yes, as a matter of fact, I do."

"And you believe that there is a perfect game."

"I do," Will replied, "but how did you know?"

Lilith laughed deep in her throat, "Did you think I would not know? Would you like to play?"

"Uh…ordinarily I would love to, but we really must be leaving. Our task…remember? And you promised me some new intelligence that you said could save us time."

"Yes, I did. The new information may even provide the answer you are looking for. But, look, your friends have fallen asleep. Let them nap briefly while we have a quick game—just one game, OK? You have time for one quick game, surely."

Will looked from Knorbert to Shilli-Shalli, both snoring soundly. Then he looked back to Lilith and the game board. "OK," he said, "one quick game."

Lilith set the pieces up on the board between them. "Your first move is always the same, I believe."

Will smiled and made his move. "Pawn-to-King-Four," he announced. He then reached for another morsel of Turkish Delight. "This stuff is great," and he swallowed another tidbit as Lilith studied the board.

Will looked over at Lilith. She looked up and said, "Now, don't rush me, Will. I must make sure I make my best move in defense of this perfect game of yours."

Will waited. Lilith sat looking at the board, unmoving. Finally, Will stood and began pacing the room. Lilith was taking so long that he started worrying about time again. *This intelligence she says she has better be good*, he thought.

Finally, Lilith made her move. "Pawn-to-King-Four" she said.

Chapter 25 – The Pleasure Palace

"I expected as much." Will sat back down. "Your play is the usual response to my opening."

"Are you mocking me?" Lilith sat back, her eyes slits. She crossed her arms across her chest. "You claim to be a chess master, but you need to learn to master your tongue. That was insulting."

Will sat back. "Oh...Lilith, I am so sorry. I did not mean to insult you. Please, forgive me. I was merely commenting on the nature of the game."

"To treat me so boorishly after all my hospitality is a double insult, a triple insult taking into account my offer to assist your efforts to solve the Riddle. Play your chess game by yourself. That way you can't lose!" She stood up so suddenly she knocked over the chessboard, spilling the pieces all over the floor.

"Lilith, I'm sorry. Really, I am." Will crawled around on the rugs, retrieving the chessmen. "Please, forgive me. I apologize. I am so, so sorry." He scooped up the last of the chess pieces and started setting them up as they were before Lilith had knocked them over.

Lilith stood with her back to Will. The handmaidens froze in place. The only sounds were the snores coming from Knorbert and Shilli-Shalli.

"I should just go, Lilith. I'm sorry I spoiled our stay. If you not too mad at me, I would like to collect that latest information. Then we'll be on our way, and we won't bother you anymore."

"You have sorely tested my benevolence, Will." Lilith kept her back to Will.

"What can I do to make it up to you?"

Lilith snorted. "Nothing. Wake your friends and go."

"Lilith, please."

Lilith turned. "I know. You want that intelligence, don't you?" She took a deep breath, her arms still crossed across her chest.

"If it's not too much to ask," Will asked, smiling slightly.

The Riddle of Riddles

"What have you learned?"

"It is not what I have learned. It is what *you* can learn."

"What do you mean?"

"I don't have the intelligence. You have the intelligence. I have a method to provide you with the means to gather that intelligence."

"How?"

Lilith leaned in toward Will. "I have a very special potion," she whispered. Suddenly her whole demeanor changed, and she giggled like a schoolgirl.

"What are you talking about?" Will asked.

"The insight you need to learn the answer to the Riddle only comes from within. I do not have any special information for you. You possess that ability. You possess all the answers. I only have this..." She smiled with those perfect, white teeth and scarlet lips.

Lilith clapped her hands again, bracelets ajangle. A Whouri entered carrying a tray cluttered with bottles and containers of assorted shapes and sizes. Lilith selected a special demi-John. Then taking mushblooms, koyote buttons, whole pink worms, roots from the mandrink plant and seeds from a triffid, she mixed them all together with a pinch of an iridescent powder.

"Now drink," she said, "and all intelligence can be yours." Her voice was soft.

"I don't know about this." Will's voice was barely audible.

"It is the only way to gain the insight you need to solve the Riddle. You don't have to drink it. It's up to you. Do you want to know or don't you?"

Will hesitated. "Of course I want to know." He took the container from Lilith and swallowed a deep draught expecting the delicious taste he had come to expect. Instead, the drink was as bitter as tongue-tip spit, and he would have spit it out had not Lilith tipped back his head and gently stroked his throat. "Swallow," she crooned.

Chapter 25 – The Pleasure Palace

Will choked. He barely managed a swallow. A Whouri stepped forward. Will instantly understood the significance of the act. One swallow was enough. Then he understood the fact that he understood, understanding his own understanding, and was dumbfounded by the acuteness of his awareness. Then he realized that it was the elixir that was making him so aware, and that realization broke through the last barrier of his closed-mindedness. He knew that he knew he knew.

With his mind wringing with fear, his understanding soared like a Willi-Nilli out of control, yet somehow, not really out of control. It soared to the very edge of an abyss beyond awareness, the very edge of understanding all there was to *ever* comprehend.

"More," Will cried. "I want more." Lilith pushed the container forward. "I want it all!" Will snorted, drinking up the remains of the drink in one gulp, fingering out every last morsel. He sucked the wetness off his fingers.

His awareness soared, soared higher than before. He could feel the climb of this consciousness and loved it. He was anxious that it continue. He saw things becoming clearer. He felt as though he was floating, though his body was more under his control than ever.

Each exertion required but the slightest effort. His vision became sharper and clearer. His ears, too, picked up every sound, every breath, and every silence. He could make out individual conversations coming from the crowd outside and was able to picture the entire scene just from those sounds. He could smell the air, taste it too, and he licked his lips.

It was coming fast now. He witnessed his own anxiety about its power and laughed at it. He was totally in control, had such clarity, and had such, such…

The Riddle of Riddles

His consciousness hung at the very edge of that abyss, his own awareness flowing all around him; infusing him with such intensity that he knew that he knew everything all at once but could discriminate nothing. He watched his brain operating as though he were a spectator watching *himself* perform. He could do it all. The thought of this magnificence made him gasp. He wept humbly, shamelessly, before its power.

He watched his tears flow as though everything were in super-slow motion. He studied their colors, felt their presence, their vitality, watched as they left his cheeks to fall with uncommon dignity onto the pillow below.

Then he was drifting back up from those teardrops perched on that pillow like radiant raindrops on a lazy, lissome leaf, drifting back up through space, back to his eyes, back through his eyes and back into his brain. He watched his brain as it blinked and stared back at him watching it. He watched it look away because it knew it was slowly dropping off the edge of understanding, off the edge of awareness, not wanting to fall but unable to stop the fall, as that superlative perception began to fade, began to leave him.

Too soon it was over. Will longed to return to the edge of that abyss into which he had been allowed but a glimpse, yearned to look deeper, not the slightest bit afraid though he did not know what might attend there.

"More!" he cried. "Give me more!"

"I will give you all you want," Lilith soothed, "but now you must sleep. You have experienced much. You need some rest until next time, and there can be a next time if you so desire. I promise. Now rest."

"Yes, yes," Will mumbled. "There is so much to know, and there is power enough to know it all, even the answer to The Riddle of Riddles."

"Yes, just as I promised you," cooed Lilith. "Next time you will have all the answers. Next time. Next time. Now sleep."

"But will I ever get to ask the question? The power is so

Chapter 25 – The Pleasure Palace

intoxicating I wonder if I could ever get beyond that. And it lasts such a short time."

"But it takes you so far and is so tiring. You must sleep."

Will did indeed feel exhausted, as though he had gone some enormous distance. He was drained, mind-weary. The soft music of the sharps played by the Whouries lulled him. The intense alertness faded into a quiet euphoria.

He slept.

The clatter of a dish awakened Will. He sat straight up, rubbing his eyes, only to fall back onto the silken cushions with a groan because of the throbbing in his head. From nowhere, Lilith suddenly appeared at his elbow, blowing electric air at him across her fingertips.

"Breathe deeply. Your friends have almost finished eating," she said, "Now you can join them."

Knorbert smiled over at Will, his lips and chin covered with some purplish goo.

"You have to try this habenerror jam," said Knorbert, "but watch out. It is sweet as maple candy but hot as an ice pick stuck through your tongue. Try it on one of those white crackers," and he pointed.

Shilli-Shalli was also busy eating, each head buried deep in a bowl, her tongues swishing round their insides.

Will's stomach was queasy. The potion Lilith had given him made his tongue feel like it was growing hair. He scraped his teeth over the top of his tongue but that did not help. "I need a glass of water," he said.

"I wandered around a bit while you slept," Knorbert commented, delicately picking his teeth with his pinky nail. "It is incredible what I saw. It is like being wide-awake inside your own dream."

Will got unsteadily to his feet. He placed one hand on a low table to help maintain his balance and he chortled. "You think you saw incredible things. I traveled all the way to the front door of nirvana and back without ever leaving this room."

The Riddle of Riddles

"You traveled without moving, moving without leaving?" questioned Shilli from across the room, her nose smeared with something brown.

"Then a Willi-Nilli you will no longer be needing," Shalli mentioned, nodding her head up and down.

"Don't be silly, Shilli-Shalli. We will always need you. Won't we, Will?"

Will stomach rumbled. His mouth felt as dry as the desert sands outside. His tongue felt like it was swollen. "I can't believe I fell asleep. How long did I sleep, Knorbert?"

"Not long...I think." He grimaced. "I do not really know. I was asleep part of the time myself."

"Here," Lilith offered, "drink this." She pushed a glass of clear liquid in Will's direction. "You must be thirsty. It is more water from the spring Thele."

Will reached for the glass and took a sip. His stomach heaved. Will took a mouthful, more slowly, and this time he was able to swallow. Then he took an even deeper draught.

"I can't believe I fell asleep," he groaned. "I drank some stupid potion that was supposed to give me insight into the answer to the Riddle but I learned nothing. The potion was powerful, too powerful. Then I fell asleep. What a waste. What a waste of time! I can't believe I was so foolish."

"Does that mean you don't want to try the potion again?" Lilith asked. "You said you came so close to learning all there was to know."

"No way! As powerful as that potion is, it cannot provide me with the answer to the Riddle. I know that now. The only thing the potion taught me was that it was impotent, that we must find the answer ourselves. No more potions for me. We've got to get out of here. Oh, the time we've lost!" He rubbed his temples between his fingers.

"Calm down. You don't have to do anything you don't want to do. Try some more water," Lilith suggested. "It will help settle your stomach."

Chapter 25 – The Pleasure Palace

Will swallowed a few more mouthfuls. He then turned toward Knorbert and Shilli-Shalli. "Get yourselves together," he said. "We're leaving."

"What is the matter with you?" Knorbert asked. "Why are you so angry?"

"I'm angry because I fell asleep, that's why. That was stupid, stupid, stupid!" Will took another swallow. "We've got the answer to a riddle to find, remember? And we have wasted so much time." He shook his head.

"OK, Will," Knorbert soothed. "Take it easy. We will leave if you want."

"I'm angry, Knorbert. I'm angry at myself for wasting time, and we have to find…uh, find…whatever it is we are looking for."

"The answer to The Riddle of Riddles," said Knorbert.

"Right," said Will.

"I'm ready. Let's go," offered Shilli.

"I'm not. I say no," differed Shalli.

Will took another swallow. "We are trying to find…trying to…What is it we are trying to do anyway?"

"What is the matter with you?" asked Knorbert.

"Nothing is the matter with him," Lilith volunteered. "He's just so impatient to get going that he's getting all jumbled up. Here's some water, Knorbert. Be sure to drink plenty of water before you go. The desert is a dry, forbidding place."

"That is a good idea," agreed Shilli, and she dunked her head into the fountain.

"Any idea is a good idea" conceded Shalli, also plunging her head into the fountain.

They all drank while Will stood by scratching his head, repeating to himself, "We're trying to find…trying to find…to find out something."

"Drink up," Lilith urged. "Make sure you drink enough water before you venture out into the desert. You'll need it."

Will lifted the glass to his lips. *"When is the riddle the*

The Riddle of Riddles

answer? When is the riddle the answer? When is the riddle the answer?" He said phrase over and over, but what did it mean? He forgot why he was repeating those words. He even forgot to drink, the glass halfway to his lips.

"Drink," Lilith urged, pushing the glass toward Will's mouth.

He turned toward Knorbert. "What is it?"

"What is what?" Knorbert asked.

"What is it that we are trying to remember?" Will asked.

"When?"

"Before," Will answered.

"Before what?"

"How should I know?" asked Will. "That's why I'm asking you."

"Asking me what?"

"What?"

"Yes, what?"

"What what?"

"I don't remember."

They both burst out laughing.

"Why are we laughing?" asked Knorbert.

"Beats me."

"If this is logic, then I'm the one with the brains," said Shilli shaking her head.

"And if we have brains, then we will need no reins," added Shalli nodding.

"Weren't we doing something?" Will asked.

"Nothing that important, I guess, if I cannot remember."

"That is it." Will nodded. "I cannot remember either, but that is it. We have forgotten to remember not to forget. We even forgot that we forgot."

Shilli and Shalli both burst out laughing.

Will shook his head. He had indeed forgotten. All he could remember was the phrase to which his mind clung desperately. *When is the riddle the answer? When is the riddle the*

Chapter 25 – The Pleasure Palace

answer? When is the riddle the answer? That he would not forget. Deep inside, some part of him rebelled. He could not, would not forget *everything*. His mind grew lazy, so he pushed it. It lumbered slowly forward, but he could not remember anything beyond that phrase that haunted him.

"Don't forget to drink up," Lilith ordered.

Will raised the glass to his lips once more. Yes, drink. Do not forget to drink. Forget to drink?

Drink to forget.

Of course! That was it.

The drink was the forget!

It was the water that was making them forget.

Will looked up. His eyes met Lilith's briefly before hers crabbed away. A flood of memories returned, memories of cheers and food, of potions and of…leeches!

"I had completely forgotten about the leeches. I drank this water to rid myself of the taste of the slimy leeches, and I forgot all about the leeches. It's the water!" Will looked at the glass in his hand. "Don't drink the water. It is the Water of Forgetfulness!"

Will flung the glass against the wall, scattering shards everywhere. They were trying to find the answer to The Riddle of Riddles, but the water was making them forget everything. He struck the glass from Knorbert hand.

"What?" Knorbert's eyes followed the glass.

Will spun around to face Lilith. He captured her eyes and as he watched, right there before him, she started to change, her own reflection in Will's eyes the catalyst for that change.

Lilith no longer appeared to be the most beautiful of women. She began aging right there before him until, almost before he knew it, she had changed into an ugly old hag with long greasy hair, and a leaking nose. Her frown revealed brown and broken teeth.

The Whouries, too, transformed. They held up their claw-like fingers, resembling a conceit of ancient felines. Shilli-Shalli screamed, streaked through the door, and was gone.

"What about our chess game?" the hag that had once been Lilith asked, her voice cracking.

"Ha!" Will snorted. "Bishop to Bishop Four! My game continues, but yours ends here. We're leaving."

Will advanced on the old hag, his eyes locked with hers. She looked away but then looked back at Will only to look away again.

She appeared to be strong, threatening, aggressive, but as Will got closer, she backed away until she was up against the wall. Will stood directly in front of her, his eyes searching out hers. Her eyes darted about the room.

Abruptly, Lilith fell to her knees. "Please," she wailed. "Please go. I mean you no harm." She raised her arms over her head defensively. Her bracelets jingled. Something dropped to the floor.

"Come on, Knorbert. Let's get out of here."

Will took a step, slipped and nearly fell. There at his feet, beside Lilith, lay the small shimmering object on which he had slipped. Intrigued, he scooped it up, and placed it into his shirt pocket.

Will ran from the room, with Knorbert wobbling along behind him, trying to keep up. They fled from the fountain, from all the soft pillows, from the intense incense, out onto the terrace where the revelers saw them. The crowd cheered and applauded once more. Down the steps and through the feasting crowd they ran. All around, the other creatures laughed and called after them, their mouths overflowing, the food dribbling down their chins. Some tried to reach out to touch them.

Will could feel the frogs beneath his feet as he ran.

Squish!

Squish!

Squiisssshhhhhh...

Out the door and down the ruby-red road they fled, never once looking back. The hags stopped at the palace doors, hissing evilly after them.

Chapter 25 – The Pleasure Palace

Cresting dune after dune, they ran, and they did not stop until the oasis and its palace were left far behind, lost somewhere in the shifting sands. Only then did they slacken their pace.

Knorbert was played out. He plopped gratefully down onto the sand. "What...what happened?"

"I don't know." Will was gasping for air. "Somehow they knew we were coming and what our task was, but that doesn't make any sense. How could they know?"

"They were very nice to us," said Knorbert. "The food and their drinks were delicious."

"Yes, that's true enough," Will nodded, but he was frowning. "They were nice enough, but...but why did they turn on us? And that Water of Forgetfulness. I just don't get it. We lost so much time, so much time. If only I had not fallen asleep." He shook his head.

"We all fell asleep, Will. You are not the only one to blame, and, besides," Knorbert looked down, "if I had not steered for this place to begin with we would not have wasted any time."

Will reached into his shirt pocket and removed the object he had picked up, the one that lay at Lilith's feet.

"What do you make of this?" he asked, holding it up so Knorbert could see.

"What is it?" Knorbert asked.

"I don't know. See for yourself," and he handed the item to Knorbert.

The Riddle of Riddles

ONE SIDE   ANOTHER SIDE

Chapter 25 – The Pleasure Palace

"What do you think?" Will asked.

Knorbert turned it over in his hands a few times, trying to make some sense of it. "I have no idea. It looks like it could be part of something, like maybe there are parts missing."

Will took the object from Knorbert and examined it more closely himself. "You may be onto something," he said. "It does look like it could be part of something, but part of what?"

Will returned the object to his pocket. "We've wasted enough time here, time we could not afford to lose." He took a deep breath, threw back his shoulders, and narrowed his eyes.

Knorbert looked off to one side. "Where do you think Shilli-Shalli went?" he asked.

They called for her several times, but there was no answer. All they heard was the hiss of the shifting sands.

"I sure hope we haven't lost her," Will said.

"Me, too."

"I thought you didn't like riding a Willi-Nilli."

"Oh my, I do not, but I was learning to control her flight a bit. Besides, she is our only way out of here. I wonder where she went. She could be anywhere by now, what with her fantastic speed."

"Try playing some music, Knorbert. See if you can attract her."

Knorbert settled himself onto the soft sand, took out Forlorn, and began to play.

Luci burned down on them, her heat reflected off the shimmering sands. The notes of Knorbert's playing drifted off into the distance, carried by curlicues of heat.

Remembering the facility with which he had once played, Knorbert's music quickly grew in beauty until it began to sound just as good as it had when Shilli-Shalli was there singing with him.

And there she was—singing as sweetly as ever, singing a tune so in tune with Knorbert's tune that, happy as they were to see her, they were reluctant to end its enchantment. The last notes drifted away on the mirages of heat waves, leaving them stranded in the vast desert silence.

"It's good to see you," said Will. "We were afraid you might have left us."

"Leave my friends? Never!" disclaimed Shilli.

"Friends for forever!" exclaimed Shalli.

"Well then, let's be on our way." Will's tone was suddenly strident.

"The answer to the Riddle abides," said Shalli.

"As time speeds by with giant's strides," Shilli said.

Knorbert was the first to mount Shilli-Shalli. He grabbed hold of the fur on each of the necks and swung himself up with more ease than the first time. Then Will swung himself up behind Knorbert.

"Not so tight, please. I'd rather be cajoled," said Shalli.

"I cannot fly, please, being so controlled," added Shilli.

So intent was Knorbert's grip that Shilli-Shalli hovered stationary, undulating in the sky.

"I think I have mastered it now," Knorbert said.

"Do you ever just not think?" asked Shilli.

"For even just an eye blink?" gasped Shalli.

Knorbert reacted like he had been slapped. "Oh me, oh my, oh no! What do you take me for, a silly Willi-Nilli?" He started a laugh and Shilli-Shalli immediately jerked forward.

Knorbert quickly pulled back on both heads.

"I have no choice but to relax my hold on you two if we are to fly, but that does not mean you can just take off. Do you understand?"

"We understand."

"Just ease your hands."

Slowly Knorbert gave Shilli-Shalli her heads. Bit by bit their speed increased, and soon they were soaring through the Void once more. But still Knorbert held on tightly. He was not about to lose control. That was never going to happen again.

CHAPTER 26 – DEEPER INTO INNER SPACE

"Let's fly, Knorbert. Let's fly. We have to make up for lost time." Will snorted. "As if that's even possible." He shook his head and then exhaled slowly.

"Ease your grip some."

"Are you sure?' Knorbert asked.

"Go ahead, try it."

Knorbert eased his grip on Shilli-Shalli's heads slightly, and before long, they were streaking across the Void at a dizzying speed.

"Whoa!" Knorbert shouted, his hands clutching fiercely at the very roots of the fur on each of Shilli-Shalli's necks.

"Whoa there girls…eh…girl. Easy now."

"It's OK. Let them go." Will kept his voice steady.

"Trust me, yet guide me and we can go anywhere," claimed Shalli.

"Sensitize yourself and the way shall be clear," maintained Shilli.

Faster than a falcon's stoop they flew, deeper and deeper into Inner Space. Will's heart pounded with excitement.

They were, once again, on their way. The speed they were traveling, the distance they were covering toward their goal, absolutely exhilarated him. On the backs of Willi-Nillies was the only way to travel. Will stared steadily over Knorbert's shoulder, encouraging him or warning him or leaving him alone, as each situation warranted.

The faster they flew, however, the more trouble Knorbert had controlling Shilli-Shalli. Their gyrations swung in wider and wider arcs, resulting in a jerky, erratic flight. Soon Knorbert could control only their general direction, steering around this or that obstacle as best he could.

The Riddle of Riddles

"Our terrible foreknowledge is not really knowledge as defined," announced Shilli.

"It's a calm surety of purpose, a righteousness refined," pronounced Shalli.

Will was concerned that they were behind themselves, behind where they should be at this late stage, behind the beat of some unseen, distant drummer who was attempting to keep them in time with the rhythm of their fate.

Will watched carefully as Knorbert fought to control the direction of their flight. When Shilli veered off wildly in one direction, Will noticed that it was taking all of Knorbert's strength to steer her back on course. The same thing happened when Shalli took off in the other direction.

"What's happening, Knorbert, is that both Shilli and Shalli know the right course to pursue but in their anxiety to get there they are overshooting their marks. Each head is battling the other, each one sure that *she* is right. Let them go but try not to be so exact with your course corrections. Try bringing each head back on course but do it slowly. Let them swing by the proper course until they stop. Then when other head takes control and veers off in the opposite direction start slowing her down, but don't try to stop her completely. Let her swing by the course heading again, but decrease the scope of that swing by a half if you can. Each time try decreasing how far we've swerved off course by half, and then by half again."

"At this point I am willing to try anything."

Shalli pulled them frantically to the left, as Shilli tugged half-heartedly to the right. Knorbert let Shalli veer left, slowly decreasing the speed of her swing, bit by bit, until Shilli demanded control. Knorbert immediately started slowing Shilli's swing, but he did not try to stop her exactly on course. Instead, he allowed her to veer past their course, slowing the range of her swing gradually.

"What a great idea, Will. I finally feel like I am exerting some control."

Chapter 26 – Deeper into Inner Space

Each time either Shilli or Shalli took off, Knorbert bracketed the scope of their oscillation by a half, then the next span by a half and then the span after that, bracketing and halving, bracketing and halving until he had gained a remarkable degree of control over their flight.

"Now we are making progress. If only I had not insisted on stopping at the Pleasure Palace we would be much farther along."

No sooner were the words out of his mouth before Shilli-Shalli reacted.

"Farther along, farther along, oh what a pitiful song," Shilli droned, pulling vehemently to starboard.

"To whom, to whom does the guilt belong?" Shalli moaned, pulling even harder to larboard.

"It's all my fault. I'm the guilty one," jibbered Shalli.

"Pity one, not pretty one, who pity won," jabbered Shalli.

"Easy there, Shilli. Now where are you going, gal? Ease up. Whoa now, Shalli. Listen you two! We are not going to make it if we do not all cooperate."

But Shilli-Shalli did not react. Each head pulled in its own direction. All attempts at bracketing and halving became futile.

"She does not respond to logic," Will said.

"You are telling me! Even brute strength only has limited success now." Knorbert pulled back with all his might but Shilli-Shalli failed to slow appreciably. "If we do not gain some kind of control we are bound to fail."

"There is no allowance for failure," Will growled.

"To fail? To fail? What a sad tale." Shilli sighed. "A tale, I rail, I cannot hail. "

"Despair we will share if we don't get there," Shalli cried. "Get where, when there, we will dismiss despair."

With each loud wail, Shilli and Shalli fought Knorbert's efforts at control. Will saw that he was tiring rapidly again.

All around, the endless Inner Space threatened, offering no solace. Behind them—nothing. Ahead—nothing. The Void was

The Riddle of Riddles

all there was.

Except...

Over there. Another planetary way station. Another place to rest.

"Look Will," Knorbert lisped through parched lips, "there is a place for a brief break." He pointed with his nose. "I am exhausted."

"Not again!" Will shouted. "We've got to push on. You said so yourself. We should not have stopped at the Pleasure Palace. That was a delay we could not afford. Perhaps, if I exert some more effort, I can ease the strain some." He pulled back harder on each of Shilli-Shalli's heads.

"I have to stop, Will." Knorbert's voice was shrill and high-pitched. "I need to stop. I am so tired. I deserve a rest. I *deserve* it! Look how good I am getting at controlling our flight. We are making great time. We can afford a short break to catch our breaths, to catch my breath. My muscles are aching."

"I deserve a guilty plea," bleated Shalli.

"Does guilt deserve such pity?" entreated Shilli.

"It is no use. I need to rest," Knorbert croaked, and before Will could react, Knorbert quickly set their course toward the way station he had spied.

Shilli-Shalli was completely out of control, spiraling down and around, spiraling, spiraling down and around, caught in a death spiral.

"Pull, Knorbert!" Will could hardly breathe, so intense were his efforts.

Knorbert tried to set them down as gently as possible, but the landing was jarring. Will's strength had slowed them sufficiently to prevent any real damage, and though no one was injured and no bones broken, all three were quite dazed.

CHAPTER 27 – MAN HATIN' ISLAND

As it was, Will bounced and rolled before skidding to a halt. He shook his head and blinked his eyes. Knorbert was off to one side trying to stand up, his butt sticking straight up in the air, arms pushing against the ground, wobbling side to side. Shilli-Shalli was unwrapping one neck from around the other, like undoing a figure eight.

Knorbert wobbled over to Will's side. "Sorry, Will," he mumbled with downcast eyes, "but I really *was* starting to get tired."

"Just as we were starting to make good time too," Will said, shaking his head.

"Speed is not everything," Knorbert sniffed rubbing his behind. "Safety counts, too."

"And so does accuracy." Will said, slapping at his pants legs to remove the dirt and dust. "I must admit you were getting better at controlling our flight, Knorbert."

"Thanks for helping me. You are obviously not as weak as you once were. Without your strength, our crash would have been a lot worse."

"Do you really think so?" Will looked at his arms.

"I know so. I was almost exhausted. You saved the landing."

"I wonder where we are." Will looked around.

"Here we are arriving almost before leaving," said Shilli.

"But push on we must if we are to be achieving," added Shalli.

"♪DE, DE, DE, DE, DEH ♪— ♪DE, DE, DE, DE ♪— ♪DE, DE, DE, DE DEH, DE, DEH, DE, ♪AH—AH ♪"

Startled, Will turned his head, looking the source of the music. A short distance behind him was a uniformed brass band lining either side of the street. Behind the band were crowds of people, clapping, cheering, and smiling. The lines the band formed led down the street to a platform situated in front of a gray office building, complete with a statue of some once-important figure sitting astride a horse with no name.

On the dais was a lectern behind which stood an unfamiliar man smiling down on them. Behind him was a row of officials all dressed in button-down shirts and three-piece suits. They were all applauding.

Tall buildings pushed in at them from all sides, tilting in over their heads at jaunty angles. Flocks of widgeons, disturbed by the clamor, took flight, disappearing somewhere in between the crowding buildings.

"Welcome!" the man at the microphone boomed. "On behalf of the citizens of Man Hatin' Island, may I extend the warmest of welcomes to the seekers of the answer to The Riddle of Riddles."

Will and Knorbert exchanged quick glances and then looked back toward the dais from which the muffled words had come.

When the band struck up another tune, Will, Knorbert, and Shilli-Shalli were all physically pushed along the pavement toward the platform by the sheer force of the windy cheers. The man at the microphone had both arms up-raised, urging the crowd.

"Step up, please. Step up," he said as they reached the platform. "Let the folks have a look at their heroes. We are *so* honored to have you with us."

Again, the thunderous waves of applause fairly lifted them up onto the dais with scarcely an effort of their own. Once they were up where the entire crowd could see them, the applause became even more clamorous.

"Ladies and Gentlemen, won't you please give a warm welcome to the Seekers of answer to The Riddle of Riddles."

The applause became deafening, echoing off the stony buildings.

"What is all this?" Will leaned in toward the man at the

Chapter 27 – Man Hatin' Island

microphone.

"You must be Will," the man said bowing, "and this must be Knorbert, and this and that, Shilli and Shalli. Why, everyone knows who *you* are. The whole wide world is in a tizzy over your exploits. It is news from one edge of the world to the other."

He stopped momentarily and cleared his throat. "Please allow me to introduce myself. I am the Mayor of Man Hatin' Island, Sidney Mitty, but please call me Sid."

Sid was of an indeterminate age. His hair was as black as night and slicked back neat-as-you-please. His face was round and very pink, his nose a sharp point. A pencil-thin moustache spread like eaves over his fat fleshy lips. He wore a three-piece suit, bedecked with medals, that was at least one size too small for his short pudgy frame. On his head he wore a black derby, which he doffed with a flourish as he bowed. Strangest of all was the small, furry monkey that sat on Sid's shoulder. It, too, wore a derby, which it doffed, imitating Sid.

"This is Dis," Sid said motioning toward the monkey. "Dis. That's Sid spelled backwards. Get it?" Sid threw back his head laughing, the medals on his chest jingling loudly. Only then did Will notice his green and rotting teeth.

Sid leaned forward so the others on the dais could not hear him. "Everybody's got something to hide except me and my monkey." He winked. His breath was awful.

Sid then introduced them to the others on the platform. There was the Assistant Mayor, Mr. Fawning; the Comptroller, Mr. Banks; the Police Commissioner, Captain Grim; the Mayor's advance man, Mr. Smiley; the head of the Department of Public Works, Mr. Pocketsful; the Consumer Advocate, Miss Graft; and then too many others for Will to keep track.

The introductions completed, Sid turned them toward the crowd. The applause, which had subsided to a low but constant muffle, again began to grow. Sid smiled over at them. Will wished he'd get his teeth fixed or, at least, not smile so much. Even the monkey, who grinned each time Sid did, had better teeth and

The Riddle of Riddles

breath.

Sid waited until the last of the applause died down before again stepping up to the microphone. "As you all know, we are gathered here today to honor these heroic individuals for their courageous deeds in pursuit of the answer to The Riddle of Riddles."

He barely finished his statement before the applause began again. Will sighed and shook his head. Knorbert blushed deeply, fidgeting nervously, while Shilli-Shalli was more interested in the widgeons, her necks craning up toward the building tops. Sid waited patiently for the applause to fade away before continuing.

"As a tribute to your continuing efforts, I would like to take this opportunity to present you with the Lock on the City." Sid turned and presented each of them a black, papier-mâché facsimile of a locked lock with no key.

He turned back to the crowd and bellowed, "**Let us all show our honored guests how much we admire them for what they are doing—Seekers of the answer to The Riddle of Riddles**."

The crowd began to grow quite mad in its enthusiasm.

"**Conquerors of the Thicket of Snags!**"

The crowd clapped and whistled, stomped and cheered.

"**Traversers of the Bog of Discouragement!**"

The crowd grew wilder still and crazier.

"**Conquerors of Mount Kneverest!**"

The ovation rose like some gale-driven wall. Wave after wave of applause broke over the platform, spraying them with such adoration that Will actually began to fear that they could drown in such worship. Sid smiled over at them with his bad teeth.

Finally, when the last of the applause had again faded, Sid turned to the three of them and said, "Come. We have prepared a sticky tape parade in your honor."

"We really must get going." Will stated with exaggerated politeness. "We only stopped here for a brief rest."

"Not yet, not yet." Sid shook his head violently. "Hang

Chapter 27 – Man Hatin' Island

with me for a bit. I have something that may help you in your search."

He led them from the platform, through the pressing crowds, to a waiting black limousine convertible parked on the centerline of Fall Street. He indicated that they should sit up on the back of the rear seat so that everyone could see them. Sid sat in front, turning whenever necessary, to point out the sights—bawdy bands, prancing politicians and flowery floats. Everywhere cheering crowds lined the streets as sticky tape rained down from the windows in the pointy buildings above.

At Assault and Battery Park, an enormous billboard showed a picture of Will and Knorbert forcing their way through the Thicket of Snags.

When they reached Men-Wench Village, there was a pansy-craze display depicting Will and Knorbert setting off from Knorbert's cabin. It was entitled, "One Small Step for Man."

Up Fraud Way, they found the Varmint District where there was a ice carving of Will and Knorbert sitting astride Shilli-Shalli. Drops of water dripped from sculpture, puddling at its base.

Everywhere crowds cheered, standing on tiptoe to get a better look at their heroes, looks, often, of open awe.

At Crimes Square, they alighted from the limousine, only to mount another stage where Sid began his acclaim all over again.

"Ladies and Gentlemen, may I present to you the Seekers of the answer to The Riddle of Riddles."

The crowd roared.

Sid went on. "All fame and fortune shall be theirs. Kings shall come bearing gifts. Wise men shall become their students and shall sit at their feet." Sid went on, and on, and on, between ovations from the crowd, telling story after story about the fame and fortune that awaited them once they solved The Riddle of Riddles. He told a great story. It was a shame about his breath.

On and on the stories went, on and on, story after story, word after word, the crowd continually roaring its approval.

At several points in Sid's dissertation, the crowd began

The Riddle of Riddles

chanting, "**TRI-O! TRI-O! TRI-O!**" so loudly that Sid was unable to continue for considerable periods. All the while, the crowd shook banners in time with the rhythm of their chanting.

Knorbert stood transfixed, lost in all the praise, lost in the hurrahs, glowing. Will tugged on Sid's jacket, pulling Sid close enough to yell in his ear, "How long do these festivities last?"

"Why, for as long as you'd like," Sid replied with a crooked smile. "Nothing but the best for fellows as valorous as you."

"But we must get on with our task. You are praising us for something we have not yet finished."

"Did you hear that folks?" Sid turned to the crowd. "They want to push on after the answer to The Riddle of Riddles. No need for mere accolades for these heroes!"

These words threw the crowd into frenzy, like sharks at a feeding. The cheers rang through the air, echoing repeatedly.

Will turned to Knorbert and Shilli-Shalli. "Let's go. We've got a riddle to solve." Then he turned back to Sid. "Thank you very much for all your kindnesses, but we must be going."

As they descended from the stage, they could hear Sid. "Let's show our heroes how we feel about them as they leave us."

The cheers came anew. The crowd pointed at them, nodding their heads in approval, pushing closer. Many reached out to touch them, some happily slapping their backs as they pushed through the pressing crowds.

"Wait! Please wait," Sid cried, pushing his way toward them, arriving, breathless, at their side. He cast the crowd back with an angry look. "I have a map for you, a map that details where to find the answer to the Riddle."

"Will stopped. "A map? Really? Let me see."

"I don't have it here. We have to go get it."

"Where is it?"

"Get back into the limousine," he said. "I'll take you there. We'll make better time that way."

The limousine lurched forward. "How far away is it?"

Chapter 27 – Man Hatin' Island

Will asked.

"Not far. I'll take you via Fall Street if you'd like."

"What for?"

"Why, to start the whole parade all over again, of course," Sid smiled. "We want you to enjoy our festivities as much as possible. You can retrace the parade route as many times as you'd like. The crowds will remain intact, as full and as loud as ever, I promise you."

Will shook his head. "No thanks. I just want to see the map."

Sid looked nervous. He smiled his bad-toothed smile. "How about just one more run around?"

"No. No, thank you," Will said, fixing Sid with an angry glare. "We do not want any re-runs. The map…please."

"Of course," Sid huffed, not quite meeting Will's eyes. "I stored the map in a safe place. In fact, you might just find that place quite interesting."

"What do you mean?" Knorbert asked.

"You will soon see," Sid replied turning to the driver. "Take us to Sin Thrall Park," he said.

With Sid directing their driver, they seemed to go in circles as they wound their way through countless side streets and backstreets until finally they drew up in front of what looked like a giant amusement park.

Stretching off in either direction as far as the eye could see, were multi-colored fabric tents with tattered rents filling every once-quite-empty lot. Games and shows crowded shoulder to shoulder with rides and food stands. Overhead, like a giant snake, arched a roller coaster from which echoed shrieks of delighted fear. The crowd milled about, pushing and shoving like cells of some enormous creature gone quite mad. Boys and girls of all ages and sizes, some with adults but most in groups of their peers, mingled unconcernedly with a wide variety of creatures, including Muggles, Hobbits and even some Knotheads. Many of the children were loaded into small wooden carts drawn by sad-faced donkeys clad in high-topped shoes. A cat strolled with a fox. A fat lady laughed. Over the din, a calliope called with the gayest of lilts, inviting them closer.

Knorbert's mouth gaped wide in the silly semblance of a smile. "Look Will," he cried, pointing at the chaos, "a circus!"

"Not a circus, m-boy," Sid corrected. "A carnalval and not just any carnalval either. No siree-bob! This here's the Mighty Gross Carnalval. Please allow me to be your personal guide. Come on, now. No sense in being shy. The magik is awaiting."

Will had never seen Knorbert move so fast. He wob-wobbled right up the Midway just as fast as his no-kneed legs could carry him. Shilli-Shalli's curiosity overcame her shyness. She rocketed from site to site sticking her noses in some of the most inappropriate places.

"The map is *here*?" Will sounded surprised.

"Yes, I have it locked away in a safe in the back. Come along, now."

Will looked around at all the excitement, and started down the Midway.

"That's the spirit," Sid crowed, throwing an arm familiarly over Will's shoulders.

He led them through the pushing crowds who now took no notice of their passing, so intent was each on his or her or its own desires. Some were plunking down piles of coins before a game entitled the "Miss Fortune's Wheel." Others were gambling on a game called "Diception," and others at a card game called "Three Card Montecarlose." There were craps shooters and moneylenders.

Spotted conveniently about were coffin-sized machines. Long lines of customers inserted plastic cards and withdrew stacks of thin stone coins needed to play the games.

Still others were watching two obeast women wrestle in a pit of a brown muck. The Knotheads had monopolized the bumper cars. There were games of improbability, musical electric chairs and a soggy "Dunk the Drunk" tank. Everyone was laughing and

Chapter 27 – Man Hatin' Island

screaming. Litter washed the Midway.

Sid squeezed Will's shoulder as he led them toward the largest of the tents. This one was fully many times the size of the others, with three poles sticking up through the top of the orange and black canvas like a hex sign. Will turned to look for Shilli-Shalli. She was still darting from attraction to attraction, almost as at home here as was Sid or, for that matter, his monkey Dis.

"Right this way. Please allow me to show you a bit of the sideshow," Sid said, pointing, "before we get the map. This will fascinate you. Right this way, please."

They entered the sideshow through a hexagonal gate ablaze with fire. Over its entrance was a sign that read:
MAGICAL MYSTERY TOUR
1215465 133 8675 75 586 55259 8595

"What are all those numbers underneath the words?" Will asked, pointing up at the sign.

"That is a simple Summation Kyptographeme." The right side of Sid's lip turned down slightly as he spoke. "Anyone who solves that cipher wins a Squeamish Ossifrage, but so far no one has been successful.

"Wins *what*?" Knorbert laughed.

"A Squeamish Ossifrage," Sid repeated, "a 129 toed, bearded scavenger hunter."

"Why would anyone want one of those?" Will grimaced.

Sid shrugged. "Perhaps you could use one in your search."

"No need for scavengers," said Shilli, poking in her head from the right.

"We're here for such portages," said Shalli, her face entering in from the left.

The heat from the hexagonal gate was so intense that they instinctively shied away from the flames around its edges. They entered quickly, keeping to its center.

Inside, the tent was dim and smoky, though the noise was as loud and raucous as ever. Various attractions ringed its perimeter. Sid pointed out the bearded-ladies, the lip-sticked men, the fire-eaters, the sword-swallowers and the snake-charmers.

There was a high stage down at the far end of the tent on which a band was playing. Will barely heard the music over the noise of the crowd. The lead singer held the microphone to his thick lips, whispering obscenely in the audience's ear. A guitar came in low-down and insinuating.

"*Who-who—Who-who—Who-who—Who-who,*
 I was 'round when Nero played his fiddle while Rome burned.
 Made damn sure he enjoyed all the sadism that he yearned."

"What do you think of this?" Sid flourished his arm in a long sweeping arc. He led them to a section of the sideshow that was garishly alight with a splash of almost-golden bulbs that blinked on and off, one after the other spelling out the words

WIT STEAMERS

The area was chock-a-block full of arcade games lined up side to side, back to back. As soon as Knorbert saw them, his eyes blazed. Shilli-Shalli cocked her heads, first to one side, then to the other, listening quizzically. Shilli looked puzzled while Shalli looked amused. Then the looks changed, and Shalli became bemused while Shilli grew still, absorbing all the noises.

"I told you that you would like this." Sid threw out his chest, and strode toward the machines.

He led them down row after row of machines blinking and winking, pinging and ponging, the lights assaulting their eyes with their colorful dance. There was one machine called *Spice Evaders* where the object of the game was to avoid being engulfed by clouds of the spice Melange. There was *Snack Man* where the object was to escape from a labyrinth, eating your enemies as you went. There was *Bally High*, and other games called *EverQuest, BattleTech, Drag-ons and Drudgeons*.

"Right this way, please." Sid led them toward the back of the tent, past machines of all types and all colors, most with some mortal frantically dancing in front as though trying to seduce the

Chapter 27 – Man Hatin' Island

machine into submission.

"We have multitude upon multitude of these machines," Sid explained, "with more arriving every day. If you don't like one, there is always another. Here we are, Knorbert. I think you'll enjoy this one. It's called *Simple Simian*. You start by…"

Before he could finish, Knorbert grabbed hold of the machine with both hands, shaking it madly. He was entranced, already possessed by the deviltry of the game.

"And here's a pinball machine for you Shilli-Shalli. It is called *Emotion Commotion*. Give it a try."

Shilli-Shalli took to the device like a hedonist to pleasure, instantly becoming one with the machine. Playing by intuition, feeling all the bumpers, she played a mean pinball.

Sid glanced nervously over at Will from a corner of his eye. His hands fiddled about in front of him, fiddled about, fiddled about as though they had something in mind but here was not the place, nor now the time.

"Let me see. We must have a game for you too, Will," he said his eyes searching up and down the rows of machines.

"Ah! Of course. Here we are," he said, finally locating a machine he thought might hold Will's interest. "This is just the instrument for you."

He led Will up to a gaily-colored video game that was already in paroxysms of delight, though Will had not even touched it. "This game is called *Infinity*," he said. "It is a very simple game, yet one of our most advanced. I have programmed it so that you will need no money. Simply press the reset button to get another incarnation. I think you will find this game reality-challenged."

"How is it played?" Will asked.

"It is played differently by different players. Some are more successful than others, depending on their strategies. I just know you will do well because you are so smart."

"Has anyone ever beaten it?"

"Beaten it? Oh no, no one has ever beaten it. It is

programmed to increase its ability as you approach its limits. That way the game goes on forever, don't you see?"

"Forever!" Will bellowed. "I don't have forever! I only have the rest of today! Where is that map you promised?"

"It's here, over there, actually. See those two big guys?" Sid pointed.

Will looked to see two huge men standing on either side of a black metal door. "Yeah," he replied.

"They guard my office. Inside is the safe that contains the map, and, of course, lots of my money." Sid threw back his head and laughed loudly. "Sorry about that video game. I should have known that a silly pinball game would not interest someone of your intellectual capabilities. But I understand you do play chess. Here, over here."

Sid grasped Will by an elbow and led him over to a table on which was a chess set made of ebony and ivory. Will recognized that the pieces were in exactly the same position as the game he had left back at the Pleasure Palace.

"This is the positioning of your perfect game, I believe. Your last move was Bishop-to-Bishop-Four. Is that correct?"

Will squinted his eyes, looking over at Sid. "How do you know about this game?"

"Ha!" Sid exclaimed. "Of course, I know. How could I not know? I believe it is my turn, is it not?"

Will nodded.

"Well then, no need for delays. Pawn-to-Queen-Three." Sid moved his pawn. "Your turn." He looked up at Will from beneath a furrowed brow, smiling his broken smile.

"This is not even close to the ideal game I am perfecting," said Will. "This is not even the proper beginning. However, in this game the next obvious move would be Queen-to-Rook-Five." Will picked up his Queen and moved it to its appropriate square. "Now, let's take a look at that map."

"What about the game?" Sid asked, looking up from the chessboard.

Chapter 27 – Man Hatin' Island

"We'll come back to it—if we have time, if the map leads us to the answer to the Riddle, that is." He paused. "The map...please."

"The map..." Sid took a deep breath. He looked at Will, and then over at the men guarding the door. "Sure. The map." He walked to the metal door, reaching for his keys.

The keys rattled loudly, as Sid fumbled with them. He inserted a key in the lock and opened the door. Then he turned to Will. "I'll be right out."

Will stepped back, allowing Sid to enter his office. The men on either side of the door ignored Will, their arms folded across their chests.

Will waited and waited. He could hear Sid inside. It sounded like Sid was moving furniture. "Are you alright in there?" Will called out.

"Yeah, yeah. I'm fine." Sid's replied, his voice muffled by the half-closed door.

After several long minutes, Sid came out. He had a big grin, and held a rolled up scroll in one hand. "Here you go."

Will snatched the scroll from Sid's hand. It was tied with a narrow red ribbon. His hands were shaking so much he had trouble untying the tiny knot. Finally, the knot came loose, and Will unrolled the scroll, holding it open with both hands. He held it up to an overhead light so he could read it. He turned it over. Then he turned it back, then over, then back.

"It's blank," he snapped. "The map is blank." He looked at Sid.

Sid burst out laughing. "I know. Isn't that hysterical? A blank map," and he laughed louder yet. The two gorilla-like men were trying not to laugh, but they couldn't help themselves. Their lips quivered. They started to smile, and then they both just started laughing loudly.

Will's face got red. "You think this is funny?"

"Of course. It's hilarious. Come on, Will. Where's your sense of humor? What's funnier than a blank map, eh, boys?" He looked at his guards. All three of them stood there laughing. "Hysterical!" said Sid. "Come on, Will. It's a practical joke. Lighten up." Sid was holding his side, gasping for air.

Will threw the scroll toward Sid, but it fell harmlessly to the ground at Sid's feet. He spun on his heel. "Knorbert, Shilli-Shalli!" he yelled.

There were no signs of either of them, just the cacophony of buzzes and bells and whistles, just the visual assault of ever-changing colors and perpetual motion. Will searched the rows of twitching backs and wagging heads.

He saw Shilli-Shalli's long necks stretched far above all the surrounding crowds. "Shilli-Shalli," Will called "over here. Come on. We are leaving."

Shalli looked up at the sound of Will's voice. She pulled to leave, but Shilli stayed with the machine. Then just as Shilli started to leave, Shalli pulled back the plunger and sent another pinball on its way. Then Shilli tried leaving the machine, but Shalli was working the flippers madly. First Shilli and then Shalli. Back and forth the battle waged until they bumped heads.

"Let's go," said Shilli.

"I say no," said Shalli

"No. I say no."

"But I want to go."

The noisy argument brought them back to Will, Shilli glowering while Shalli smiled sweetly. Another bump of their heads left Shalli scowling and Shilli happily humming.

Will spied Knorbert's large head bouncing back and forth as he rocked In front a machine called *Hokey Mon*.

"Knorbert," Will cried. "Let's go!"

Knorbert did not answer. "*Bingo! Ringo! Zingo! Zang!*" his machine sang. Will grabbed Knorbert by the shoulders, spun him around, and shook him. "Knorbert," he said. "Come on. We're leaving."

"What is the matter, Will?" Knorbert eyes were glazed over. "Why are you shaking me?"

Chapter 27 – Man Hatin' Island

"We've got to go. We can't stay here playing these silly games. We have a task to complete, and Luci is well on her way down."

"Oh my, yes, of course. I got so interested in my game that I forgot all about the time." Knorbert glanced back over his shoulder at the blinking lights. "Can I just finish this one game?"

"No! *You-cannot-just-finish-that-one-game!*" Will spat the words out. "Let's go."

"But I was nearly up to 100 trillion googooplexes. After that I get a free spin."

"I think you've had one free spin too many. You look dizzy to me as it is." He grabbed Knorbert by the belt, and dragged him off, leaving the machine sighing lonesomely in the background.

"Where do you think you're going?" Out of nowhere, Sid was suddenly standing directly in front of them. On either side of Sid, completely blocking the aisle, were the two gargantuan men. Sid was standing calmly, a fat cigarette clamped firmly between his rotting teeth. He folded his arms across his chest.

"We've got to get going," Will said in a quiet voice. "We would like to thank you for your hospitality—in spite of your practical joke." Will watched for Sid's reaction, but he showed none. "As you know, we have a task to complete before sundown, and it is getting late."

"Nonsense," Sid said, puffing fiercely on his fat cigarette, enveloping them all in billowing clouds of a sweet smoke. "You're not really mad at me for playing that little joke on you are you?"

"That was rude," Will said, "especially since you know how helpful a map would have been."

"That's what made it so funny, Will. Come on, lighten-up. It was just a joke." Sid drew heavily on his cigarette.

"What about the map, Will?" Knorbert asked.

"There is no map, Knorbert. It was all a joke, just one big joke," Will answered.

The Riddle of Riddles

Sid puffed away, a broad smile on his face. "And quite a funny joke, don't you think, Knorbert?"

The clouds of sweet smoke filled the air, filled their lungs each time they breathed.

"We're leaving," said Will. "We must...we must...uh...we must do something important. I forget what it is but I do remember it is important." Will shook his head. "Oh yes, I remember now. We are looking for the answer to The Riddle of Riddles. How could I have forgotten?"

"So, what are you worried about?" Sid asked.

The smoke grew denser. The scent from the smoke was so sweet that Will did not mind it at all. He enjoyed it.

"I am worried about...about what? Oh, yes. We have to leave. We have a riddle to answer."

"I understand," Sid blew a billowing cloud of smoke in Will's direction.

"I keep forgetting," Will stopped. "I keep forgetting something. I think it's supposed to be something important, but I can't remember what. Oh, yes, The Riddle of Riddles."

Sid's security guards stood on either side of Sid. They pushed in, closer to Will, completely blocking his way.

"I must not forget!" Will kept repeating the last thing he rightly remembered, *"When is the riddle the answer?"* The words made no sense to him, but he kept repeating them over and over to himself anyway.

Sid leaned forward, and blew another huge cloud of the sweet smoke right in their faces. The medals on his chest jangled loudly.

Then it came to Will. Of course! It was the smoke! The smoke was making them forget. The Smoke of Forgetfulness!

Will shook his head in a desperate effort to clear it. Sid's face, smiling ever so sweetly, wavered before him, first close, then distant, and then close again. The sweet smoke hung like a thick curtain between them.

"We have to get out of here." Will pushed through the

Chapter 27 – Man Hatin' Island

thick curtain of smoke until his face was but inches from Sid's pointy nose.

Sid tried desperately to avoid Will's eyes, but Will would not let his quarry escape. His eyes locked with Sid's eyes. The chilling horror of nothingness stared back at him.

Dis screamed and fled to the top of the nearest machine.

At the sound of the monkey's scream, Shilli moaned and Shalli groaned. She bolted for the door, and was gone in a blink. The sudden void left Will feeling particularly vulnerable.

"Please," Sid wheedled, his smile completely gone now. He recoiled from Will's eyes. "*Please* go. Here take this with you. Take this and go." He held up something shiny before Will's eyes.

Will's mind was fixated on the phrase—*When is the riddle the answer?*—though the words meant nothing to him. He focused his mind on the words like a compass needle pointing home, and kept repeating the phrase. He was afraid, afraid that if he did not, he would forget everything forever and would be forever lost.

Slowly, his eyes focused on the shiny object Sid was pushing toward him.

"PLEASE!" Sid was shouting. "Please go." He stuffed the object into Will's shirt pocket. "Consider it a present."

Will stumbled forward. Knorbert's shocked face stared dumbly back at him. "*When is the riddle the answer?*" he repeated.

He grabbed Knorbert's hand, and lurched between the unmoving, gorilla-like men, toward the fiery entrance.

In the background Will was barely aware of music, the song from the band on stage ringing in his ears.

"*Not pleased to meet me? That is plain to see.*
But what's puzzling you are games without boundaries.
Who-who—Who-who—Who-who—Who-who..."

They lurched through the circle of fire, spinning as they went. The fire singed Will's hair, its pungent burnt-bone odor barely registering on his consciousness.

Outside the air was fresh and clean. Will breathed deeply,

The Riddle of Riddles

filling his lungs, trying to clear his mind.

"When is the riddle the answer?" Will said again, only now did the words begin to have meaning. "Now I remember what I had almost forgotten. Now if I could only forget Sid, Sid and Dis, Sid and his bad teeth and worse breath."

They pushed through the crowds, still eagerly pressing forward to get in for the show. They wended their way away from the noise and confusion, away in no particular direction, unsure where they were, uncertain where they were going. They pounded their way down several hard, gray concrete avenues, then down a couple of more blocks, zigzagging across corners to avoid the mess of traffic.

They came upon a vacant lot overlooking a river. Will stopped, out of breath. He bent at the waist, his hands flopping at his sides. Knorbert, head down, wobbling side to side, bumped into Will, and then quickly reeled back. Will grabbed Knorbert by an elbow to keep him from falling. He took some more deep breaths and then squatted down.

Knorbert put a hand on the ground to ease himself down. "I wish I could do that, he said." He sat, puffing, legs stuck straight out in front of him. "Hunch down like that I mean," and he pointed at Will's knees.

"Oh, so now you like my collapsible legs, huh?" Will grinned.

"Oh so?" Knorbert asked. "Quite so...if you say so," and they both looked at each other and laughed.

The vacant lot overlooked a blood-red river. Its waters glugged by sluggishly. There were dilapidated warehouses, abandoned breweries and even an outdated tannery all crowded against groaning, grayed-out wooden pilings. A sign, hanging from a tenement building near collapse, was supported on one corner by a single rusty bolt. In peeling red paint, it read *"Hell's Kitchen"* in large block letters with the words *"Me_gid_an Cu_s_ne"* centered below in smaller type. Will struggled to read the sign, but had difficulty because of the missing letters.

Chapter 27 – Man Hatin' Island

A breeze caught the sign. "*Eeyczaw*," it groaned as it swayed on its rusty bolt. "Sounds just like Eeyore," said Will in a slow, sad tone.

"Eeyore?"

One corner of Will's lips turned up. "Eeyore is a pessimistic, stuffed gray donkey who wears a pink bow tied to his tail. He lives in Hundred Acre Wood, far, far, far from here."

"And why is that important?"

"It's not. That sound just reminded me of a story from reality, that's all."

"Reality?"

"You remember reality, don't you? It's the next dimension in the direction of Outer Space." Will paused. "I don't really mean reality. It reminded me of the imaginary part of my reality."

"Imaginary reality?"

"Yeah," Will sighed. "There is even an imaginary world in my reality. I guess I must be getting homesick."

The wind caught the sign again, and it brayed once more. "*Eeyczaw*."

"What did Sid give you, Will? What was that thing he put in your pocket?"

"I'm glad you reminded me. I forgot all about it."

Will reached into his shirt pocket, and pulled out the item that Sid had thrust upon him in leaving. It was a black and white hourglass-shaped object.

The Riddle of Riddles

ONE SIDE   ANOTHER SIDE

Chapter 27 – Man Hatin' Island

"UAMIMAU!" Knorbert exclaimed. "That looks just like the other object, the one you found at Lilith's feet."

"It sure does." Will reached back into his pocket and removed the first piece. "They do look similar, but they are not exactly the same. Some of the parts do seem to align. Here," Will passed the items to Knorbert, "take a look. What do you make of them?"

Knorbert examined both pieces closely, turning them over several times in his hard-callused hands. "You are right. They are not exactly the same. I would say they are related somehow, but I am not exactly sure how."

"Can you fit them together?" Will asked.

"Well, yes, they do kind of fit together, but it appears as though there is another piece, maybe pieces, missing."

Will sat back. He returned the pieces to his pocket. "It is getting late, Knorbert, and the later it gets, the faster time seems to go."

"Doctor Kneinstein's theory proven correct," Knorbert nodded.

"Play some music. Knorbert. See if you can attract Shilli-Shalli. Let's hope she is close enough to hear you play."

Knorbert had barely put the pipe to his lips when there was Shilli-Shalli singing beside him, their music as refreshing as a summer sip of sweet water. The music surrounded them until the air was thick with it. Even the wind stopped to listen before it snatched up the last few notes as mementoes and hurried off.

"You play so well," Will said, "that I could listen to you forever."

Knorbert blushed.

"But we don't have forever," Will reminded them. "Let's fly."

CHAPTER 28 – DEEPER AND DEEPER INTO INNER SPACE

Their gyrations on past flights had been wild, but bit by bit, Knorbert was managing to increase his control. Those wild swings were, now, not nearly so catastrophic. However, time was running out, and neither potions nor blank maps had brought them any closer to the answer they so desperately needed.

"Urge Shilli-Shalli to fly faster, Knorbert," Will suggested.

Knorbert leaned in closer to Shilli-Shalli's heads, whispering in all her ears, "Go, girls, go! Go Shilli. Go Shalli. Go girls, go"

Will peered over Knorbert's shoulder. It was all clear up ahead as they rocketed deeper and deeper into Inner Space.

"You're doing great, Knorbert," Will said. "Try lighter touches."

"Lighter touches? Are you kidding? I am having enough trouble controlling Shilli-Shalli using all my strength."

"Try it. Knowing how far out of control we dare go without really threatening our safety gives us some latitude to experiment. Try to encourage whichever head is constructive, whichever head is positive, while reining in the head that is destructive and negative. Maybe you'll be able to pick up some slight feeling that will tell you when the negative head is about to try to take control. Watch for the slow, gradual changes. They are the most difficult to identify."

"I do not know, Will. That sounds a bit reckless to me."

"Here, let me help." Will placed his hands directly over Knorbert's so their hands worked as one. "OK, let's ease up some."

Will felt Knorbert slowly relax his grip.

Shilli-Shalli rocketed forward at a bewildering speed, but

Chapter 28 – Deeper and Deeper into Inner Space

Knorbert kept his touch light. Will's hands on Knorbert's could feel each time Knorbert tightened or loosened his hold.

"Easy, Knorbert," Will coaxed, as he felt Knorbert's hands beginning to tense. "Keep the touch light. Let's see if we can feel anything."

Together they felt for that first twitch that would indicate in which direction they might next be led.

But they felt nothing.

No, nothing.

"Perhaps I was wrong." Will exhaled. "A bit lighter? I thought…Wait! What was that? Did you feel something, Knorbert?"

"Yes, Will. Yes, I did!"

There it was again. There was a definite feel to it, a sense that could be detect only with the lightest of touches, and pinpoint concentration.

At first it was difficult to detect, so when Shilli took off in a depressed mood, they veered far off toward misery before Knorbert was able to exert just enough light manipulations to swing them back. Then Shalli became manic, and they veered off in the direction of volatility.

With a heavy hand at first, followed by lighter and lighter touches, Knorbert turned them away from hyperspace. Soon their flight became smoother, less jerky—a succession of long sweeping arcs, first in one direction, followed by another long swooping arc in the other.

Knorbert bracketed, and then halved the scope of each wide arc, diminishing their range. He bracketed and halved, bracketed and halved. Their arcs of flight grew tighter and tighter. Their direction straightened.

Their speed increased, increment built on increment, but they had no method of gauging their speed. There were no currents in the vacuum of Inner Space, nothing pushing back against them with an ever increasing force to indicate their speed. Occasionally, a piece of space debris rocketed passed, but its speed and trajectory only added to their lack of orientation.

With his hands laying lightly on top of Knorbert's, Will could feel the lack of tension. Knorbert kept his touch as light as he dared, feeling for each initial impulse. Soon Shilli and Shalli started working together. Even the sounds they were making approached a near harmony. The flight grew steady, almost completely under control, all beginning to work as one.

First Shalli, and then Shilli began pulling frantically, like the arms of a swimmer trying to catch a wave. Before anyone could react, their flight neared perfection. Shilli and Shalli were now pulling together, almost as one.

Knorbert's hand tensed and they lost the synchronicity they had come so close to achieving. They were no longer an operative force working together for their common good.

It was gone. Will sensed that they had missed something extraordinary—though what it was, he could not say. They had been part of something. Whatever it was had passed through them, and then out of them, something very powerful, something too fleeting.

Knorbert was back in control.

"Knorbert," Will shouted, giving full vent to his feelings of loss, "we've lost it. We lost the speed. We've lost that certain oneness we were approaching."

"What are you talking about, Will? Nothing has changed. I did tense slightly, but I quickly regained the light touch."

"Didn't you feel it? Didn't you sense the power we had tapped into? That moment was so momentary. It fled so quickly after such effort and, harder still, such restraint, such a holding back in the face of such desire. Now we've lost it. What made you tense up? "

"I became a bit concerned that I was not using enough strength once Shilli-Shalli took off like that, and I got a little bit afraid, I think."

"Afraid of what?"

"I do not know exactly, afraid of going too fast maybe. I

Chapter 28 – Deeper and Deeper into Inner Space

do not know how to control Shilli-Shalli exactly. Was I using too little control or too much? No, no, that is not it. It is just that…oh, I do not know. I was just afraid, that is all."

"Could it be that you are afraid that if we go too fast that we might crash, Knorbert? And if we crash, we will fail and that it will be your fault? Or maybe you are afraid that if we go so fast, we will succeed, that we will win. Is that it? Are you afraid to win? Are you afraid of succeeding?"

"Afraid to fail, what a depressing tale," Shilli moaned.

"Afraid to win, a discouraging sin," Shalli groaned.

The speed they were traveling was fearsome. The closer they had gotten to achieving that state of oneness, the faster they had flown, the lighter the touch, the greater the speed. Only when Knorbert had tensed, had their speed begun to diminish. Still, they streaked through the ether faster than ever before.

The battle for control between Shill and Shalli resumed with an unvacillating vengeance.

In the distance, out of nowhere, a tiny speck appeared, dead ahead on their present course.

"Look Will," Knorbert cried, "up ahead, a place where we can collect out bearings. Let us make for there before we get lost forever, somewhere here in Inner Space."

"No way. Get control. Get control of yourself."

"We are flying too fast, way too fast." Knorbert sounded as if he were about to cry. "Maybe I did over-steer Shilli-Shalli. We will have to stop somewhere eventually, anyway. Why not up ahead?"

"Why not stop now?" asked Shilli.

"We will anyhow," sassed Shalli.

"Guilt has shackled all free flight."

"Pity strangles with all its might."

"Shilli-Shalli is right, Will. We are no longer flying freely. We are out of control. I just cannot go on. I must stop."

The battles between Shilli and Shalli intensified, Shilli twisting one way while Shalli twisted the other. Around and around they went. Shalli's neck got wrapped once around Shilli's neck, but in the attempt to untangle themselves, both necks got tied in a glob knot from which they were unable to free themselves.

They spun off into a death spiral.

"Guilt triggers pity," said Shalli.

"Pity triggers guilt," said Shilli.

"Pity and guilt, guilt and pity, twin deceivers," Shilli and Shalli intoned together. "Guilt and pity, pity and guilt, success defeaters."

"Pity drags down."

"For guilt to drown."

"Spiraling pity."

"Spiraling guilt."

"Spiraling, spiraling, spiraling down."

"Spiraling, spiraling, down, down, down."

"Pull, Knorbert!" Will yelled, pulling back on both Shilli and Shalli. "Do not give up! Do not give in. Pull, Knorbert, pull."

But the death spiral in which they were caught twisted them down and around, through a thin layer of clouds toward its inevitable destination in the emptiness of that black vacuum.

Without Will's efforts, this death spiral might have been their last, but his mounting strength was now a growing factor in their survival. He sucked in his breath, and pulled back with all his might.

CHAPTER 29 – THE WEB AND THE PIT

The Island was a barren place, dominated by a single large volcano that clawed its way through the clouds, high into the sky. Its sides were ravaged, twisted sheaves where once-molten lava had flowed, sputtering and hissing, down to the sea. Nowhere were there signs of life, as though some Lord of the Island had decreed no living thing be permitted to take root.

The top of the volcano was a smoldering black hole. A thin stream of lava wept out a narrow vent in its rim. Far below, deep within the crater, red fire winked out at them from the blackness, stared at them like the single lamenting eye of some hideous monster, beckoning them. Intense heat and acrid smoke billowed up out of the volcano, blinding and choking them.

Shilli shrieked and Shalli screeched as their death spiral carried them right into the eye of the volcano.

They crashed onto a shelf of gray shale that gave way beneath them, sliding with them in a long and bumpy ride until they came to a stop on a wide, jagged ledge of cold stone in that hot inferno.

It was dark. Overhead, the bright blue of the sky contrasted violently with the black smoke that billowed up from the pit below. The walls of the volcano sloped down from the ledge on which they had come to a halt, falling away more and more precipitously as it neared its center until, finally, emptying into the fiery red pit below.

Several worries of large wrats let go of their perch on the stone ceiling and took flight on their fleshy wings, swirling up and out of the volcano. A low hiss of lava could be heard as it oozed over cheeks of hardened magma.

"Nice going, Knorbert. You did it again," Will whispered hoarsely. "Some place you picked when you changed our course! This place looks so…sinister. Do you find yourself attracted to

The Riddle of Riddles

such places?"

Before Knorbert could answer a loud voice boomed, "**YA DON'T HAVE TA WHISPER.**" The words reverberated off the stony walls.

Shilli-Shalli trembled, as did Knorbert, and it did not take Will long to realize that he was trembling, too.

"**WELCOME**," the Voice thundered. "**WELCOME TA MY HUMBLE HOME.**" A deep laugh bounced crazily off the stony walls.

The Voice was so loud Will drew back his head, turning it side to side, trying to lessen the pain in his ears. Knorbert clapped his hands over his enormous ears, completely letting go of Shilli-Shalli, who lurched back, away from the deafening sound.

The tone of the Voice became softer and mellower. "Please, ya gotta forgive me. I see I'm scaring y'all. I'll speak softer. I ain't here ta scare nobody. I am here ta help ya."

"You're makin' da most amazin' progress gettin' ta ya goal. I congratulate y'all. Yep, I know all about cha, all a y'all. But chu probly guessed dat. Your successes are already da stuff a legend. We are all so proud of y'all."

The Voice inhaled. "You don't need ta be scared a me or dis place. Un-uh. Like I said, I'm here ta help y'all." Once again laughter bellowed forth, in waves so loud they shook rocks loose, rocks which bounced and rolled, and then careened silently into the black depths below.

Help us? Will shook his head in wonder. *Help us?* Like we've been *helped* before?

"Why ya hidin'?" the Voice asked. "Come on. Come on down. I'm waitin' on ya." The Voice was deep yet soft, loud yet soothing, demanding yet pleading, charming and quite hypnotic. Shilli-Shalli eased forward.

"Yo, Shilli-Shalli," the Voice crooned, "you're goin' down in da history a da Willi-Nillies as some kinda hero. Mm, mm. Yep, you *dared* ta approach a Knothead—and him wid a creature from anudda **di**-mension. Mm-mm. And you even made

Chapter 29 – The Web and the Pit

friends wit dos two strangers, allowin' dem ta ride on ya back. Now, dat's what I be calling courage!"

"Whoa, Shilli-Shalli." Will pulled back on Shilli-Shalli as she eased forward, apparently drawn by the timbre of the Voice. "Knorbert! Grab hold. Rein in Shilli-Shalli."

"And beautiful! Whoo-whee, you are da most beautiful creature in flight, fast *and* graceful."

Shilli-Shalli continued to drift forward. They moved over the edge of the ledge, moving down the steep shale slope.

"Stop!" Will yelled, grabbing handfuls of Shilli-Shalli's fur. "Knorbert, help! Shilli-Shalli is being influenced by the Voice. We've got to stop her."

They both pulled and together managed to rein her in, to stop their decline.

The Voice chortled. "Knorbert, Knorbert, Knorbert! What can I say ta begin ta do justice ta your *magnificent deeds*? When speaking of courage, you are *da man*. Your name goin' down in history, too. What kind of courage it must have taken ta drop everything in order ta help a total stranger? Um-um! Yours is an un-common courage, a courage ta step out, ta step out onta unknown paths, da courage ta do, ta be! You da man!"

Knorbert sighed, loosening his hold on Shilli-Shalli, who then proceeded to start gliding forward again.

"Watch what you are doing, Knorbert," Will hissed. "We are drifting again."

Knorbert sat back, and pulled back on Shilli-Shalli.

"But cha got a lot more 'en just courage, Knorbert," the deep, resonant Voice continued. "Your mind, ho, ho, ho…now dere's a mind. You got you a mind, a no grind mind, a no behind mind, no sir. You got a fine mind. Your intelligence already legendary, a courageous intelligence. You got da mind *not afraid* ta take da risks, *not afraida* being wrong, *not afraida* ridicule. What can I say? It's an honor ta be here wit cha."

A gentle smile crept across Knorbert's lips.

"Knorbert, snap out of it! We're drifting toward the pit

again. Don't listen, Knorbert. Don't listen. The Voice is trying to seduce you. The walls are getting steep, way too steep. We must be careful. We've got to turn around and get out of here."

"Easy breezy, Will. No need gettin' all jived-up. Com'ere. Come on down. Come closer. I tell ya dere's nothing ta be afraida. I praise all ya do, *especially* you, Will," the deep, bass Voice intoned, nearer now. "Don't tink for a thin-sliced minute dat I'd forget y'all, Will. Man, oh man, you got it *all*. You got da rarest combination, mind and heart and conscience all workin' together. Look at you undertakin' such an adventure! Your mind so sharp, you know when ta listen and when not. And dat heart, Will? WOW! Now dat's a heart so big you sacrificed praise, pleasure *and* potion, sacrificed fame *and* fun, ta pursue da goal."

Will suddenly realized that he, too, had started listening to the Voice, had fallen under its seductive sway, and that they were, once again, drifting toward the pit.

"Rare, Will, you're one rare cat! An I-N-D-I-V-I-D-U-A-L, individual. I can't believe I'm da lucky one, lucky enough ta be meetin' y'all. Yes sir, y'all cool cats," and the Voice laughed.

"That's enough!" Will cried, digging his heels into the loose shale while pulling back on Shilli-Shalli. "We've heard all of this before. We do not need your praise, whoever or whatever you are. Surely, you must know this about us since you seem to know so much else." Will's voice rang through the stony chamber, his heels slipping in the loose shale as he tried to prevent them from slipping forward toward the pit.

"I know dat," the deep Voice spoke once more. "My admiration for ya is so deep and genuine I forget myself. I'm beggin' your forgiveness. Y'all don't need no empty blather from me but..." and the Voice paused a long moment, "I do have something you will be needin'."

"And what might that be?" Will asked, a sharp-edge to his voice.

"Come on. Come on down, and see for yourselves."

Chapter 29 – The Web and the Pit

"We are staying right here, thank you very much," said Will. "No, no we're not. In fact, we're leaving. We have important matters to finish, and our time grows short."

Will spurred Shilli-Shalli, trying to turn them around toward the light so far above.

"Don't be too hasty," the Voice wheedled smoothly. "Da last thing in da world I wanna do is keep y'all from finishin' da job. I'm on your side, remember?" The Voice paused. "Ya gotta, have time for one quick peek at treasure though, doncha?"

"Treasure?" Knorbert came to life. "What kind of treasure? How much treasure? Is the treasure for us? Do you mean money? Let us go look, Will. Let us at least look," his eyes stretched wide.

"We don't have time, Knorbert, and you know that. We've got to keep moving." But even as he spoke, they began sliding forward again. Will's heels scraped against the shale, his muscles aching from the strain of trying to halt their dangerous slide toward the black hole. The walls were incredibly steep, one momentary lapse of attention away from oblivion.

They skidded to a halt as Shilli-Shalli shied away from the intense heat that wafted up out of the pit, a pit into which they could now peer.

Deep, deep down in the blackness, glowered a red-hot furnace that sent up clouds of acrid smoke and intense heat. Wavering in that heat, between them and that everlasting fire, sat a big black spider-like creature fully as large as the big-top back on Man Hatin' Island. Its eyes glowed as red as the coals far below. Its body was completely covered with short, stiff black hairs, including the scorpion-like stinger that curled up over its head. On its forehead were three livid scars, mean red slashes like misshapen sixes. An amulet hung from its neck. It sat motionless on a vast web of sticky, wrist-thick strands that stretched completely across the opening from edge to edge.

Surrounding the creature were bags and bags full of gold and silver coins and glittering gems, bags woven from the same sticky substance as the web. They hung from the web, jiggling with each of the creature's movements.

"Oh yeah! Dere you be. So good ta finally see y'all. Welcome. I'm Scorpideior, your host." The creature's voice was syrupy smooth. "Didn't I tell ya I had da treasure for y'all?" It touched the bags with this and that hairy leg. They jingled with their heavy loads. "And more," Scorpideior crooned, "much, much more. Dis is but da beginnin'. Look 'round. All of dis here treasure is for y'all, yours for da takin', whatever ya want. Look, over here. Check out dis here bauble."

Will tore his fascinated eyes from the hideous creature to look where it pointed. Hollowed out into the stonewalls surrounding the web was a chamber, and in it was a chest overflowing with jewels. On top of it sat the largest single diamond Will had ever seen. It was nearly as big as Knorbert's head, its facets sparkling in the dim red light from the fires below.

Knorbert gasped audibly. It was truly a magnificent gem, an empire's ransom.

"Over here," Scorpideior said, pointing with another foreleg to another chamber, "we got some more playtings."

There was chamber after chamber carved into the walls surrounding the web, each filled with priceless treasures. Besides mountains of money, there were beautifully carved music boxes. There were magnificent statuary, ancient scrolls, beautiful paintings, rare books. There were pearls, sapphires, and jade.

Atop a nearby chest, heaped over with all manner of jewelry, Will spied a delicately crafted gold crown, richly encrusted with precious stones. It looked like it would fit his head perfectly, as if it had been made specifically *for* him. He longed to reach out, to touch it, to try it on.

"Treasure! Yours for da takin'," said the creature. "As much as you guys can carry."

"I see ya checking out dat silver flute, Knorbert," Scorpideior chucked. "Cool, huh? And look over here, Will. Here's a chess set for y'all—and not just any chess set. Dis here

Chapter 29 – The Web and the Pit

chess set is one of a kind. Its made a negrasanguinium and blancaqua. Da board is made a alternate squares a glacial and trachyonic temporium. It's as beautiful as it is rare."

The chess pieces were typically black and white, but, Will swore, he could actually see *through* them. They seemed to hover above the board while actually sitting on it. Will had never seen such artistry.

The shiny amulet swung from the creature's neck as it sat unmoving in the center of its web. "I understand ya play," Scorpideior said. "I play too. Matta a fact, I'm good, real good. But tell me, If you were in my position, Will, what move would ya make?"

Will looked back at the exquisite board, and noticed that a game was in play, that same game that continued to chase him no matter where he went. He looked from the board up to Scorpideior. "It's your move. Let's see how good you really are."

"Oh?" Scorpideior glared down at Will. "Ya don't really tink ya can beat me, do ya? I'm the *Masta* Gran'masta."

"Well then, Master Grandmaster, make your move."

"OK, den." Scorpideior giggled, a strange, interior-deep snicker. The creature hesitated…continued to hesitate…until finally… "Knight-ta-Bishop-Three. *Gardé*." It plucked the knight with one of his large hairy forelegs and moved it to the appropriate square. "I'm threaten ya Queen, doncha see."

"I know what *gardé* means." Will glanced briefly at the game board, but something nagged at him. Something more important than this chess game haunted him. He was not quite sure what it was, hovering in a twilight just out of insight.

"Why are you offering us all this treasure?" he asked.

"Ya Queen's being attacked. Doncha care?" Scorpideior asked, unmoving on its web, unmoving that is, except for its barbed tail, which it continued to slowly curl and uncurl above its head.

"I can see that, but I did not come all this way to play chess. Don't change the subject. Why are you offering us all this

The Riddle of Riddles

treasure?"

"Dat's da way it is," Scorpideior replied. "Those who strive as hard as y'all get rewarded. Simple as dat."

"How do we know it's real?" Knorbert interjected.

"Oh, da treasure's real awright. It's da reward for all y'alls efforts. Da deeds of da valorous always precede dem," Scorpideior answered, continuing the slow, seductive motion of its tail. "It's da way. Simple as dat. Da praise is just my humble way of recognizing ya worth because a all y'all done. Da treasure's da real reward. It's da desire for wealth dat drives all a us, ain't it? Come on now. Y'all know I'm right. I'm standing guard over dis treasure so someone don't steal it. Come on, pick out whacha want. I'll weave some sacks fa y'all, sacks ya can carry da treasure in as you go on ya way, sacks as large as y'all can manage." The heat shimmered up with the words.

Knorbert turned to Will. "Come on," he said. "Let us grab some treasure for ourselves, and then we can be on our way— three bags full, three *big* bags full, one for each of us. No, make that four big bags full, one each for Shilli and Shalli. She is plenty strong enough to carry a heavy load of treasure. It won't take long." His eyes darted back and forth between Will and that silver flute.

Will's eyes strayed to that magnificent crown, the chess set. Perhaps they did have time to grab a few bags of treasure. They certainly deserved some kind of reward for all their efforts. His eyes swept over all the sparkling wealth before them, the crown, that enormous diamond, all those gold and silver coins. They sure could fit a lot of treasure in three…make that four bags, four *big* bags. Did they dare spare the time? Perhaps if they made it quick. How long could it take?

"Listen, ya want da answer to dis riddle of yours, right? Well, I know how y'all can find dat answer."

"You do?"

"Sure I do. Da answer is right dere," and Scorpideior pointed to all the treasure surrounding them. "Believe me, dis is

Chapter 29 – The Web and the Pit

how y'all get da answer to dat riddle."

"What do you mean?" Will asked.

"Doncha get it, Will? Wealth! Wealth is da answer. Dis treasure is da answer, not ta da Riddle, but ta how ta get de answer. You buy it! You buy da answer with da treasure. I know ya know what I'm talkin' 'bout, Will. I know ya got a li'l larceny in ya soul. Remember ya greedy wish? Dis is da same ting only smarter."

Will's face got red. He heard Scorpideior's slow, heavy breathing. The walls of the cavern seemed to breathe with the creature. He looked at all the treasure. Then he looked back at Scorpideior, and snorted. "Thank you for reminding me of my mistake. I know how foolish I was then and, I don't intend to remain foolish. I've moved on. I've learned from my mistake."

A beam of light from the mouth of the volcano far above broke through the black smoke like sunshine in the middle of the night. It shined on them ever-so-briefly before darkness swallowed them up again.

In that instant Will realized exactly where they were, how close to the edge they had come. He saw the absolute hideousness of their host. The treasure, which glittered and sparkled in that light, looked fake, real though it might have been. He heard the tinny clinking of the coins as the creature twitched nervously in that brief beam of light. The sulfurous gases that wafted up from below filled his nostrils.

"**We don't want your treasure**," Will yelled so suddenly that Shilli-Shalli gave a start and nearly pitched them into the pit. "We will earn our own treasure. We need no empty praise, no undeserved riches. We will be on our way. Come on, Knorbert. Come on Shilli-Shalli. Let's get out of here." Will nudged Knorbert, and together they managed to turn around, back toward the light far above. Slowly, they inched their way away from the web and the pit.

Voluminous clouds of smoke billowed up from below, impairing their vision. Will looked for the light, but saw only darkness. He panicked. Was he even moving in the right direction?

There was the brief jingle of the coins before the creature struck. Three times that tail lashed out, three times, striking each of them once.

The barb entered Will's back, right between his shoulder blades. It struck deep. Will nearly fainted from the pain as its poison was pumped, pumped, pumped into him.

He began to fade. What strength he had, began to ebb from his body. He began forgetting himself, forgetting where they were, forgetting everything they were here for, forgetting, forgetting, forgetting...

He fought to remember. Through the billowing clouds of smoke, he could see faint light above, so far, far away. He gasped for a breath in that smoky murk.

They slid backwards, losing what precious little ground they had gained before the creature struck. Will's ears rang with the chorus of a thousand voices welling-up as one from the pit below, howling wolf-like across the blackness.

"Come down. Come down," the voices resounded. "It's sweet, so sweet with every treat, and sleep, sweet sleep with dreams replete. No fares, no cares," the wails did creak.

Will choked on the heavy smoke. He was tired. Even his mind was tired, a physical tiredness he had never before experienced. He could taste all his past treats, all the sweets that now encumbered him, all that Turkish Delight. He still wanted the treats, even though he choked on them now. He was so weak, so slow, so fatted. He felt sorry for himself.

"*I don't care*," he thought with such deep emptiness that they suddenly slipped all the way back down to the very edge of oblivion. They bumped to a stop and hit bottom, at the very edge of never-having-been. There was no longer any worse place they could go....except....the Web or the Pit that awaited, happily, patiently, below. The Web or the Pit were ends too near, one mistake away.

One mistake.

Chapter 29 – The Web and the Pit

Will glanced sluggishly over his shoulder. He tried to dig his toes in the loose shale to keep them from sliding, but he could find no secure footholds. Then he wondered why he was even bothering. He was so tired. His muscles ached. His fingers, knotted in Shilli-Shalli's fur, hurt even between the knuckles. His thighs burned. Every movement was an effort, every movement the possibility of that final slip. His hands were slippery, slick. He wiped one, then the other, sitting shock-still, poised on the very edge of final failure.

Will dared not think about anything other than where he was and what he was about. He was here, now. There will be no tomorrow. There was no yesterday. There was no daylight above, no abyss below. There was only *here*—only *now*. There was only being present, only being here now.

He was in a battle with himself. There was no longer any room for lying. He fought for control of his destiny, fought the pain and the poison, fought forgetting and letting go. He must not forget.

The question, *When is the riddle the answer?* marched through his mind like the ticking of a clock inside a crocodile. Tick. Tock. Tick. Tock. *When is the riddle the answer?*

He took a single breath.

Then he took another.

"You will fail," the wailing voices sang magnetically. "You are afraid, and that will make you fail." The walls trembled with the tumult of the wailing.

"**You fools!**" Will yelled at the unseen voices. "**I am not afraid. Fear is like wind in a vacuum.**" Now it was Will's turn to laugh, and laugh he did, like a man crazed, teetering on the edge of that great void—insanity.

"Never! Not me!" Will imbibed in his emotions. "You are the ones who can never succeed. The very best you can do is to cause others to give up while there is still life. But you will never beat me as long as I am alive, and I intend to live. Life! I choose life!"

The Riddle of Riddles

Will spurred them forward. "Come on, Knorbert. Come on Shilli-Shalli. Let's get out of here."

Slowly, they inched away from the edge.

"Tink a all da treasures, all da pleasures y'all be leavin' behind," Scorpideior hissed. "Tink a dem, all a dem."

Then it screamed. "**Ya still wan 'em, doncha, doncha, you pigs? Ya still want da treasures and da pleasures. Doncha?**"

Will inched them forward, veering side to side, dazed and confused. He was so tired. He wanted to rest but knew he dared not, not for even a moment. He could remember nothing, nothing but the phrase *When is the riddle the answer* which replayed itself, like a mantra, over and over and over in his mind.

Will looked up and saw the light. It looked so far away. The way up looked so distant, so narrow, and so unattainable. The way down looked so wide and inviting.

"Y'all never gonna make it," Scorpideior hissed, moving toward them, the web jingling. "Besides, y'all really don't wanna succeed, do ya? Your darkest dreams, da ones ya desire da most, da wickedness dat would delight cha most, none a dat will ever be yours if ya leave, I promise ya, will never be yours if you leave!" Its voice was a coarse, rasping whisper.

Will's muscles twitched. He kept breathing as steadily as he could, slow, deep breaths. They had gotten themselves in deep, much deeper than Will realized. The way up was so steep with so few footholds. One false step and it was a quick chain of events to the bottom of the bottom.

"Life! I choose life, free, spontaneous, unlimited life." Will spurred them forward.

He turned to see how far they had advanced, and as he did, they lost some of the precious distance they had gained. The creature was right behind them, at the very edge of the web, looming over them, its barbed tail twitching menacingly as though ready to strike again. The amulet around its neck swung to and fro, tantalizingly familiar.

Chapter 29 – The Web and the Pit

Will's eyes met those of the nemesis, and in that one brief instant, Will saw the emptiness that filled its heart. With a horrible groan, Scorpideior tore its eyes from Will's.

A hand reached out. It closed around the amulet. With a quick tug, the amulet came free. Scorpideior shrieked, crabbing clumsily back across the jingling web into the darkness.

With one last mighty effort born from that look of despair in the creature's eyes, Will spurred them forward once again, slip-slip-sliding away as they advanced.

But advance they did.

First by inches.

Then by yards.

Faster and faster they moved.

Faster and faster still, until, oh so blessedly soon, sooner than they had ever dared to hope, they saw the light above, wide and bright.

They flashed out into the light, out of the darkness, out of the clouds of caustic black smoke, back into the light, back into the clear freshness of possibility.

CHAPTER 30 – WHO IS IN CONTROL?

Up from the volcano they rose, circling, circling without direction.

Slowly, the cleanliness began rousing them from their deadly stupor.

Luci hung perilously close to the horizon. A blood-red moon rose slowly before them. The bright blue of the day was slowly giving way to the deep blue-black of twilight. It was almost dark enough for stars.

Stars!

Will quickly scanned the sky. He squinted and searched again, this time more slowly.

Nothing…nothing…oh yes…

Way over there…yes! A star. A pulsating star. Will's star! Lost for so long, but visible once again in the dimming light, beginning its ascent above the horizon opposite the sun.

"Put our backs to the sun, Knorbert," Will directed. Shilli-Shalli was hovering in one spot, one set of wings propelling them up and forward, while the other set propelled them down and backwards.

"But Will…" Knorbert protested.

"This is no time to argue, Knorbert. Put our backs to Luci. Put our backs to the sun!" Will repeated in a louder voice. "I can see my star. We must follow my star."

"But Will, I cannot."

"Why not?"

"Because that creature poisoned me that is why. Let us just hover for a bit. I need time to recover."

"That's exactly what we do not have, Knorbert. Time! Look at the Luci. Do you see how late it is?"

"But Will, I deserve a rest."

Will sat back. He took a deep breath. He did not say a

Chapter 30 – Who's in Control?

word.

"One short break will not hurt," Knorbert went on, "just one. I will get us moving soon. Just let me clear my head. Let me get my strength back."

Will remained silent.

"We need rest," Knorbert added. "Why not now?"

Silence.

"Besides I just do not feel like it," Knorbert whined in a squeaky voice.

"*I don't feel like it,*" Will mocked. "*Once won't hurt. I deserve it. I'm so tired. I'll do it eventually anyway, so why not now.* Alibis, Knorbert. All alibis. You've been full of alibis since we left, since you hesitated to step off your porch. I am in charge now. There will be no more alibis, Knorbert, you hear? No more alibis."

"Those are not alibis," Knorbert huffed. "Those are rationalizations, perfectly logical appreciations of the facts, I would say."

"Would you now? Would that include your own complicity in your own failure?"

Knorbert's eyes darted side to side.

"Am I right, Knorbert? Am I?"

"Right about what?" Knorbert locked his eyes straight ahead, avoiding Will's eyes.

"Right that there always is an alibi."

"Oh me, oh my…well, that is…" Knorbert stammered, flustered by the directness of Will's accusation, by the anger in his voice.

For a brief moment no one spoke.

"Well?" Will demanded.

Knorbert dropped his head and sighed.

There was another period of silence.

"You are right, Will," Knorbert blurted out. "You are absolutely right. Alibis. All alibis. I did not mean to…" Knorbert stopped. "There I go again." He shook his head. "Another alibi!"

"And who is in control here?" Will continued. "Who?"

"Why…why, you are, Will. You are, of course."

"And you will not forget it, right?"

"Right, Will. Right. You are in charge. No more alibis. I am lucky you ever came along, lucky you asked me to join you in your adventure."

Will's anger vanished like a Willi-Nilli at the sound of laughter. "Oh, Knorbert, I'm sorry. I'm sorry I had to be so hard on you. We all have failings, Knorbert. All of us. Now, look at Luci. Time has nearly run out. Luci is nearing the horizon, and I have no idea of what to do now except to follow my star."

"Right, Will. Right." Knorbert turned Shilli-Shalli toward the pulsing star. "Come on Shilli-Shalli. We must follow our star! No time for alibis. It is time to fly."

And fly they did, slowly at first, but more and more rapidly as Knorbert refocused his attention on flying, flying toward their star.

CHAPTER 31 – THE RIDDLE AND THE ANSWER

Using all the skills they had learned in controlling their flight, they rocketed through the dimming light.

"Don't forget to use light touches," Will reminded Knorbert. "Bracket and half, maintain course and give some purpose to our flight."

"Aye, aye, Captain!"

Will took a deep breath. He looked down into his hand. The amulet he had snatched from Scorpideior's neck was still clasped tightly in his fist. "Well, I'll be a Knothead," he exclaimed.

"What it is, Will?"

"Somehow I grabbed the amulet from around Scorpideior's neck without even realizing it. It looks almost exactly like the other two pieces we got before."

Will removed the first two pieces from his pocket, and spread them carefully on his lap in front of him.

"Hmmm," he said. "They *are* almost alike. They are definitely related somehow, like the puzzle you said they might be. Here, take a look for yourself, Knorbert. I'll steer."

Will handed the pieces to Knorbert. Then he turned his attention to Shilli-Shalli, stroking Shilli's neck, urging her on, while coaxing Shalli to relax.

The Riddle of Riddles

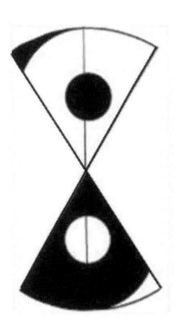 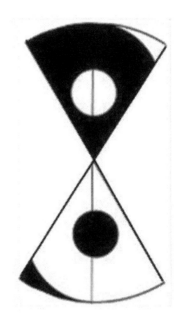

ONE SIDE   ANOTHER SIDE

Chapter 31 – The Riddle and the Answer

"Yes," Knorbert said, fumbling with the pieces. "This looks like the piece we thought was missing. Now, if only I can just figure out how they all fit together." His voice trailed off.

Knorbert tried putting the puzzle together first one way, and then another, not knowing which side was up. He had difficulty holding the pieces, his fat fingers so clumsy, their strength so unnecessary now. He flipped the pieces over and over in his lap, first one way and then the other. It looked so simple, but he could not get them all to fit together so it looked right.

Will encouraged Shilli-Shalli, praising her progress, chastising her when she went negative.

He coughed up some of the black soot he had inhaled from the volcano. He still felt dizzy and disoriented. He glanced over his shoulder at the sun. His heart fell to the bottom of his stomach. The sun was falling toward the horizon so rapidly that he swore that he could actually see it moving. They were running out of time, and they had no answers, none. Was it already too late? Had they already failed?

He coughed up more black soot. "I can't get rid of the smell of that smoke back there. Its stink will be in my brain forever."

"**THAT'S IT!**" Will was thunder-struck. "Of course, that's it!" He threw loud laughter up at the stars. "It was Belvidere, the master of disguise, all the time!

Knorbert started at Will's sudden outburst, but he stayed hunched over, concentrating on the puzzle in front of him.

"It's all so obvious now, Knorbert." Will grinned. "Scorpideior's lair smelled just like the low tide that Belvidere tried to blame for his own stench. In fact, so did Sid's breath, now that I think about it – and even Lilith's perfume couldn't completely hide it. Hidden, disguised, obscured, but unmistakably the reek of Belvidere. Ugggh, that ugly, brain-piercing odor! And the jingle of Lilith's bracelets, the jangle of Sid's medals, the jingle-jangle of the bags of coins on the web. How could I have overlooked the obvious? It was Belvidere all the time. Belvidere

The Riddle of Riddles

the Master of Disguises, trying to waylay us, delay us, keep us from completing our task. Belvidere thought he was so smart, smart enough to defeat us, but he certainly is no scholar. His disguises need help, and so does his chess game. Scorpideior blundered badly."

Will sat back. "Queen takes Bishop Pawn. **CHECKMATE!**"

"UAMIAMU! I got it!" Knorbert turned to Will. "Look, Will. I finally got the handle of it. Look!" Knorbert held up the assembled puzzle.

In one of those moments of clarity that comes only when the mind lets go of itself, Will groked it all.

"The Riddle and the Answer all in one. How obvious!"

Cannons of laughter resounded across Will's universe, from edge to edge, from bottom to brim. It was so obvious. Will wondered why he had not understood from the very beginning.

"Home, Shilli-Shalli. Take us home as fast as you can fly."

CHAPTER 32 – RACING WITH THE SUN

Will looked over his shoulder at the sun. Luci seemed drawn to the horizon by some powerful magnet, picking up speed as it fell.

They flashed for home across the darkening sky, toward their star.

Will was giddy with excitement at their accomplishment—and with the deadly concern over their lack of time. They still had to get the answer to Lou, and there was precious little time left.

Will grimaced, glad Knorbert was so focused on their flight, he never noticed. They had so little time left, so little time.

Shilli-Shalli streaked through the sky with only the lightest of touches from Knorbert guiding them. Faster and faster they flew, racing the sun, flashing across the sky as the sun dropped closer and closer to the horizon.

Faster and faster they flew.

Faster and faster the sun fell.

Will was flying as high inside as they were outside, but his heart was twisted in knots, fearing that they could not possibly make it back in time.

Knorbert was urging Shilli-Shalli on.

Shilli-Shalli was humming.

Each of them was at once aware of self and, at the same time, aware of the self of the others, all working together.

Then some gigantic, invisible wave grabbed hold of them. They were lifted high, being swept along on level flight like they were surfing—like a wave was sharing its power with them, was helping them, pushing them along at speeds exceeding that of light.

"We've got it! We've got it!" Will yelled. "We've caught

The Riddle of Riddles

a wave of Grace!"

Will was buoyant, in harmony with his rhythms. Together they had again achieved that grand state of Oneness. He felt completely alive, sensitive to every nuance of his being, to the very center of his being, living totally in the world of the immediate present. Will felt humble, unworthy of such assistance.

But it was so late.

They slipped off the wave.

"Focus," Will whispered in Knorbert's ear. "Focus on the moment."

Together they concentrated only on the present—aware of the intensity of each moment, without singling out any single aspect of the moment.

Another wave of Grace caught them, lifted them high. They crested speed.

Far, far off in the distance, Will could make out other mounted trios flying as they were flying, each flashing in its own direction, each intent on some unknown purpose all its own. An arrow of longing left Will's heart aimed at Knumerator.

Behind them, the brilliant orange and red sun donned a purple mantle as its lower limb met the horizon and crossed it.

Luci was almost gone.

Beyond the speed of light, on waves of Grace, they rocketed into the growing darkness.

So great was their speed that the space through which they traveled took on the shape of a tunnel. They flashed through that tunnel toward the circle of blackness at its end. So focused was Will's attention on the immediacy of the moment, that the black circle at the end of their tunnel grew smaller and smaller as they got closer and closer, smaller and smaller, until Will found himself focused on a circle of black no larger than the period at the end of this sentence.

CHAPTER 33 – BIRTH DAY

Will stared at this book in his lap, at the period at the end of the last sentence.

He was home, in his room, seated quietly, this book—open here.

He sprang to his feet. Through the window, he could just make out a thin purple sliver of sunlight on the horizon. He ran to the mirror.

"**Lou!**" he yelled. "**Lou!**"

But Will saw only his reflection yelling back at him.

"Lou, where are you? Lou!"

There was a green flash of light as the horizon squeezed out the last lick of sunlight.

The sun had gone down.

"Lou," Will cried, tears flooding his eyes. His fingertips pressed against the cold mirror face. "Lou! Where are you? You were supposed to be here waiting for me."

Through flooded eyes, the glass in the mirror got all-soft like gauze, turning into a sort of silvery mist. The glass melted away.

His tears blurred his vision, blurring the image in the silvery, misty mirror. The image ran before his eyes like a watercolor in the rain. His pale forehead ran down over his cheek. His mouth twisted—familiarly.

And there was Lou, staring back out of the gauzy mirror.

"Lou," Will cried. "You *are* here. I've done it, Lou. I've solved The Riddle of Riddles!"

Lou smiled a frown. "It's too late, Will. The sun has gone down. You were to bring me the answer before sundown. I'm sorry."

"But… but," Will stammered. "I was here before sundown. I was here, Lou. I was. You weren't!"

"I was here, Will. I am always here. I watched you call for me."

"Then why didn't you come?"

"I did come, Will. Here I am."

"But you came too late."

"No, Will. You came too late."

"But I do have the answer, and I was here before sundown."

"But you didn't bring me the answer before sundown, Will, and a deal is a deal."

"But I assumed that I would see you immediately," Will pleaded, tears rolling down his cheeks.

"There are many things in this world we cannot assume, Will. You know the consequences," Lou stated matter-of-factly. "You did not provide me with the solution in the allotted time, so you must forfeit your life."

"That's just not fair," Will howled. His blood was running so loudly through his veins he could barely hear Lou.

"Fair? " Lou raised an eyebrow. "Life is not fair, Will. Life just is."

"Exactly, Lou. That is it."

Lou stared out at Will. "That is what?"

"That is the answer."

"What answer?"

"The answer to The Riddle of Riddles."

"Really, Will? When is the riddle the answer?"

"The riddle is the answer. Life is both the riddle and the answer. The journey is the destination. Life is the answer!"

Lou peered at Will out of the mirror, across the narrowly-wide expanse of mist separating them. "Oh, you humans..." He shook his head. "Why do you continually make false assumptions, half-baked theses, and unnecessary laws? Why must allowances always be made for you?"

Will stopped breathing.

"Since you have proven yourself to be a Noble Warrior, to

Chapter 33- Birth Day

say nothing about a brave and honest lad," Lou began, "a lad who pursued his task diligently in the face of great and unknown challenges, and since you are, after all, only human..."

"Yes, yes!" Will let his breath out slowly, his heart pounding.

"The taking of your life *will* be postponed for now."

"Oh, thank you, Lou. Thank you. Thank you."

"This is your childhood's end. Your life will not be taken today, but make no mistake about it, Will, someday, any day, your life will be claimed. You may never know when. You are not immortal, Will. You never were. That was just another of your childhood assumptions. You are mortal, *ever so mortal*."

"Ever so mortal." Will took a deep breath. He had succeeded in his task, and, suddenly, time took on a new, singular dimension.

Lou continued. "Each year, on the anniversary of this day, henceforth to be known as your birthday, you will grow one year older, and on your birthday, you will be granted one wish, though, of course, not the Wishful Wish. I hope you have learned to wish wisely."

"Oh yes," Will bubbled. "Yes, I've learned a lot. I will make each wish as though it were my last."

"That's an excellent idea. It just might be. "

"Thank you, Lou. Thank you so much for understanding." Will wiped away the tears from his eyes, watching his image wipe away its tears as the visage of Lou faded away in the silvery, gauzy, misty mirror.

Will stepped back, turned, and took a step.

From that day forth, Will was never again bored. There was just so much to do and so little time in which to do it all tha Will did his best to fill all his days with happy tasks .

Will got to celebrate many, many, many birthdays. He knew he was no different from any other boy or girl. He was no different, but he was still special. Each birthday he spent in the company of his dear friends, Knorbert and Shilli-Shalli, who never

The Riddle of Riddles

left his side, having become so close, they were now as one.

Each year Will marked his birthday with a celebration of life, his life, his one and only life.

PART III

THE WRITER OR THE READER

That on-going flood of déjà-vu continues to sweep me along as I continue reading here.

So…

Am I the writer

or

Am I the reader?

If the truth be known, watching myself now reading *this*, I realize that this **now** really is our "**Once** upon a time…"

THE END

AFTERWORD

The following are the answers to Knorbert's riddles:

1. "What number, other than zero and infinity, yields the same result when it is either added to itself or multiplied by itself?"

ANSWER: The number "2"

2. "The begetter of alpha and the end of omega.
Seen not in any mirror, though I'm seen in every face.
Begetter of allusions, end of every enigma.
I cannot be found in here though I am found in every place."

ANSWER: The letter "A"

3. "Not every riddle is solved by clues.
Some are solved simply be spelling.
Tabulate numbers, each line a cue,
For letters found therein dwelling,
To see what you will find so dignified."

ANSWER: "Noble"

Line 1 – letter 1 is "N." Line 2 – letter 2 is "O."

4. "Behold the righteous man blessed with children and substance.
Till he who came from going to and fro on the earth,
Taketh away all to leave him to writhe in the agony of sore boils.
There came three friends to comfort him,
But, instead, they mocked him and accuseth him of wickedness.
But a voice spoketh out of a whirlwind to lay low the proud,

And he repented and was restored much greater than before."

ANSWER: "Job" from the *Book of Job*, The Bible

5. "Here I am,
   What I am.
   What am I?"

ANSWER: A "riddle"

6. "Four digits have I,
   One 'pposable friend.
   Applaud you I do,
   Who grasps this pun's end."

ANSWER: A "hand"

7. "Questions are pleaded,
   The replies come nigh,
   Solutions needed?
   The response comes by.
   Process completed
   By me. Who am I?"

ANSWER: An "answer."

8. "Our of the eater, came forth meat.
   Out of the strong, came something sweet.
   For love of nectar, I labor long.
   Stinging dances to buzzing songs."

ANSWER: A "bee"

Note: The Bible (Judges 14) tells the story of how Samson killed a lion, and later found a swarm of bees with honey in its carcass. From this event Samson put forth a riddle (Judges 14:14) which comprises the first two lines of the riddle above. Samson's enemies discovered the answer to his riddle by deceit, but Samson had his revenge by killing a thousand of them with the jawbone of an ass.

9. "OB-LA-DE
   OB-LA-DA
   What goes on, bra?
   LA-LA What goes on?"
   ANSWER: "Life" from the Beatles song.

The answers to these nine riddles form a literary rebus as follows:

* * * * * * * * *

The answers to the questions posed in the Forward are:

1. This book begins on the title page.
2. Here is the puzzle assembled:

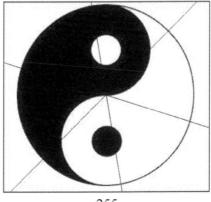

3. Three of the anagrams are: Thele = Lethe, Thal Ajam = Taj Mahal, WIT STEAMERS = Time Wasters.

4. This work is divided into three parts. There are 33 chapters and numerous other number combinations associated with the number three.

5. The solution to the Kryptographeme (cryptogram) is quite simple. If "A" is "1" and "B" is "2", what is the quote? If you have not yet solved it, go back and try again – or you can go to the end of this Afterword and find the answer there. *

6. The hidden names of members of a certain rock music group are:

"By George ..." Harrison
"Paul bearers..." McCartney
"demi-John..." Lennon
"Bingo! Ringo! . . ." Starr

7. The titles of 33 songs written and recorded by The Beatles are hidden in the text.

8. The lyrics/poetry sampled are: *Tambourine Man* by Bob Dylan; *OB-LA-DE OB-LA-DA* by Lennon/McCartney and *The Divine Comedy* by Dante Alighieri.

9. The games began right there in the Foreword. The words that are capitalized, with the exception of the first word of the sentence (which is always capitalized), spells out the phrase BE HERE NOW

OTHER ALLUSIONS

Some of the other allusions included (look for others) are:

a. *"A hint the scent of violets dusted the air."* St. Teresa of Avila recounts in *The Interior Castle* that at moments of inspiration she would catch a scent of violets.

b. "An elephant that had been swallowed by a boa constrictor . . ." is a reference to *The Little Prince* by Antoine Saint Exupery.

c. Quidditch, Nimbus Millennium prototype, and Muggles are all from the Harry Potter books by J.K. Rowling.

d. Sapientiopolis comes from the word "sapient" which is defined as wise, discerning, usually used ironically.

e. The five gateways into Sapientiopolis are the five senses (wits).

f. A hookah smoking blue caterpillar is from *Alice in Wonderland* by Lewis Carroll.

g. Jubjub and Bandersnatch are from *The Hunting of the Snark* by Lewis Carroll, as are the quotes: " . . .a shriek fleet and deep...," and "....snicker-snack."

h. The wording of the silvery, misty gauzy mirror in which Will encounters Lou both at the beginning of the story and at the end is a paraphrasing of Lewis Carroll's words in his *Alice Through the Looking Glass*.

i. "In the Beginning was the Word." The Bible John 1:1

j. Ada is sometimes regarded as the first computer program. It was written by Countess Byron Lovelace, daughter of the famous poet Lord Byron and Anne Isabella Milbanke Noel-Byron.

k. Game have already begun in the FOREWORD "... Brain-teasers, Enigmas, Hints, Epigrams, a literary Rebus, Equations, Numerology, Observations, and What-nots." The capitalized letters of the above words spell out the phrase BE HERE NOW

l. What Bird is This? The bird referred to is Dante

Alighieri.

m. The poet valued dearly is Virgil.

n. Dis is the name given to the Devil in Dante's *Inferno*. The reference to "spotted leopards, she wolves, and lions" is, likewise, from the same source.

o. "Pawn to King Four" begins the simple chess game known as Scholars Mate.

p. Lilith is an evil female spirit in ancient Semitic legend that haunts deserted places and attacks children.

q. Three children's books are directly quoted: *Peter Pan, Pinocchio,* and *The Little Prince*.

r. "Children loaded in small wooden carts drawn by sad-faced donkeys clad in high-topped shoes. A cat strolled with a fox" are from *The Adventures of Pinocchio* by Carlo Collodi. "Cocagne" is the island of the damned in *Pinocchio*.

s. "Three-headed dogs, creatures that looked like fish with the heads of eagles, and horse-like creatures with the head of a lion and the tail of a snake" are all taken from The Book of Revelations, The Bible.

t. Mitty is from *The Secret Life of Walter Mitty* by James Thurber about a man living in a fantasy world.

u. A Houri is a beautiful virgin who inhabits Paradise according to The Koran. Whouri is a corruption of that word.

v. A "Squeamish Ossifrage" is part of the phrase, "The magic words are Squeamish Ossifrage," which was the solution to a challenge "ciphertext" posed by the inventors of the RSA cipher in 1977. The cipher was solved in 1993/4 by 600 volunteers and 1600 machines over a period of six months. The prize for its solution was $100 dollars, which was donated to the Free Software Foundation.

w. References to various body parts are intended:

Headlands, Heartland, Kortextium (cortex), brain, Interior, Inner Space .

x. The three parts of the human personality are represented by the three main protagonists. Will represents the will, the conscience. Knorbert represents the brain, the mind. Shilli-Shalli represents the emotions, feelings.

y. When is the riddle the answer? The riddle is life and life is the answer.

z. In each of these three chapters, The Pleasure Palace, Man Hatin' Island and The Web or the Pit, the sequence of events is the same. First our heroes are offered fame (holograms, parades, and praise), than the subject is changed, first to pleasure (food & drink, leeches), than to diversion (video games), than to money. Next, they forget whatever it is that they are doing, (Water of Forgetfulness, the Smoke of Forgetfulness, and the Poison of Forgetfulness.) Then they get a reward—pieces of the puzzle.

This is a sequence of events our consciousness goes through when we attempt to complete a difficult task, one requiring long, hard periods of concentration.

As we first begin to solve the problem, at the first glimmer of a real solution, we feel pleasure, happiness at being on the right track. We have a tendency to pat ourselves on the back, to congratulate ourselves for our accomplishment. This can be the end of our progress unless we diligently push on towards the solution.

Then finding the endeavor taxing, the mind will change the subject; change its focus to something that each individual finds interesting, and we lose track of our focus.

Then if we drag the mind back to the original problem, it will rebel. The mind will forget the problem that it is pursuing and go off onto other thoughts.

Having recognized this pattern of mental behavior, I dealt with it in the following manner. When I realize that I'd forgotten whatever it was that I was doing, I would repeat to myself the last thing I remember before I forgot – even if it did not appear to have any meaning (in this book I used a mantra – *the riddle of riddles*). This enabled me to refocus my attention on solving the original problem.

Then, having refocused and reapplied myself to my task, my mind gave up something of great value, usually something to do with the original problem but not necessarily. Sometimes the mind offered a solution to a different problem that has been plaguing it. Note that prize, and then refocus (the three puzzle parts). These solutions are unusually weighty, and of great value.

The sequence described here is only one manifestation to the tricks the mind plays. The sequence is most likely distinct to each individual, but my guess is that there will be a commonality to the patterns.

* The answer to the Kryptographeme is taken from Dante's *Inferno*. The phrase is "Abandon all hope ye who enter here."

CREDITS

Grateful acknowledgement is made for samplings of the following for copyright material:

Warner Bros. Inc.: For portions of the lyrics from Mr. Tambourine Man by Bob Dylan. Copyright 1964 Warner Bros. Inc.

" . . .like some ancient empty street . . " and " . . .spinning, swinging madly across the sea . . "

" . . .with one hand waving free . . "

" . . .there is no where I am going to. I have no one to meet "and you must forget about today until tomorrow . . "

Charles Scribner's Sons: For the quote from Peter Pan by J.M. Barrie. *"Second on the right and than straight on till morning."* Copyright 1911/Copyright renewed by Charles Scribner's Sons, New York, NY.

Apple Records, Inc.: For lyrics quoted from OB-LA-DE, OB-LA-DA by Lennon/McCartney Copyright 1968

"Ob–La–De, Ob–La–Da

Life goes on, bra . . "

W.W. Norton & Company, Inc.: For portions of the verses from *The Divine Comedy* by Dante Alighieri; translated by John Ciardi. Copyright 1961/Copyright renewed.

"Oh you who wish to learn about these things,
Have followed thus far in your skiff–like boats,
The wake of my great ship that sails and sings,

Turn back and make your way to your own coast.
Do not commit yourself to the main deep,
For losing me all may perhaps be lost."

Harcourt, Brace, Jovanovich, Inc.: For the quotes from *The Little Prince* by Antoine de Saint Exupery. *"The eyes are blind. One must look with the heart,"* and *"The thing that is important is the thing that is not seen."* Copyright 1943 by Harcourt, Brace, Jovanovich, Inc., Orlando, Fla.

ABOUT THE AUTHOR

Thomas McGann is a native of Long Island, NY, a graduate of Bishop Loughlin MHS and the U.S. Coast Guard Academy.

Beside a military career that included a tour in Viet Nam, Tom has been involved in several business ventures. He was the owner/operator of Maguire's Bay Front Restaurant in Ocean Beach, Fire Island and Seasons Restaurants in both East Moriches and Speonk, NY. He was also the CEO of Seafarers Construction Company and a managing partner in Seafarers Investing Company that had vested interests in numerous business ventures.

In addition, Tom spent ten years digging clams on the Great South Bay and was a self-employed house painter for another ten. Other stints have included tending bar, waiting tables and driving trucks.

His real passion is writing. He wrote an online political column for three years for examiner.com and is the author of this young adult fantasy, several plays, numerous short stories, essays and reams of poetry.

Sailing, motorcycling and reading are his hobbies, but family is his life.

Made in the USA
Lexington, KY
29 March 2015